UNDEAD GIRL GANG

a novel by

LILY ANDERSON

RAZORBILL

RAZORBILL

An imprint of Penguin Random House LLC, New York

First published in the United States of America by Razorbill,
an imprint of Penguin Random House LLC, 2018

Copyright © 2018 by Penguin Random House LLC

Visit us online at penguinrandomhouse.com

THE LIBRARY OF CONGRESS HAS CATALOGED THE HARDCOVER EDITION AS FOLLOWS:
Names: Anderson, Lily, author.
Title: Undead girl gang / by Lily Anderson.
Description: [New York] : Razorbill, [2018] | Summary: While investigating the supposed
suicides of her best friend, Riley, and mean girls June and Dayton, sixteen-year-old Wiccan
Mila Flores accidentally brings them back to life.
Identifiers: LCCN 2018012918 | ISBN 9780451478238 (hardback)
Subjects: | CYAC: Murder—Fiction. | Wiccans—Fiction. | Zombies—Fiction. |
Witchcraft—Fiction. | Overweight persons—Fiction. | Mexican Americans—Fiction.
Classification: LCC PZ7.1.A526 Und 2018 | DDC [Fic]—dc23
LC record available at https://lccn.loc.gov/2018012918

Printed in the United States of America

This edition ISBN 9780451478245

1 3 5 7 9 10 8 6 4 2

Design by Corina Lupp.
Text set in Kepler Std.

"I'm the witch. You're the world."

—Stephen Sondheim, *Into the Woods*

For Anna-Marie, Candice, and Tehlor,
las Chicas Malas, who make me braver and kinder
and better than I thought I could be.

ONE

THE PROBLEM WITH your best friend dying is that there's no one to sit with you at funerals.

It's not the number one problem. Obviously, my best friend's bloated, waterlogged corpse being lowered into the earth for the rest of eternity is currently at the top of my list of Emotionally Debilitating Things That Will Take the Rest of My Life to Recover From.

But sharing my pew with strangers while Ms. Chu, the principal of Fairmont Academy, drones on and on definitely ranks high on the list of reasons why my friend being murdered is the pits.

Everyone is crying. It's standing room only for a sea of red-eyed, sniffling Fairmont Falcons. Their bodies are pressed to the familiar floral yellow wallpaper of the Greenway Funeral Home's reception room, their hair ruffled by the dusty air the heater is pushing through the ceiling vents.

The girl who slut-shamed Riley for dating a senior last year.

The guy who punted Riley's lunch across the quad just to prove he could.

The girl who slapped Riley in the face for cutting in line for class schedules.

The Nouns clique.

The principal's stepson.

The sole reporter for the Fairmont Academy newspaper.

All crying. Wailing. Stifling sobs into each other's shoulders. Eyes puffy to the point of closing. Snot ropes trailing from noses to sleeves. Mouths twisted into grotesque gargoyle shapes. The video montage of Riley from birth to sixteen really broke them, despite the fact that none of them were in the pictures. None of them were her friends.

To be fair, they did have a pretty long dress rehearsal for this the day before yesterday.

I hug my jacket closer to my chest, pressing my cheek to the denim collar. I've cried so much in the last forty-eight hours I think my organs have started to shrivel. My face is numb. I'm sure people have noticed. The people sitting nearest me—Riley's second or third cousins and some members of her parents' church—must be wondering why the fat girl is glaring at the front of the room instead of weeping prettily with everyone else. They'll think I'm an asshole, not understanding that I've spent two days screaming myself hoarse. That my eyes ache from use.

Two days is a long time when you can't sleep or eat because remembering that your best friend is gone slams into you whenever you think you're safe from it.

"Now more than ever, the community of Cross Creek must look to its young people," says Ms. Chu, the words leaden with politician-like fake gravitas. She even gives a soft, wagging fist with it, her thumb pointing toward the front row of mourners. "We must do more than see their struggle. We must hear them with open ears. Fairmont Academy will lead by example. The Fairmont family will not allow harm to come to another of our own. We will do everything we can to preserve the memory of Riley Greenway..."

Open ears are not a thing. Neither is the "Fairmont family," come to think of it. Fairmont is about as bloodthirsty as an artsy charter school can be.

But that's problem number three—behind Riley being dead and me sitting alone. No one believes that my best friend was murdered.

Despite our town being named after its twin bodies of water, no one in Cross Creek actually goes near the creeks. They're disgusting pits of algae and giardia. So when Riley's body was discovered floating and bloodied at the right fork of the creek, I knew something shady happened to her. If nothing else, Riley would never risk her dye job with creek water. She lived in fear of her bleached-blond locks turning even kind of greenish and avoided all non-shower water as a result. She wouldn't even use conditioner that wasn't opaque.

More importantly, Riley and I had already squished together in the back pew of the funeral home this week. June Phelan-Park and Dayton Nesseth, two of Fairmont Academy's most notable and obnoxious, hanged themselves in the park on Saturday night. Since Riley's dad is the town funeral director and June was Riley's brother's ex, we got guilted into going to their service. Double suicide, double funeral. Tragic as fuck.

But also kind of a scene-stealer if you were Riley and planning an outdoor suicide of your own.

I'm not trying to be glib or heartless about it, but really: Why would Riley let herself get lumped in with June and Dayton's honor society suicide pact? Riley was a lot of things, but copycat was not one of them.

"And now," Ms. Chu wraps up, inclining her head, "Riley's brother, Alexander Greenway, would like to say a few words."

Mr. and Mrs. Greenway did not invite me to speak at today's memorial. I'm pretty sure that my mom warned them about my "feelings" about Riley's death—i.e., the murder thing. It's easier for everyone to blame Fairmont Academy, to put the weight of tragedy on academic pressures and stress, the uptick in anti-anxiety prescriptions in the student body. And maybe that's why June and Dayton decided that they couldn't hack it on this plane of existence anymore—they were both involved in way too many extracurriculars, and all their friends were trash people. They were on the fast track to peaking in high school.

But that wasn't Riley. Riley breezed through Fairmont. Last

year, she literally slept through twenty minutes of her history final, woke up, and jotted down an A-plus paper.

She didn't need a way out. She would have told me if she did. I'm sure of it.

My parents and my sisters—who came to show support for the Greenway family in their time of need—made it very clear upon arrival that they didn't want to "encourage" me to "continue acting out." Which is what they call not believing that the Cross Creek police did any sort of investigation before they told everyone that Riley died by suicide.

They're sitting right behind the Greenways. Izzy looks over her shoulder at me as Xander stands and makes his way to the pew. Even in times of absolute tragedy, you can't stop an annoying little sister from making a face when your crush is around.

Xander spoke at June and Dayton's service, too. He was blindingly beautiful in a crisp black suit that made him look like an actor pretending to be eighteen rather than an actual high school senior. Today, he's in a formal black sweater and slacks that crease along the lines of his calves. The son of the town funeral director never wants for black clothing. Normally he'd call them work clothes. This week has been different.

As he sets his hands on either side of the podium, the crowd shifts. The sobs tone down. The sniffling mutes. People lean forward, waiting. Even the picture of Riley frozen on the flat screen above Xander's head seems to dim its light. This is what most people came for, to hear the most popular boy in school grieve aloud. The room is packed with rubberneckers. And I'm literally no better than them.

I imagine what it would feel like to comfort him, to run my nails through his thick brown hair, following the arch of his part. To have his head rest on my shoulder, his breath on my neck. Is his sweater as soft as it looks? The Greenway kids inherited expensive taste from their mother, so there's a chance that's real cashmere. It could slide under my palms, slippery soft . . .

Focus, Flores. Don't be a letch right now.

"My sister," Xander says, his voice wrung tight, "was the best person I've ever known. She was so funny and so smart and . . . There's so much she never had a chance to do. She never went to a school dance. She never owned her own car. She never beat me at Uno."

People laugh nervously, unsure if they're allowed to be even kind of happy on such a sad day. Xander pauses with a wince, cheeks flushing. He's doubting the joke, too. His cool blue eyes flutter closed. He has two sets of eyelashes, the same genetic mutation that Elizabeth Taylor had. Tears slide between them now.

My crush on Xander predates his painfully handsome phase. When we first met, he wasn't much taller than me and his knees and elbows stuck out like doorknobs from his pale skin. But it was unrequited love at first sight. Mortification stabs my guts as I remember talking endlessly about him over dinner back in middle school. My sisters have never let me forget this. I had to start paying Izzy five bucks any time Riley was over just so she wouldn't start blabbing about it in front of her.

Should I have told Riley about my crush? It wouldn't have

saved her life, but it's weird to have secrets from her now. I always figured I would tell her about it someday—when it was funny instead of pathetic. But I always figured that someday was coming, and, God, it sucks to be wrong.

"The world sucks without Riley," Xander finishes heavily, echoing my thoughts. My heart beats faster. "The world is darker without her. My life will be worse off for not having my little sister to share it with. And I'll never—" His voice breaks. He was so poised when he spoke at June and Dayton's service. Sad, but recognizably himself. But today he's unraveling. His spine curves and his shoulders pitch forward as his sobs echo around the room. One of his graceful hands comes up to his face, and he presses the heel of his palm to his wet eye. Even from the back of the room, I can see his fingers shaking. "I don't know why she's gone. I'll never understand why . . ."

He turns away from the microphone, almost boneless. His father appears beside him, wrapping his son in a steadying hug as they weep on each other. I wonder when the last time was that Mr. Greenway cried at one of his own funerals. He's usually so unflappable, full of dad jokes and rarely seen without a can of sparkling water in his hand. But he can't even lead the service. He steers Xander back to their seats. Mrs. Greenway joins their group hug as Ms. Chu reappears at the podium, reclaiming her position as the emcee.

"And now," Ms. Chu says, firmly redirecting the audience's focus to her steady voice, "Fairmont Academy's award-winning show choir will perform a final tribute to Riley's memory."

Wait, what?

I scramble a little, looking for the program I shoved under my butt when I sat down. The picture of Riley on the front is less than a week old. The last picture she'll ever post to Instagram. And it's a bathroom selfie, heaven help us all. I flip open the paper, scanning down the itinerary. Sure enough, the Fairmont show choir is scheduled as the penultimate presentation. They performed at June and Dayton's service, too, but at least Dayton had been *in* the show choir. Riley didn't give a shit about their a cappella shenanigans.

Out of the standing mourners, the members of the show choir file toward the front of the room. I should have recognized them in the crowd. They're noticeably less upset than everyone else, their shoulders squared, their eyes shining with the thrill of performing. Soulless freaks.

As they shuffle themselves into rows in front of the podium, I flip over the program. On the back, there's a quote from the Bible—nice try, Greenways, but Riley was pagan—and a poem that Aniyah Dorsey wrote about her feelings. Riley would laugh until she cried if she could read this poem. It rhymes. *Riley. Shyly. Wryly.*

The show choir warms up, a series of menacing *ooh*s. The soloist standing at the center of the group aggressively taps out a four count on her leg. There's a collective intake of breath, and they start the same damn song they sang at June and Dayton's funeral. "I'm Always Chasing Rainbows." They must be competing with it this year. They should rethink that. It's terrible. A public domain rip-off of "Somewhere Over the Rainbow" that's somehow even more of a bummer. The soloist—a senior girl who is rail-thin and short-haired—starts the song.

"I'm always chasing rainbows. Watching clouds drifting by. My schemes are just like all my dreams. Ending in the sky."

God. So nasal. It's physically painful to my ears.

I won't give them the satisfaction of looking at them. I turn back to the program. Riley smirks up at me, blond and effortless, with the kind of athletic build that everyone subconsciously registers as healthy. She should have been the queen of Fairmont. Considering she was Xander's sister, she could have been. But she was happy—*seemed happy*—to hide in the background with me.

In the picture on the program, she's wearing a beanie with round bear ears on top pulled down almost to her dark eyebrows. Her roots were growing out. It was only just starting to feel like real autumn, but she swore she was going to hide her hair under a hat until she got a chance to buy a box of bleach this weekend. And now she'll never have the chance. She'll have half an inch of dark brown growth on display until it decomposes from her scalp. If she knew, she'd be pissed.

Fuck a duck, she'd say in her raspy voice. She didn't smoke, but she always sounded like she was getting over bronchitis. I can hear it so clearly in my head, it's like she's with me, making commentary in my ear.

Where she should be.

Where she never will be again.

My head spins. I can't do this anymore. I can't be here. My body is too exhausted to cry, but if I stay I might start screaming over the show choir. And while I don't care if I ruin this garbage performance, I don't think it'll disprove my parents' theory that I've lost my mind.

"Some fellows look and find the sunshine."

I stagger to my feet, turning my back to the performance and the crowd. It's not like I can blend in. I can't pretend like my body doesn't take up space. The only thing to do is lean into it, to do what Riley would do and not give a fuck that people can see me leaving. The sounds of my boots are muffled against the carpet as I stride down the aisle. I keep my head up, letting everyone I pass see my makeup untouched by tears, letting it confirm their worst fears about the fat witch of the junior class.

I see Aniyah Dorsey, amateur poet and school newspaper reporter, standing near the door. She's in plus-size leggings and a black flannel. Tears fog the silver glasses perched on her dark brown nose. She whispers after me, "Mila?"

"Your poem fucking sucks," I growl at her.

Her chin snaps back. I can't tell if she's offended or indignant, and I honestly couldn't give half a shit to stick around long enough to find out. I don't need fat-girl solidarity right now. I don't need anyone's solidarity. Ever.

"I always look and find the rain."

I pop the collar of my jacket, stuff my hands into the pockets, and step out into the friendless world.

TWO

I'M NOT READY to be back at school, but here I am, balanced on a stool at the center table in third-period chemistry while Mr. Cavanagh wipes last period's notes from the whiteboard. People filter into the room, their voices like mosquitos buzzing. I can't seem to stop myself from flinching when they pass too close to me.

According to the internet, only 20 percent of homicides are committed by strangers. Which means there is an 80 percent chance that the last thing Riley saw was the face of someone she knew, staring down at her through the murky water of the creek. There is an 80 percent chance that it was someone like Dawn Mathy of the Nouns clique, who is sitting daintily in front of me, smoothing her short bangs. She gets belligerent whenever someone questions the need for a speech and debate team. Or Dan Calalang, a senior stuck in junior-level chem. His forearms are scary beefy from CrossFit, the better to drag you to your death with.

It could be one of the janitors or Ms. Chu or someone whose name I've never bothered to learn. Someone who took my best friend from me and is still going to class and taking notes and looking forward to cafeteria chicken nuggets.

I feel sick to my stomach. I'm not ready to be here. Everyone seems so normal, but they can't all be—normal people don't drown girls in the creek.

"Hey, Mila."

I look up and immediately wish that I had a bushel of bay leaves. (They're good for banishing—although Riley's mom kept them in the spice cabinet to use in her spaghetti sauce.)

Caleb Treadwell, Ms. Chu's stepson and my lab partner, is climbing onto the stool next to mine, wobbling a little as he tucks a silver chain into the collar of his T-shirt. I should have smelled him coming. He starts every morning by drowning himself in cologne that smells like leather and moss, but it can't quite smother the tang of clinical-strength face wash. He stinks like a chemical fire.

On the surface, he's almost painfully nondescript. His hair is too khaki-colored to be considered brown or blond, and it's cut into the same short-on-the-sides, long-on-top style that every other guy in school has. His chapped, mauve lips are so puffy that he has a near constant pout.

"It *is* Mila, right?" he asks, even though there's no chance he doesn't know my name. We've been lab partners for almost two months. He just wants me to feel bad for not immediately saying hello. He smiles when he's angry. The insincerity makes his eyes look dead. His teeth are as big as my thumbnails.

"Hi," I say shortly. I plant the sole of my boot on the bottom rung of my stool for balance and lean a little farther from him.

"I saw you leave the funeral."

"Oh yeah?" I say, digging through my backpack and retrieving my chem notebook and slapping it down on the counter. "Which one?"

He wheezes a laugh. The sound slides over my skin, making the hairs on my arm stand on end. There's no one thing that makes Caleb creepy. It's not that he licks his lips until the skin shreds or that he talks incessantly about being "one of the nice guys" or even his habitual sweatpants boners. Rather, it is all of these things as a whole that lends to his overall air of Total Fucking Creep. An aura of Men's Rights Activist. Eau de Internet Troll. Musk of Mansplainer.

And his mouth looks *a lot* like a vagina. That doesn't help.

Knowing Caleb means that my respect for Ms. Chu is lessened at all times, since I believe she is at least partially responsible for not buying him pants that would curb his public erections.

Huh. Maybe there's a spell for that. Why didn't Riley and I ever investigate this? Forced impotence would make the world a much safer place.

"I saw you at both funerals," Caleb says, undeterred by my lack of interest or eye contact. "You're hard to miss, ha ha."

Caleb loves to slip mentions of my weight into conversation to see if I'll snap. If I do, he'll throw his hands up and say he's just kidding loud enough for everyone around us to hear, so that it sounds like I have no sense of humor and he's hilarious. *Fatphobic asshole.*

"It's a shame about all this," he continues. He flexes his hands against the edge of the table. His fingers are long and tapered and so solidly white it's like they're made of yeasty dough. I expect them to engorge to bursting. Or sprout powdery green mold. "June and Dayton. They were both in the honor society with me, you know. Dayton never seemed like she should be—God, she was a flake, just so, so stupid—but her grades were good. And they were neck and neck for the Rausch Scholarship, too. Whoops. Bad choice of words. Neck and neck." He mimes a noose around his own neck, pulling the imaginary knot sharply to the right. "Hanging's a rough way to go out. Big rope burns cut into their skin, their necks distended . . . They'd have to drop pretty far for the force to knock off one of Dayton's shoes. Did you hear that they never found it? It could still be stuck in a bush in Aldridge Park."

I shudder. June and Dayton's caskets were both closed at their funeral. I didn't give any thought to why. Now images of their mangled bodies swim in front of my eyes as Caleb continues to talk about postmortem bloating of the corpses.

"What do you think the last thing they saw was?" he asks abruptly. "I've heard that people shit themselves when they're hanged, but that's probably just a myth. I mean, anyone *could* shit themselves when they die. The muscles loosen and . . ." He trails off. The spit in his cheeks makes a burbling fart noise. What is it with dudes and sound effects?

"After June and Dayton, Riley Greenway probably would have been next in line for the Rausch Scholarship," he says, reaching down to scratch his leg. I make a fist, ready to punch him in the temple if his hand starts to stray crotch-ward. "Even though she didn't belong to any clubs. Xander said that she was going to write her essay on working in their funeral home. That's how he won last year. The committee really eats up the humanitarian angle."

I wish I could scrape Riley's name out of his mouth with my fingernails. I hate that people like Caleb Treadwell feel like they can talk about her like they knew her. Riley wouldn't have cared if she'd won the Rausch Scholarship. She would have entered just to take the prize away from people like Caleb and June Phelan-Park.

"But she's gone, too," he says with a shrug and a giggle. "So the road to the Rausch Scholarship is clear for me."

"Excuse me?" Aniyah Dorsey stops next to our table, her books hugged to her chest and her eyes staring over the tops of her round glasses. Her hair shines like lacquered paint, the natural curl pressed flat and straight. "Are you implying that your life is better off after the suicides of three of your classmates? Can I quote you on that? I'm writing an article about the impact of grief on the school, and your lack thereof would make a great lede."

"Move along, Rita Skeeter," Caleb says, waving her off. His rage-smile stretches so wide that it wrinkles the corners of his eyes. "No one gives a shit about your newspaper."

He's not wrong. Fairmont Academy only has a newspaper

because Aniyah won't let it die. I don't know anyone who reads it. But I don't think she cares. It'll look good on a college application regardless of how many people read it when it's passed out on Fridays.

Or is it Mondays?

I picture Aniyah down at the creek, her hair pulled up high to avoid being splashed. In a boring town like Cross Creek, it must be hard to find newsworthy happenings. Would it be worth it to her to make her own story? She's about my size, more than strong enough to hold Riley's narrow shoulders underwater.

"You're not next in line for the Rausch Scholarship anyway. It's given to students who embody the Fairmont mission statement, and there's nothing in there about being a fuckwit," Aniyah says, glaring down at Caleb. "Besides, it's an alumni-awarded scholarship. If they gave it to the principal's son, it'd look shady as hell."

"Stepson," Caleb corrects loudly. People wandering to their seats pause and look over at our table. The attention feels predatory. More eyes, more suspects. "Don't worry. I'll make sure that there's a moment in my acceptance speech that commemorates the three girls who couldn't keep up anymore. Or maybe I won't. Everyone will have forgotten about them by the end of the school year anyway."

He starts to laugh again, looking around at the other tables for people to join him.

I know he's mostly talking about June and Dayton. They weren't nice when they were alive. They used to make fun of Riley for living above a funeral home. And they made fun of me for being fat and Mexican. They found the things about other people that made them different and highlighted how that made them shitty. It was like they learned how to be popular from TV and didn't understand that being known didn't have to be synonymous with being a dick.

Last week, I probably would have sat back and made a note to try a new curse to see if I could make Caleb fail all his classes so that he'd never get the stupid Rausch Scholarship.

But my fuse is shorter than it was last week, and Caleb said *three* dead girls, which, by my count, makes this more personal.

My boot shoots out, connecting with the bottom rung of Caleb's stool with enough force to knock it out from under him. Arms waving in panic, he topples over into Aniyah and some people who were walking behind her. Textbooks clatter to the floor with gunshot-loud bangs. Aniyah's legs waggle in the air, her backpack holding her to the ground like a felled turtle. Caleb is holding his face and screaming curse words into his palms. There's no blood. For a second, that bums me out. At least he's stopped smiling.

I turn and see Mr. Cavanagh hanging up the phone on the wall. He jerks his head toward the door. "Not okay, Mila. They're expecting you in the office."

I leave the classroom picturing Cavanagh's disapproving frown lines filtered through creek water. Riley had him for fifth-period chem.

"Miss Flores?" The secretary stops me as I reach for Ms. Chu's doorknob. "You're here to see Dr. Miller."

I pause, turning around. There's a second door in the office that I've never paid any attention to. It's not as fancy as Ms. Chu's frosted glass with her name etched into it. The one on the other side of the room is the same metal door as the ones leading to the classrooms, painted institutional cream. The sign to the right of it says: *Dr. Miller, school psychologist.*

I bite my lip hard and dig my nails into my palms. I should have seen this coming.

I look back at the secretary. Her eyes are pitying and liquidy.

Oh God. She knows.

Part of me is really tired of being pitied. But part of me doesn't feel like I've been pitied enough. I mean, my mom has been accusing me of being psychotic this week because I haven't been able to instantly bounce back after my best friend died. The secretary—Ms. Pine, if her nameplate is to be believed—is close to my mom's age, but her brown skin is papery and her curls are starting to fade to gray. She looks like she's going to be someone's super-loving grandma someday. I bet if she wouldn't be immediately fired for inappropriate conduct, she would totally give me a hug right now.

No one has hugged me since Riley died.

But Ms. Pine doesn't know that I'm supposed to be hard as nails. When you earn a reputation as a grumpy witch, there are no tender hugs coming your way, no matter how sorry people feel for you. You don't suddenly get to be squishy when bad shit happens.

"Go on in, sweetheart," Ms. Pine says. She sounds so sincere that I can't even be mad at her for being part of this nightmare.

I step into Dr. Miller's office. One step is about all I can take because it's a glorified closet. Actually, it might have been a real closet. It has no windows.

All four walls are painted lavender. Directly across from me is a giant vinyl sticker that reads: *Life isn't about waiting for the storm to pass. It's about learning to DANCE IN THE RAIN!*

The font is very aggressive.

Dr. Miller is a thin white woman with fluffy blond hair like goose feathers. There's a pad of paper, a plain red folder, and a cup of steaming tea in front of her. Her computer is turned off.

Was she just sitting here, staring at the door, waiting for me to show up? That is terrifying.

"Camila Flores?" she asks with a slight tilt to her head. She has a neck like an ostrich.

"I go by Mila," I say. I realize she's waiting for me to close the door behind me. I do, and it thunks into place. The walls reverberate, making the vinyl words wiggle.

"Please have a seat." She points at the only other chair in the room, which happens to be directly next to my leg. It's a standard school chair—maroon plastic, the same as in most of the classrooms. It doesn't go with the lavender walls at all. I'm starting to think that Fairmont doesn't spend a lot on the school psychologist. Does Ms. Chu even know that this isn't a broom closet?

"I'm Dr. Miller," says Dr. Miller. "I'm so glad you could take the time to meet with me today."

"Uh huh," I say, hooking my boots around my chair legs. The metal is cool through the fabric of my jeans. "I'm sixteen. I pretty much go wherever they tell me to."

She smiles at me tightly. I recognize the look. It's very similar to the way Mrs. Greenway looks at me. It's the *"Oh no, you think you're funny and I'm a humorless old snatch"* look. There goes any chance I had at making a new middle-aged psychologist friend.

"I've been wanting to speak with you for a few days now," she says, possibly also sensing that we aren't going to be bosom friends. "I understand that you were very close to Riley Greenway. This must be an awfully hard time for you."

I wonder what it would be like if I said no. Like *"Nah, dog, my bff is dead but otherwise it's been a super-chill week."* That seems needlessly combative, so instead I say, "Yes. It's hard."

She glances inside her red folder. I spy last year's yearbook picture—the one with the uneven eyeliner and bulky Disneyland sweatshirt—paper-clipped to the corner of what I can only assume is my permanent record. Shouldn't that be digital? Is Dr. Miller a Luddite?

"You only took two days off from school?" She gives me an exaggerated frowny face as though doing her best to actually become an emoji. "That's not long at all. Do you feel ready to be back?"

"Again," I say, slowly because I'm starting to think this woman might be even dumber than Dayton Nesseth, God rest her soul, "I'm sixteen? My parents told me to come back today, so I'm back. Kind of like 'Ready or not, here I am.'"

I'm actually here because my walking out of the memorial service did not go unnoticed by my mom. She decided that disrespecting the dead—her words—was a sign that I was healed enough to learn. I think she's actually punishing me for telling Izzy and Nora that if they kept trying to talk to me, I'd curse their tongues to rot out of their skulls.

"Right," she says, in a way that makes me think she's not listening. She's peeking inside the folder again. I wonder if my life is really so complicated that she needs a cheat sheet. "Do you still believe that you're a witch?"

People say *witch* the same way they'd say *fairy princess*. Like it's a game that Riley and I should have outgrown. But to Riley it was a religion. And to me . . . well, I don't know. Maybe it was make-believe?

Wicca came to me through Riley's excited whispers shortly after I moved to Cross Creek. Choosing a new religion seemed so grown up, so definitive. I was eleven and had never realized that you could choose to be different from your family. We could be different and *powerful*. Which does sound a little like make-believe now, but Riley made me believe it in one sentence: "We're gonna do great things together."

So I went from elementary school on the coast, where I was mostly known for reading in class and making Post-it origami, to middle school in Cross Creek, where I was Riley's friend and a witch. I don't know if I'm ready to be either.

Is it possible to be a pagan agnostic? I'm open to the idea that there are more things in heaven and earth than I've dreamed of and all. I just don't know if I'll do magic now that Riley's gone. The whole witch thing was her deal. She's the one who started reading books on Wicca and making supply lists for spells. I was kind of along for the ride, mostly for the incense and crafting part of things. Riley never had the patience to join me in making jewelry, so we switched to spells.

Plus, when people know you spend your free time hanging out at Lucky Thirteen, the Wiccan store downtown, they tend to leave you alone. And I like anything that encourages people to give me a wide berth.

We'd mostly done spells for minor acts of vengeance—bumps to test scores, zits on the chins of people who talked shit in the halls, making sure that show choir never won a single competition, not that they needed our help there. Sometimes, we messed around with love charms—talismans that Toby, the owner of Lucky Thirteen, swore increased attractiveness or lust. We spent most of sophomore year trying to get crushes to reveal themselves, which worked in that Riley had a series of boyfriends and I quietly pined for Xander, the same way I had been doing since seventh grade, when I moved to Cross Creek.

I've never seen magic really work. But, as Riley would point out, I've never seen it *not* work. She was always vocally against my confirmation bias.

I don't feel like I owe this explanation to Dr. Miller, especially since someone has fed her private information about me. I don't think that's how therapy is supposed to work. I wonder who spilled my secrets to her. My parents? Xander? I guess it was common knowledge that Riley and I hung out at Lucky Thirteen. Anyone could have mentioned this to the school psych.

"*Witch* is the word for a follower of Wicca," I say airily. "Although, if you were going to be politically correct, you'd say *wix*. It's gender-neutral."

She picks up a pen and makes a note on her pad. Oh my God, she literally writes down *wix* and nothing else. When she's done, she looks up at me again, her long neck stretched threateningly forward. "Do you believe that you're capable of magic?"

"That question infringes on my religious freedom."

"Mila." She flattens my name like it's a bug under her shoe. She doesn't want to play with me anymore.

"I'm serious. You can't legally try to talk me out of my religion. Church and state. The state is your employer, right? Technically that's where your salary comes from?"

Her mouth snaps shut. She's trapped, not that she'll admit it. I watch her brain switch tactics. "Your best friend killed herself."

"She's dead, yes."

Dr. Miller clasps her hands on top of the Red Folder of Mila. "She killed herself. Your parents seem concerned that you haven't come to terms with this. It's understandable. Denial is the first stage of grief, and there's no rushing—"

My parents. Of course. Additional retribution for me threatening Izzy and Nora. Additional distance between them and me. This week I've finally tipped into feelings so big that all they can do is deny them entirely. Feelings so big that they've made my parents scared of me. Who knew that you could be so sad that no one would even be able to look at you out of fear of contracting your feels?

"Either way, Riley's dead," I say. "Why does it matter how it happened?"

"Are you familiar with the concept of a paranoid delusion?"

I suck the spit off my teeth. Now she's pissing me off. "Do you talk to everyone you counsel like this or just the grieving ones?"

She ignores me. "Your belief that Riley didn't take her own life is understandable. As her friend, you might feel responsible, like you could have done something to save her—"

"I probably could have saved her from being murdered, yeah—"

"—or that maybe something you said or did caused her to—"

I slam my hands down on her desk. A small wave of tea splashes over the side of her mug and starts to seep into a corner of the notepad that's blank except for the word *wix*. The smell of spicy ginger—as biting and hot as my temper—fills the small space.

"I didn't do anything to her. We went to a funeral, split up to do homework, and then someone drowned her in the creek. She had no history of self-harm, she wasn't a depressive, her grades were fine, and she wasn't even PMSing! All she did was cross the wrong person. And no one is doing anything about it. There's a fucking murderer walking around and no one cares!"

"Language," Dr. Miller chastises as she opens a desk drawer and retrieves a box of Kleenex. She whips out a tissue and blots the tea spill on her desk. "Riley's death was ruled a suicide by the Cross Creek Police Department. Why do you think that you would know better than the professionals what happened to her?"

"Because I did the research." I don't tell her that I did the research at four in the morning because I haven't been sleeping. Because every time I close my eyes, I can taste the creek filling my nose and throat, pulling me down with Riley. "Thirteen percent of teen deaths are homicides. Only eleven percent are suicides. It's statistically more likely that she was murdered."

She pitches the tea-stained tissue into the trash can under her desk. It lands with a hollow thud. "Except we were told that she wasn't. Unfortunately, the likeliest solution isn't always the correct one."

A thought lights up my brain. "Then what about June Phelan-Park and Dayton Nesseth?"

Her eyes stray back to the red folder in a flash of panic. "Were you friends with June and Dayton, too?"

I snort at the idea. Me, friends with Nouns. "No. They were awful. But the police said they were suicides, too. What makes more sense? Three unrelated suicides or three connected murders? Have three people ever committed suicide within a week in Cross Creek before?"

"I don't have those statistics for you." Her upper lip twitches. She's getting worse at hiding her disdain for me. "But I can tell you that Cross Creek has never had a serial killer before either. It's not as common as movies make it look. I understand that this is a traumatic time for you. And it's not unusual for someone to create a scenario that would be more palatable to them when faced with something awful. But your friends and family are worried about you."

I lean back in my chair, flexing my shoulder blades into the hard plastic. "I don't have friends. My only friend was fucking murdered."

"The truth is that Riley took her life, and we may never understand why."

I think of Xander at the memorial service: *I'll never understand why...*

Xander is the only person who knew Riley as well as I did. Neither of us understands because it literally doesn't make sense. She wouldn't do this. She wouldn't leave us. She'd stay, she'd rail against the system. If she were here instead of me, she'd get justice even if she had to burn the world down around her to do it.

She'd do a spell to find the killer.

THREE

I'M SURE THE school—probably kind-faced Ms. Pine—
will call my parents and tell them that I disappeared after third
period. But I think I get to keep pulling the "my friend is dead"
card for a bit longer. Like the next couple of years? Besides, since
every adult in my life now agrees that Riley's death has pushed
me into a paranoid delusion—thanks for the cool new vocab, Dr.
Miller—I might as well lean into it and say that my first counseling session sent me to a dark place. Which isn't even a lie. The
Yarrow house is hella dark.

The old boarded-up farmhouse at the edge of town is mottled
green with patches of brown where fifty winters have washed
away the lead paint. There are a couple of raccoon families that
live underneath what's left of the wraparound porch. The woods
that frame Cross Creek back up almost all the way to the house's
unlocked back door.

When Riley and I first started hanging out here, neither of us had any idea what we'd find between the rough-barked oaks and bushy maples that wept milky, obscene-looking sap. We didn't even know to look out for the thick patches of poison oak until a sticky summer afternoon when we ducked into the woods for shade, our sandals clacking so loud that we startled the birds out of the trees. By the time we limped back to my house, we were both covered in balloon blisters and scaly red rashes up to our knees.

Stretched out on holey beach towels on the floor of my bedroom, covered in calamine lotion and oatmeal up to our thighs, we watched hours and hours of Disney movies, hoping the happy endings would distract from the fire-hot pain and explosions of yellow goop down our legs. As the sun went down, I looked over at Riley and asked why she was still with me when she could go home and recuperate alone. And she laughed and said, "You can't get rid of me now. We're blister sisters. Blisters before misters."

And it wasn't *that* funny, but the pain and the grossness and the stupidity of it made us laugh so hard that we couldn't breathe, and Izzy started banging on the wall to tell us to shut up, and eventually my mom came in with more cold oatmeal and her disapproving head shake.

After that, I found my boots and baggy denim jacket at Goodwill and stared wearing them in all weather, and Riley made sure that she always had on long pants and high-tops. The next time we went to the woods, Riley shimmied up to the top window of the Yarrow house and broke the lock on the back door so we'd have somewhere to go if we ever wanted to wear sandals.

The Yarrow house had been abandoned for years. According to Mrs. Greenway, the town council has been trying to find a way to tear it down forever but can't get around the fact that it is, technically, a historical landmark.

"This is the problem with Californians," she'd say in her sharp Michigander accent. "They think anything older than a hundred years is priceless. The Yarrow family hasn't lived in Cross Creek for fifty years."

For Riley and me, this meant that there was no chance that the house's owner would come sniffing around, wondering why the house smelled like raccoon shit and incense.

Most of the rooms inside the farmhouse are wrecked with disuse. The floor droops in the living room. The ceiling sags with water leaking from the bedrooms above. The stairs are missing planks. There's a basement that I've never been brave enough to explore. But the kitchen is solid as long as you aren't skittish about seeing the occasional mouse or wolf spider. It's the brightest room in the house since it has a whole window with no boards. The October breeze isn't strong enough to slip through the hairline fractures snowflaking in the corner of the glass.

It's hard to believe that it has only been a week since the last time I was here. Riley wanted to drop off a bag of new white candles for a spell that had to be completed on the full moon. The candles are here, lined up carefully in the sagging cabinetry. None of the cabinets have doors, so all our magical inventory is visible.

Chunks of pastel stones, candles in all colors, brown vials of essential oil, herbs drying in bundles, cast-iron pots from

Goodwill to contain anything that needed burning, Riley's entire magic library—from the first Silver Ravenwolf book she ever read, still adorned with the Cross Creek library barcode, to the handwritten spells she bought off Toby at Lucky Thirteen. A glossy blue full moon chart is tacked to the wall where a fridge used to be.

There's a shelf just for Riley's fortune-telling supplies—multiple packs of tarot cards and polished gem rune stones and bags of muddy-tasting tea next to a chipped teapot. She loved the instant gratification of divination. Knowing what was coming was half the joy for her. The rush of expectation that makes me want to puke.

There's a dollar-store broom propped in the corner, its bristles weak and basically useless for anything but swatting moths away. I pick it up and try to clean a square for my backpack. If I come home dirty, Mom will flip out and make me spend the weekend shampooing the carpets.

Mr. and Mrs. Greenway wouldn't let Riley keep anything related to paganism in their house. They're good Christian morticians who thought Riley was inviting the devil into their home when she bought a box with the Celtic Green Man painted onto the top. Mrs. Greenway smashed it with a hammer and tossed the splinters into the yard. After that day, we'd started sneaking anything witch-related to the Yarrow house. Xander had helped, carrying loads over on his bicycle since we'd all been too young to drive.

Magic makes my parents vaguely annoyed and uncomfortable; it made the Greenways livid. When Riley had asked her mom about the idea of Jesus as the embodiment of love rather than a literal, physical being, she'd been gifted a slap in the face and some emergency weekday church.

Wicca doesn't mind if you work in metaphor. Wicca never minded that Riley and I didn't really know what we were doing. The only vengeful deity in witchcraft is yourself. Do bad shit, get bad shit. Do good, get good. Or be like me and Riley and do almost nothing but giggle over incense and get perfumed smoke in your nose in return.

The floor is still dusty with old chalk circles and sigils. Riley and I have only been here a couple of times since the school year started. The last big spell we worked was the end of last month for the autumnal equinox. We'd spent an entire day running through the woods, picking up the first fallen leaves and acorns off the ground and dragging them inside. The decorative squash Riley had stolen from her parents' mantel is starting to decay in the corner of the kitchen. I can picture her setting it victoriously in the center of the chalk circle, the sunlight winking against the rose quartz necklace she never went anywhere without. There is nothing flashy about an equinox spell, and there was something about its simplicity that made it feel realer.

"Most magic is just telling the universe you're thankful to be here," Riley had said that day before closing her eyes to light the first candle.

I hope that I've been thankful enough to have built up some brownie points with the universe. I need a big favor right now.

After lighting a stick of incense—rose, for luck, and because it's the best for covering the rodent stench—I yank down the books by the handful, making a stack on the floor. I know that it's unlikely that I'll find a way to use magic to uncover a murderer in *Sexual Sorcery: Lust Spells for the Hedgewitch*, but I'm not going to leave a single stone unturned here. I sit on my backpack to keep the dust off my jeans and turn on the noise-canceling app on my phone that I normally use for studying. It makes the house sound like it's trapped in a rainstorm, which kind of adds to the whole Hogwarts library vibe of the day. I flip through every page of every book, reading carefully. I understand that finding a "Hey, Here's Who Killed Your Friend" spell might be a bit of a stretch, but I'm not above patching together a variety of spells. I make a list of stones and herbs that inspire people to tell the truth, and I dog-ear a spell for opening your third eye to see into the past—though that one only works in dreams, which would require me to actually sleep.

I wonder if I should track down a Ouija board and just let Riley herself guide my hand . . .

I squeeze my eyes shut, dizzied by how stupid this feels. Maybe my parents and my sisters and Dr. Miller are right. Maybe I'm delusional. Maybe I snapped the second my mom shook me awake and whispered, "There's been an accident," in my half-dreaming ear. I hadn't believed her. I clung to her shoulders until her forehead crinkled in pain and her brown eyes started to leak tears. My mom isn't much of a crier. She prefers to choke down all her feelings and let them out in fizzing bursts.

She had left me alone in my room. The first thing I did was roll over and grab my phone, the impulse to text Riley and ask if it was true so strong that it momentarily wiped away my reasoning. And then I dropped the phone onto the carpet. My nails clawed into my sheets. My body writhed, possessed by blinding pain. That's when the screaming started, rising out of me without my permission. Guttural screams tore through my throat until I was sure my esophagus would crack and bleed, leaving me permanently silenced.

Maybe that's the moment I snapped.

I could go home now, change into my pajamas, and hunker down with a steady stream of Disney movies and hot cocoa until I can stand to face the world without my friend. I could drag out my old jewelry supplies—abandoned when my crafting turned to spellwork—and count seed beads onto string. How many bracelets could I make before I successfully brainwashed myself into ignoring everything I know about Riley and buying the lie the police fed us about the Fairmont Academy suicide pact?

Something thumps outside, yanking me back to the here and now as my skin ices over with fear. I realize that I have never been in the house alone before. Normally, I'd look to Riley. She's the one with a plan. Without her, I'm aimless.

I swallow. The air is thick with floral smoke. It sticks in the back of my throat as my boots creep across the floor. It's probably raccoons under the porch or the wind rattling through the shutters. My fingers start to tremble, but I open the door anyway, swiftly, ready to run past whoever is lurking on the other side and straight on until I make it back to my car.

But there's no one there. The porch rattles under my feet, and in the distance, a car radio fades up the winding road. No one ever drives all the way out here. Even Riley and I have always been careful to park up at the top of the long tree-lined driveway and walk down so that no one spots us trespassing.

Something catches my eye. Under one of the boarded-up windows near the front of the house is a white box. It stands out starkly against the porch.

A FedEx box.

Of course. I've never been here for a drop-off before. I forgot that I'm supposed to be at school. The world is a different place between eight and four.

It takes some balancing to get from one side of the porch to the other. The wood creaks under my weight, and I think of Riley's rough laugh when we first started exploring the house. "It's old as hell, Mila. It doesn't care how much you weigh. It'll screech under any weight at all."

I pick up the box. It's addressed to Serafina Pekkala, care of Yarrow House.

Serafina Pekkala is the witch from *The Golden Compass*, one of Riley's all-time favorite books.

My pulse quickens. Riley bought almost all her supplies at Lucky Thirteen. But every now and then she'd find something online that Toby didn't have in the store, usually from the Hoodwitch or the Wiccan superstore in the Bay Area. And she'd have it delivered here under the name of whatever famous witch she thought of while she was checking out. There had been a book of sigils for Strega Nona, a bottle of pure cardamom oil for

Winifred Sanderson, and a set of *Alice in Wonderland* tarot cards delivered to Pansy Parkinson—Riley was firmly pro-Slytherin.

The box clutched in my hands, I run back into the kitchen, not remembering to be mindful of the loose planks. The door rattles shut behind me. My head swivels as I push aside the bric-a-brac on the shelves, searching. Cold metal touches my palm, and I give a squeak of victory as I pull the ceremonial dagger off the shelf. Its handle, inset with a gigantic fake ruby, glints in the dim light. Despite its six-inch-long blade, Riley and I never used it for anything except cutting twine off the dried herbs. Toby gave it to us as part of a Black Friday sale last year. It's a silly thing, basically a gigantic fancy letter opener. But the edge is sharp enough. I plunge it into the tape holding the box together, slicing open the cardboard and peeling it back.

Inside is the oldest book I've ever seen. The cover is smooth, like the most worn parts of my Doc Martens. The spine is rough red fabric. There is no title anywhere to be seen. And no receipt to give it away.

Letting the dagger and the box fall to the floor, I settle the book gently into my lap. It is massive, almost too wide for me to hold in my hands. The pages smell like a thousand used bookstores as I turn them. The font is as absurdly ceremonial as the dagger— faux German-looking, as though every single page should start with *Once upon a time . . .* Except they don't say that. Instead they say things like *Coax the Rain from the Sky* and *Draw the Rot from the Heart of Your Enemies.*

Each spell is more dramatic than the last, with ingredients

lists longer than any I've ever seen before. I don't know how many spells I read through before I get to the last one. Nothing else matters once I reach the page that says, *The Seven-Day Breath of Life*. In spidery handwriting, there's an annotation next to the spell's title in rust-colored ink. It says, *Lazarus*.

Hot tears spill out of the corners of my eyes for the first time in two days. I know wherever Riley is, she sent this book to me. She gave me something more valuable than her killer's name. She sent me the key to bringing *her* back. If magic is about being grateful, I'm more grateful than I've ever been before. There's hope. For the first time since Riley went down to the creek, something other than darkness cracks open in my chest.

"Thanks, friend," I whisper.

FOUR

ON THE OUTSIDE, the magic-supply shop is a cute yellow Victorian house with wisteria vines dripping down from its white gingerbread trim. It's in the middle of a row of similarly pastel houses, a block over from the heart of downtown Cross Creek. Most people wouldn't notice it at all except there's usually spillover parking from the movie theater in front of it. Even then, they'd have to notice the small sign in the window: *Blessed Be, We're Open.*

Or they'd have to do what Riley did when we were in middle school and Google "Wiccan supplies near me." That's the only way we even knew to call it Lucky Thirteen since it isn't written anywhere on the outside.

My eyeliner is smudged from my quick cry at Yarrow House, but I rub it under my lashes with my thumb until it's punk-rock smudgy instead of sad-girl runny. It wasn't that neat to begin with. My hands have been wracked with lack-of-sleep tremors for the last couple of days. The adrenaline coursing through me isn't helping. My heart is racing like it's Christmas morning.

I can bring her back. I can fix this.

I leave my backpack in the trunk of my car so that my truancy is less obvious. My parents haven't called my phone yet, so I figure I've got until the end of the school day until Fairmont tells them that I left. I might as well make the most of my free time.

The moment I'm through the door with the bells tinkling behind me, I'm crushed into Toby's sharp freckled collarbones. Every day, no matter what, she smells like medical marijuana and sandalwood, although when Riley and I first started hanging out at the store, we'd only been able to identify one of those scents.

Toby doesn't look like the owner of a yellow Victorian house or a Wiccan store. She's half a wrinkle away from looking more biker grandma than biker chick. Her skin is saddle-leather, pre-melanoma tan and covered in tattoos done by different artists. Her long hair might be white with bleach or age.

"Oh, Mila," she says, stepping back but squeezing my shoulders to hold me in place. Her eyes scan my face wildly. "I'm sorry I didn't go to the service. I knew I wouldn't be welcome. But you haven't left my thoughts."

I flinch a smile at her. "Thanks. I'm okay."

She releases me and starts to weave between the round tables set around what had once been the living room of the little house. I always wondered if Riley felt comfortable here because she also lived in the same building as her family's business.

Unlike the Greenway Funeral Home, not much has been done to disguise this room's original use. A velvet rope is stretched across the bottom of the staircase next to the door, keeping people from wandering up to Toby's bedroom. The long glass case with the cash register blocks the path to the hallway leading to the rest of the house; packs of tarot cards and handblown glass wands sit inside the case, obscuring the view of what's beyond. The fireplace is uncovered, stacked with wood waiting for the cold to deepen. There are expensive statues lining the mantel and the windowsills. The books on the built-in bookcases sit face-out with neon orange price tags stuck to their covers.

There are no other customers. There rarely are.

Toby scoops small gemstones into her palm and opens a tiny velvet sachet to pour them into. I recognize the beginnings of a charm bag. I have one in my underwear drawer to summon my true love to me—*way to ignore the call, Xander*—and one in the glove compartment in my car that's supposed to increase my luck—which it failed to do the day that Dan Calalang dinged my side door.

"Now would be a good time for you to come join my circle," Toby says, pivoting toward the farthest wall. A scoop of dried rosemary goes into the bag, followed by salt. Sometimes, magic looks a lot like how my mom prepares chicken. Riley would say that's because food is magic, too. "I always worried about you girls practicing on your own, away from a guiding hand. Too many prepackaged, inorganic spells. Plastic will choke your magic like soda-can rings around a duck's neck. The Goddess can't reach you through fossil fuels."

Says the biker.

"Toby, most of our store-bought spells came from you."

"*Most*," she underlines. "You have so much unfocused power inside of you. It's a gift and a curse in someone so young."

I try not to roll my eyes. Toby's campaign to get me and Riley to join her coven has been long running. Riley thought she was probably lonely. There couldn't be that many other witches in the area. I agreed, but was still not down with the idea of hanging out with a bunch of strange adults, working spells together.

I mean, I like Toby, but I don't know her well enough not to have some stranger-danger alarms go off at the idea of hanging out alone with her and her friends. The risk of there being some kind of nudity or blood ritual seems way too high for my comfort level. At the very least, I never want to get high with someone older than my parents.

"I think I'm going to stay solo for a while," I say. "I'm not really a group-worship person."

I focus on the nearest table of gemstones. For the resurrection spell, I need a stone strong enough to help ground my magic and open the link between me and wherever Riley is. There's a beautiful iron rose hematite on display that would empty out my bank account, leaving me a pedestrian until my grandma sends my yearly Christmas cashier's check. But I can't really put a price on bringing Riley back, can I? Plus, the petals are naturally formed, not carved like the polished quartzes and trashy ambers next to it. If that isn't real-life magic, then I don't know what is.

Toby nods, looking crestfallen as she slips a white candle into the charm bag. She draws the strings closed and ties them in a loose knot. "It's an open invitation. We're here whenever you want company, even if it's just for the holidays."

I run my fingers over the iron rose's petals. They are rough and sharp. "Like my family only going to church on Christmas?"

"Hopefully less grudging than that." She hands me the charm bag, her face softening as much as its sun damage will allow. "Here's a little something to help you rest. You can always come to me for magic help. Any questions at all. You know you can't trust any of the spells you find on the internet, right? Most of it is rhyming bullshit made up by tweens and people trying to make us out to look like Satanists."

"I know." I laugh. "You made me and Riley swear never to use untested spells."

"God damn right," she says, pointing a finger at me. It's a hilariously cliché witch pose, very *Wizard of Oz*.

I tuck the charm bag into the pocket of my jacket and feel the cold screen of the phone. All the ingredients I need to bring Riley back are saved to my photo gallery. It seemed more practical than dragging the giant old book around. Especially since there's literally nowhere in my room that my sisters wouldn't be able to track it down. The last thing I need is Izzy and Nora accidentally drying up the town's water supply because they burned the right series of kitchen herbs at the right point in the moon cycle.

I wonder if I can trust Toby. Bringing someone back from the dead—even for only seven days, if the title of the spell is to be believed—could cause a fuss. But the book is old enough that there's no way the spells are untested. Riley was too smart to buy bunk. And if I work the spell without telling Toby, it could hurt her feelings. She's only ever tried to help me and Riley. She said herself that she would have gone to Riley's funeral if the Greenway parents wouldn't have gone berserk.

"Actually," I say on a shaky exhale, "there is something that I need your help with. Before she—well, it doesn't matter when—Riley bought a really old grimoire. It has some really intense spells in it with the longest ingredients lists I've ever seen. But it has a resurrection spell in it. They call it *The Seven-Day Breath*—"

I start to reach for my phone to show her the pictures, but her hand shoots out and stops me. The tips of her nails bite into the soft skin at my wrist. Her grip is at least three times as strong as I would have guessed. I can feel my bones bruising as the muscles in her forearm strain against the faded dream catcher tattoo she got at whatever point in the past appropriating cultures eternally onto your skin was the cool thing to do. The pain forces me to make eye contact with her, falling deep into the unfamiliar fury that has replaced her wizened stoner sleepiness.

"Is that a joke?" she hisses.

I swallow, attempting to pull my arm back an inch. I can't budge it. "No. I'm serious. The grimoire is hand-lettered, and there's no copyright, so I'd guess it's pretty old." I make a fist and her nails dig deeper. "You're hurting me."

She doesn't appear to hear me. Or she doesn't care. "The dead do not walk. Not ever. Not even for a moment. In metaphors or allegories, maybe, but never literally. It's against nature. It defies the will of the Goddess."

"You don't understand." I yank my arm back and cradle it against my stomach. Red crescent welts stare up at me where her nails cut into me. "Riley didn't kill herself, Toby. She was murdered. The police aren't investigating it because they think she's just another Fairmont Academy suicide, but it's not true. There's a murderer loose in Cross Creek. And Riley needs to tell us who it is. She needs to come back."

"Whatever magic you work comes back against you times three," Toby says, her face pinched into a possum sneer. "You know that! I've told you that a thousand times. What do you think the price of bringing back the dead is? Of working in opposition to nature? Did you ever think that maybe that's what happened to your friend to begin with? She always had designs on magic too big for her capability and dragged you along with her. Always wanting to see the future, throwing money into magic like she could bribe a better result out of the Goddess."

"That's not true!" My voice echoes off the walls. Hurt, inside and out, is starting to singe at the edges of the gratitude I felt at Yarrow House. I think back to the moment that the book fell open to the Lazarus spell, the moment of pure clarity. That had to be a sign from Riley. It's too big for coincidence.

"Then where did this grimoire come from, huh?" Toby's voice hatchets into my thoughts. "Any book that purports to have the answer to death isn't Wicca, I'll tell you that much. This is some dark shit. You are inviting the devil to your door."

"Wiccans don't believe in the devil," I snap back at her.

Her eyes narrow. "Don't tell me what we do and don't believe. I've been a practicing witch since before your mama dropped her first egg. And I know damn well enough not to go around trying to tamper with death. If you go rummaging around in the darkness, you'll only bring more darkness down on yourself. Do you hear me? People need to stay dead. And some people have to go early." She presses her lips together until the blood runs out of them and they're stark white against her face. It makes her look ancient, skull-like. "I know what it's like to have your life ripped open by grief. I know how it can make you do things you'd normally have the sense to fight. Don't let it take your sanity. Stay in the light, Mila. Please."

I know now that I've lost another one. Another adult who looks at me and only sees crazy. No one is going to understand that I have to try to bring Riley back. The only person who could understand is the one who needs my help.

As much as I want to set every bridge in my life ablaze, I will still need ingredients from here. When Riley is back, she'll want to be welcome here. So, I swallow down the vitriol in my throat, self-poisoning instead.

"You're right," I hear myself say. "I'm being stupid. Childish."

"It isn't childish to miss your friend," Toby says, her voice sliding into the same register Dr. Miller had used with me at the beginning of our meeting. Placating and distantly afraid. Of me or for me, I don't know. I don't care.

I promise to come back another day when I'm ready to work a minor spell again. Something light, I say. A devotion for Samhain.

When Toby turns her back, I scoop up the iron rose hematite and slip it next to the velvet bag in my jacket pocket.

Rosemary for remembrance, salt to ward off negativity. It's a mourning bag.

But I'm done mourning.

FIVE

I HAVE A notebook open on my bed. The iron rose I took from Lucky Thirteen is balanced on the corner where I normally write my name and class period. My phone is tucked between two pillows, showing the list of ingredients so I can copy it down. Unlike the spells Riley and I were used to, the grimoire demands fresh supplies. Lucky Thirteen and Etsy won't cut it this time.

Beeswax candles. A trip to Walmart. Easy!

White petals that bloomed in the shadow of the full moon. Harder.

The question that needs answering. Hardest. And possibly a riddle.

Everything else is mostly what you'd expect from a resurrection spell, blood and bone and breath. Spiderwebs damp with dew. Salt to open up the earth so that Riley can step out without ruffling the party dress they buried her in.

On the other side of my closed bedroom door, I hear the sounds of family dinner. Plates tinkling against the table and cups being filled with water, voices mingling together in a well-trod dance.

For a second, I wonder when they will talk about me. They obviously notice that I'm in my room instead of sitting in the empty chair next to Nora. It's never acceptable to miss family dinner. I can't count how many times my phone rang while I was studying at Riley's after school, Mom's voice on the other end. "*Dinner is in twenty minutes,*" she'd warn. Enough time to make it back, roll out the placemats while Izzy put down paper towels and Nora counted out silverware.

Not tonight, though. I heard the warning knock on Izzy and Nora's door, but mine never came.

It's not that I'm not hungry. I'm just not hungry enough to sit still and listen to my sisters recount every minuscule detail of their days—the trials of middle school and the meaningless con-versations with all their totally alive friends. I don't want Mom and Dad to ask me anything about my day, but I also know that it'll hurt like hell if they don't.

There's no winning. So, I'm going to stay alone for everyone's sake.

Turning my attention back to the spell, I notice that one of the last ingredients is "a heart to beat for each day he walks." The spell is written in masculine pronouns, but that's not the crappi-est part: All the "hearts" need to be buried alive in the grave dirt, sort of like life jumper cables. Which means I need seven crea-tures small enough to be buried alive.

Shit. I don't feel great about killing seven things.

But the spell isn't specific about what needs to be buried. I could get some bugs into a jar. Or I could outsource the job so that I can focus on the bigger stuff.

Despite all of Toby's warnings, I've done some deep Googling to try to decipher the spell's wording. Like when it says that I need an "anchor" to Riley's physical body, I'm afraid that it means her hair or spit or other organic material. Exactly zero of my possessions have Riley's DNA floating around on them, which is great for not being a murder suspect but turns out to be a real hindrance when it comes to bringing her back to life.

Blood pounds in my ears, the rumble of a breakdown getting closer and closer—the thunder preceding a storm. I try to cling to the feeling I had when I first opened the grimoire, or when I could hear Riley's voice so clearly at the memorial service. That feeling of her nearby, nudging me toward the right answer.

The next full moon is Saturday, so I have one shot to find fresh, lunar-light-infused flowers or else I'll have to wait a whole month before I can perform the spell. And I don't know if Riley can wait that long. The book doesn't say anything about how fresh she'll be when she wakes up, but I figure a month from now her body will be past the point of resurrection: rotten and deformed and smelling so bad that not even her cotton candy perfume could cover it. And who knows how many other people could be dead by then?

There's a knock on my door. I have just enough time to slap my notebook closed before the knob turns, revealing Nora's nose sneaking around the corner a moment before the rest of her body follows, a plate of chicken and rice in hand. Izzy hangs back in the doorway.

I sit up, feeling a wave of terror as Nora moves to set the plate in my hands. There has literally never been a plate of food in my room before. It's one of my parents' house rules. Eating alone would mean that you weren't eating with the family—a cardinal sin, according to Mom—and you could be attracting ants, Dad's greatest nemesis. He flipped his shit when they got into the garage over the summer. And the garage is basically outside.

"I'm not allowed," I start to protest, but the plate is in my hands and Nora is dropping a fork and a paper towel onto the bed next to the iron rose.

"Tonight you are," she chirps. Her voice is high and soft, making her sound younger than she is. Sometimes, when I hear her talk, I expect to look up and see a round-bellied preschooler instead of a sixth-grader with a braces-lisp and bra straps constantly falling down.

"We could get ants," I say, looking over Nora's shoulder at Izzy, who shrugs.

"Then you'll have to cast a spell to get rid of them," she says blandly.

I choose to ignore this, picking up the fork from the sheets and starting to scoop rice into my mouth. It's obviously the end of the pot—too few chickpeas, oilier than normal—but I can't complain since I'm getting special treatment. Plus, since I walked out of school before lunch, I haven't had anything to eat since this morning.

My sisters watch me eat, showing no signs of leaving. Nora looks around the room greedily, a burglar scouting her next score. I don't know why she thinks that my stuff is any better than what's in her and Izzy's room, except that she doesn't see it quite as often. I slide the iron rose under my pillow. I don't want her getting any ideas about taking it. Riley needs it to live, and I worked hard stealing it for myself.

"I need a favor," I say, swallowing hard and wishing I had something to drink. Bits of rice and chickpea skin cling to the back of my throat. Dad must have cooked tonight; he never shucks the chickpeas. "Can you catch seven to ten moths for me? Big monstery ones. Like from the front porch light."

I quickly go back to eating, sawing into the chicken breast on my plate and ignoring how the temperature of the room changes. I didn't think it was possible for my sisters to look at me any harder, but curiosity sharpens their attention. I think if they could, they'd carve my secrets out of me with the side of a spoon like guts from a pumpkin. I don't think they would like what they found, though. Other than one plan to resurrect my dead friend, it's mostly sex dreams about Xander and wishing I had cool clothes from Torrid like Aniyah Dorsey.

"Is this for magic?" Nora asks, still too young for tact.

I remember being eleven. At eleven you still tell everyone everything. At eleven I told my whole family how cute Riley's big brother was and how I wanted to go to Fairmont Academy just like him. I'm sure Nora has told the entire sixth grade that her sister is a witch. I hope it doesn't get her ass kicked.

"No," I lie blithely, helping myself to another bite of chicken.

"Mom doesn't allow magic in the house," Izzy says. She sweeps her hair over her shoulder and looks toward the kitchen. It feels like a threat.

"That's why there isn't any," I say, my tone cultivated to be the height of blasé. I've had more practice than either of them.

Nora has nervous hands, like me, and they fidget and twitch against her stomach. She's been learning origami, but she presses her seams too tight without checking for clean lines.

"I'll do it," she says.

Thank the Goddess. I would let out a sigh of relief, but I don't want to spew dinner all over my sheets.

I start to say thank you, but Nora cuts me off, pointing at my dresser.

"I want your *Moana* doll."

My head snaps toward the precious stuffed pig standing guard over my seldom-used retainers. "My Pua?"

"You're too old to have so many stuffies," Izzy says from the door.

"Whoa," I say. "I don't police your toys."

"That's because I don't have that many toys," Izzy says. "They're for babies."

"Pretty snarky for someone who put out cookies for Santa last year."

"I did that for Nora!" she snaps.

"I'll get your moths," Nora interrupts, louder than I want. I check the door for signs of Mom or Dad but only see Izzy's eyes roll. "But I want Pua. You don't even sleep with it."

She's right. And it's a small price to pay.

"Fine," I say, heaving my shoulders like this is the greatest of burdens. Nora likes to feel like she's really triumphed over the rest of us. "But you'd better keep those moths alive until I need them. Make sure they have air and food."

"Okay." She skips over to the dresser and yanks down the stuffed pig. Is it my imagination or does he look sad to leave with her? "If Mom asks, tell her it's for science."

"It kind of is," I say to her back as she shoves past Izzy to go put her prize pig in a place of honor in their room.

Izzy hovers in the doorway, watching as I dig back into dinner. She flips her hair to one side. The yellow highlights one of her friends bleached into the black glint in the light from my ceiling fan. I wish the highlights didn't look so good. They make me question keeping my hair its natural color.

"You waiting to take my plate?" I ask her.

"No." She snorts and folds her arms over her chest. I know everyone is a snot in the eighth grade, but as the second-born Flores, Izzy has had this too-good-for-everyone attitude from the moment she was born. She has already informed our parents that she has too many friends to follow me to Fairmont next year. She wants to go to Cross Creek High. And, really, good for her. I wouldn't want to follow me to school either.

"So?" I ask, my cheeks bulging with rice. Not that they need help. Looking at Izzy is a reminder that Mom's chipmunk cheeks are an inescapable family curse. I could keep two days' worth of food stored in these babies. "I'm not going to bribe you into not blabbing to Mom and Dad about the moths."

She casts a sneering look around the room, eyes darting from my Stay Weird poster to the collection of washi tape above my desk to the pile of eyeliner pencils on top of my nightstand. Her gaze finally lands on my rumpled purple sheets. "I don't want any of this stuff," she says, before pushing herself off the wall and walking over to me. She reaches into the pocket of her pants and pulls out a black ponytail holder. She holds it out, within my reach.

"Um," I say, deeply confused. It is not the first time that Izzy has complained about my hair—according to her it's too long and thick and straight and boring—but it *is* the first time she has interrupted a meal to insult me. I set down my fork with a sigh. "Thanks?"

"My friend Emma wears one of these when she gets depressed," she says, the words too fast, like she rehearsed them and her speech isn't going according to plan. One of her front teeth digs into her lower lip. "She snaps it against her wrist when she starts to feel numb. I thought . . . I don't know—here." She thrusts the piece of elastic into my hand. "When you scream—even when it's into your pillow—it freaks everyone out. Nora, mostly. But also all of us? Just try something else, okay?"

I take a second, the band pinched between my thumb and forefinger. Anger flares in me, as hot and fast as a lighter blazing against a candle wick. Shame sweeps in behind it. I imagine my sisters on the other side of my bedroom wall, hearing every scream and sob of the last week. Mom and Dad forbade me from talking about Riley's death in front of Izzy and Nora because the topic was "too mature." I didn't consider that they might not be scared of death as much as they're scared of what's happening to me.

"Yeah, okay," I say quietly. I roll the band over my wrist. There's a long black hair attached to it, and I don't know if it's Izzy's or Nora's. Or maybe it's mine, a ghost of ponytails past. I pull it off before it can fall onto my plate. As it floats down to the floor, a jolt of inspiration hits me.

I know where to get a piece of Riley's DNA.

SIX

THE DRIVEWAY AT the Greenways' house curves up the side of the lawn, the concrete immaculately smooth and wide. It ends under a carport with stone pillars next to a set of double doors that, when open, lead either to the showroom on the main floor or to the morgue in the basement, depending on how alive the passenger is. Today, the gleaming black hearse is missing from the top of the driveway. Mr. Greenway must be out—retrieving or delivering, I'm not sure.

Xander's car, a silver Honda with a license plate number I may or may not have memorized, is parked beside the neighbor's red elderberry tree. In the branches, I spot the white fur of Binx, Riley's outdoor cat. I make a quiet clicking sound to see if I can lure him out of the tree, but his eyes watch me with lazy disinterest. *Ungrateful asshole.* I've fed him so often over the years, even though wet cat food smells like dumpster custard.

The Greenways' neighborhood is covered in a blanket of dead leaves that crunch and squish under my boots. I don't know how many times I walked this block with Riley—shuffling between our houses before I got my grandpa's old car, coming back from Lucky Thirteen with contraband in our pockets. Laurel Street has always been the road to Riley.

I look up at the house, a rush of pain passing through me as I realize that she won't be on the other side of the door. Instead, she's underground in one of the caskets from the showroom—the best one, the one made from high-gloss cherrywood and lined with cream-colored velvet. She's empty, her body purposeless without the essence of her inside.

Heart hammering in my chest, I grab the hair band on my wrist, pull it back as far as it will go, and release.

"Shit, shit, shit." I can't help but yelp out loud as the elastic snaps against my flesh. Tears sting at the corners of my eyes, but at least they're tears of pain. Sadness is my enemy now. It means admitting defeat. And I am not defeated yet.

I hustle past the large street-facing GREENWAY FUNERAL HOME sign that fences in most of the perfectly maintained front lawn, which—regardless of drought or season—is Crayola green. I open the front door and step inside before I can chicken out.

I know it's been just days since the last time I was here, but the main floor of the house looks so different. The wallpaper is still covered in yellow flowers tangled together in endless loops, but the color seems brighter with the light coming in from the big front windows. The heavy burgundy carpeting is homey, but it's freshly vacuumed and seemingly untouched. There's no cheesy music playing or people shedding tears over someone they didn't even know.

There's also no sign of the Greenways.

The showroom, with its neatly buffed caskets and dust-magnet display urns, is empty. I can't say that I'm disappointed not to find Mrs. Greenway behind the service counter. I really didn't want to have to talk to her, knowing that she'd likely derail my plan. Or ask why I'm not in school.

Xander has been out all week. Not that I blame him. People were already starting to act like vultures at the funerals. There's no way he'd be safe in the Fairmont halls, where the rules of decency are nonexistent and the prying questions and shitty comments are endless.

He is safe here. Riley always said that when she and Xander were younger, no one ever wanted to play at their house because they lived above the funeral parlor. They couldn't have birthday parties in the apartment because other kids would refuse to come past the showroom. I've never seen anyone other than the Greenways on the third floor. Xander stopped inviting people over after Chloe Wellington, one of Fairmont's resident pseudo-goths, tried to convince him to fool around in the morgue.

Could Chloe Wellington have killed Riley to punish Xander for embarrassing her? June Phelan-Park did tell the entire school about how Chloe had a secret Tumblr full of poetry about Xander rejecting her.

The door to the third floor is locked to keep out unexpected guests and to alert the Greenways to the presence of customers. I press the doorbell. The chimes are ominous and loud enough to be heard in every single room of the three-story house. I stuff my hands into the pockets of my jacket, pushing past the empty plastic sandwich bags hidden inside. I dig my nails into the creases of my palm, one by one. Life line. Head line. Scar from burning my hand on the stove in second grade. Heart line.

There's a pitter-patter of footsteps. The deadbolt shifts. The door opens, and Xander is on the other side, guilelessly handsome in a gray T-shirt and blue plaid pajama pants. My brain momentarily short-circuits, imagining him rolling out of bed to answer the door, his long limbs tangled in the sheets, his arms stretching out the knots of sleep, his shirt riding up his stomach.

"Hey," he says, resting his shoulder against the doorframe. He doesn't sound unhappy to see me. His eyes flick toward the carpet for a single bashful moment as he combs his nails through his hair and it falls into a perfect part. His geometrically impossible cheekbones flex with a smile. "Is everything okay? You aren't here for business, are you?"

What a tactful way to ask if anyone else at school is dead.

"No," I say with a sharp shake of my head that spills hair into my face. I brush it away with itching fingers. "I, um—this is kind of awkward, but I left some stuff in Riley's room? Before she . . ." I trail off, praying he won't ask what I'm looking for. This is a recon mission of the sketchiest variety. I need to stuff my pockets with as much loose hair and other random Riley-samplings as possible. Fingers crossed for fingernails.

"Of course," he says hoarsely. "Come on up."

After making sure to lock the door behind us, I follow the sway of his hips up the narrow staircase to the family's apartment. The stink of pollen and petals on the edge of decay and old flower water coats the inside of my nose, making my head ache. Bursts of lilies and irises and white roses in vases wrapped in black ribbons line every flat surface we pass: the entryway table with the labeled key hooks mounted above it, the china hutch in the dining room, the long wooden table, the mantel in the living room, covered in stiffly posed portraits of the Greenways smiling in a field or sitting on their couch or piled into the back of the hearse.

I catch sight of a card nestled inside a spray of carnations. *To Xander*, it reads. *You're in our prayers. Love, the Fairmont Show Choir.*

The vase next to that, filled with roses, has a card signed *Dr. Cora Miller*.

These aren't touching tributes to Riley at all. They are offerings to the King of Fairmont Academy from his loyal subjects. June's friends. Staff members taking breaks from writing his college recommendation letters. More people clamoring to be close to Xander.

Because now he isn't just the hot guy with a dead girlfriend. He's walking, talking tragedy porn. People will claw their way toward him the same way they watch Lifetime movies or read Nicholas Sparks novels—enraptured with the pain clouding his formerly perfect life.

No one who sent these flowers cares about Riley at all.

The thought makes me want to start smashing things. To yank fistfuls of petals and shred them down to white mulch. To crunch vases under my heel.

Would Xander help? Does he hate these symbols of false grief as much as I do? I'm scared to ask in case it makes me look jaded. Maybe he truly appreciates everyone keeping his family in their thoughts, even if they never did when Riley was alive.

Thankfully, the back hallway is devoid of flowers. The long wall of beige paint is broken up by doors—Mr. and Mrs. Greenway's bedroom, Xander's room, the bathroom, and, finally, Riley's room. The door is closed. Maybe they like it better this way, the hope that maybe, just maybe, she's on the other side.

Xander doesn't hesitate before walking into her bedroom, but I do. I wasn't expecting him to stay. Instead of looking for the items I'm here to steal, I watch him sit on the edge of Riley's day-bed. The comforter wrinkles under the weight of him.

He looks up at me. His eyes are ice blue. Not the color winter *is* but the color winter *feels*. The color behind your lids when peppermint floods your sinuses. The color the guy who wrote the *Pocahontas* songs meant when he made up the phrase *blue corn moon*.

Other people would call it *sky blue*, but the sky has never made me want to strip off all my clothes and rub myself against it, so I'm not convinced that's the right term.

He shifts to the side, making space for me. Not an offensive amount of space—some people eyeball me and think I need yards of room to sit—but enough that I won't have to brush by him to get comfortable.

"You left the funeral before I could talk to you," he says, his tone light and nonjudgmental.

I settle down next to him and fold my hands in my lap. I peer up at the string of lifeless twinkle lights hanging above the bed. I remember how Riley used to leave them on at night, yellow pinpricks casting shadows against the pale turquoise paint. "I know. I'm sorry. I couldn't hang anymore. It was too—"

"Fake?" he supplies. The corner of his mouth lifts in a sad smile. "Dad says that funerals are for the living, but, man, Riley really would have hated the whole thing."

My heart flutters with a lightness I haven't felt in days, and it takes me a moment to recognize it as comfort. "Yes, exactly. It felt like she was missing from it, you know? I mean, come on, who invited the show choir?"

He huffs out a breath that sounds a bit like a laugh. "My mom, of course. She thought they were a nice touch at June and Dayton's service." Invoking his friends' names washes the glimpse of happiness off his face. Deflecting, he throws the heat to me. "You haven't gone back to school yet?"

I twitch a shrug. "I made it about halfway through yesterday and then walked out of a meeting with the school psych. She called my parents and said that I might not be ready to interact with the public yet."

"I don't think *she's* ready to interact with the public. She's kind of a trip," he says. His shoulders roll back, stretching his chest.

The soft crackle of joints and bones makes his insides sound like a campfire. "She cornered me after Riley's service, tried to get me to have a session right there. I told her that we have our own grief counselor—we're a funeral home, you know—and she still went to my parents, asking permission to have daily meetings with me when I go back to school."

"I don't recommend even one meeting with her." I shudder at the thought. "Are you coming back to school?"

"Ever?" he teases, and I'm living for the flash of teeth he gives me. "Of course. I'm going to finish my senior year. I need to graduate. And there are people depending on me—honor society and the Rausch Committee. I'm a peer counselor, too. But my parents don't want me to rush into going back. They've already gone back to work, but they'll come up here randomly during the day and just . . . *look* at me. Like they're checking to make sure that I'm still here. They didn't know she was out when she died." He closes his eyes. His lashes are unfairly long. Of course, he's never had them snap off while wearing three coats of waterproof mascara. "They never knew where she was. They kept pushing her away, making her pretend to be something she wasn't. I keep thinking if they'd just let her be Wiccan instead of pretending like she quit because they forced her to, would she still be here? Would she have told them where she was going that night? Would she have told me? I was with June's family, at the funeral reception. When I came home, she was gone, and my parents had no idea."

"I didn't know either," I say, my voice suddenly working hard to be more than a whisper. I haven't been able to say this to anyone yet. There hasn't been anyone to hear it. "I left her here after June and Dayton's service. I had a paper to write, so I told her that I'd talk to her in the morning and warned her not to text me unless it was the biggest emergency. I don't even know why she would go near the creek." My sinuses burn, and I scrub under my eyes to keep the tears from spilling. "And maybe if I hadn't told her not to bother me, she would have told me why she was going down there. I could have saved her—"

I almost divulge my theory about Riley's murder and the spell that could bring her back. But I stop myself mid-breath. Xander is burdened with enough right now. If I succeed in raising Riley from the dead, he can reap the benefit without having to know how it happened. I lost my best friend, but he lost his friends *and* his sister. I can't complicate that with thoughts of murder and revenge.

"No." He leans toward me, his face open and imploring. "No, you can't think like that. You can't blame yourself for her death. Don't even think it for a second."

He reaches into the foot of propriety between us and scoops up my hand. His fingers brush against the elastic on my wrist, scorching my skin. I swallow, hypnotized by a half-healed scratch on the curve of his thumb. Paper cuts are as common at Fairmont as racism and Adderall addictions. But the line is jagged and swollen, an odd imperfection against his flawless white skin. His hand squeezes mine, and I can feel myself shiver from the tips of my boots all the way to the roots of my hair.

Focus on his giant forehead, I tell myself. It's large enough to almost be a flaw. But it's also ample space for a single lock of hair to coil seductively. Fuck. I wonder if I rubbed my face against his face, memorizing the texture of his skin and the curve of his bones, if I could finally shake loose from this pathological jonesing. Or would the flames roar higher and swallow my entire life?

"Mila," he says, branding this moment to my brain forever. What is it about hearing your name on the lips of your crush that makes it seem like an utterly new sound? In Xander's mouth, my name is a dark flower blooming. "You were the best friend my sister ever had. She was so lucky to have you."

The idea settles over me, a drizzle of ice water that turns to a downpour. Thank you, Alexander Greenway, for finding the off-switch to my lust—good old-fashioned guilt. Here I am, sitting on my dead best friend's bed, being comforted by her grieving, tortured older brother, and I'm trying to write a letter to *Penthouse* in my head?

"Thank you," I whisper, sneaking my hand out of his grip. I finger the elastic band, longing to give it a tug. "I really needed to hear that. I just . . . I miss her so much. Every place I go without her is worse because she's not there. She should be here and at Yarrow House and at school. And when she's not, I feel like it makes me shittier. I've been totally unbearable to be around."

"I doubt that." He kicks one of my boots with his toes. "I'm bearing it pretty okay, I think."

"Then you're immune to my venom."

"Maybe I've got too much venom of my own."

I smile at him. I can't help it. Xander is so the opposite of me.

He has that alluring Greenway personality that makes people want to be near him even when they can't pinpoint why. People are literally drawn to him, to his easy smile and winking blue eyes.

He's not a fat witch who freaks out his own family. Dr. Miller would never be snotty with him. She literally begged to treat him, while I walked out of her office with zero complaints.

I glance around the room. Riley wasn't the neatest person, but Mrs. Greenway is one of those moms who snoops and tidies in equal measure, and she was always on constant high alert for anything that could be vaguely magical.

"She's already starting to throw it out," Xander says, following my gaze. "The first load has already gone to Goodwill."

I snap my attention back to him. "Seriously?"

"You know my mom." He sighs. "Now that no one is using it, it's clutter. It's not right. It's like she's erasing Riley, one box at a time. I tried to stop her, but she wouldn't listen. She and my dad are at a service right now, so if there's anything you want—" He pauses and jumps to his feet. "Wait here for a second, okay?"

I blink up at him, startled. "Okay. I'm not going anywhere."

"Great." He smiles like he really means it, like my words are a strike of genuine pleasure. Then he darts out of the room.

I jump to my feet, deciding to grab the oddest memorabilia while I'm alone. The trash can is empty, ruling out nail clippings or used tissues. There is a hairbrush small enough to fit into one of the sandwich bags I brought. I don't know how much of Riley's physical body is enough for the spell—there's no measurement included in the list of ingredients. I grab a pot of Carmex and a tube of expensive lip gloss that I don't recognize and a chewed pencil covered in washi tape that we decorated the week before school started. I hope her travel toothbrush is in the bathroom. I think the family would notice if I stole her Sonicare.

Xander reappears in the doorway, and for once I can't focus on his handsome face or tight muscles. A silver chain dangles from his fingers. The pendant, a blush-pink piece of quartz shaped into a point, moves in tiny circles. It's a punch to the gut seeing it anywhere except on Riley. She was literally never without it. It was the first thing I noticed about her when we met. Every day, no matter what other jewelry she was wearing or what outfit she was in, the rose quartz was around her neck. She had purchased it from a street fair and blessed it herself. It was the first magical object she ever owned and the only one she was allowed to keep in the house. She'd convinced the pastor at church to explain to her parents that there was nothing inherently Satanic about quartz.

Not that Wicca and Satanism are anything alike, but there's no convincing Mr. and Mrs. Greenway of that.

"My parents didn't want her buried in it," Xander says, walking toward me and holding the necklace out. "Pagan jewelry, Christian burial. It's bullshit, and she'd be pissed if she knew, but . . ."

He's offering it to me, I realize.

I don't think before I blurt out, "I can't. It's Riley's."

"If my parents find it," he says patiently, "they'll throw it out again. I can't hide it forever. Riley would want you to have it."

I don't know if that's true. Riley wouldn't want to know that she had been parted from her necklace. She showered in it. She slept in it. She would have wanted to be buried in it. But I'm touched that Xander saved it for me. That he thought of me when he definitely didn't have to.

He takes my silence as consent and unclasps the necklace. I start to panic as his fingers brush my hair away from the collar of my jacket. He flourishes the chain around my neck. I can feel his breath slipping over the tip of my ear. Despite the warmth of his exhale, my spine breaks out in almost painful shivers.

The rose quartz settles above my cleavage. It looks smaller against my chest than it did on Riley.

"There," he whispers, one more puff of air against my skin. "It needed a good witch to keep it safe."

SEVEN

CREEK WATER MAKES my socks squish. I expected my boots to be more waterproof, but as I balanced on a wide rock, one arm of the Cross Creek flooded between my shoelaces and pushed past the leather tongues, drenching my feet. Shock almost made me lose hold of the mason jar I'd brought down to the shore. I can hear it sloshing inside my backpack, and I pray to the universe that none of the water spills onto the red grimoire. Or drowns the moths. Or washes the spit off the toothbrush.

I'm really wishing that the spell didn't call for "steel from the blade that felled him." Water could really fuck this thing to hell. Plus, now my clothes smell like creek.

I left my car at home. I couldn't risk the roar of the old engine waking up my parents. After days of planning and gathering up the ingredients, something as stupid as a long walk won't stand in my way. The streets of Cross Creek are empty. The waning gibbous moon turns everything I walk past a shimmering silver-white.

The cemetery gate is locked. Thankfully, Riley and I snuck out here for Samhain last year, so I easily find the short kissing gate hidden behind a willow tree. For a small town, Cross Creek has a lot of dead people. The cemetery lawn rises and falls in hills that don't feel like much in a car but have me sweating under my jacket by the time I make it to Riley's plot on the left side of the lawn. The horizon dips downhill, another couple hundred head-stones standing between me and the back gate.

There is no tombstone for Riley yet. The dirt is slightly hilled and stark brown against the grass that surrounds it. It looks exactly the way fresh graves look in the movies, poised to have an undead hand shoot up through the soil.

Oh God. I hope her hand doesn't shoot up through the soil.

Skin close to steaming, I slide off my jacket and fold it neatly to the side. I carefully pick up and set aside a giant bouquet of wilted lilies left behind from the funeral, accidentally snapping off a brittle petal when I place my backpack on the ground beside them. I have plenty of time to set up, so I take a second of silence. The stars wink at me as I hold on to the rose quartz pendant at my neck.

"Okay, Ry," I whisper into the ether, "get ready to come home. We really need you here."

The wind slides through my hair, lifting wild strands like black flags. It feels like a sign to get started.

With the grimoire propped open to the page with the Lazarus spell, I start unpacking my bag. Curved honeysuckle branches unfurl in my hand and I set them in a circle on top of the grave dirt. I pour salt inside the circle from the big Morton's container we keep at Yarrow House. Salt is integral to most spells. Four brand-new beeswax candles—*lights from a local hive*—are planted at the north, south, east, and west corners of the branches. I empty the sandwich bags of Riley-ness at the north quadrant of the circle—a mass of hair and lip gloss and a toothbrush and an old piece of gum, lumped together like the nastiest bird's nest. A pair of flip-flops—Izzy's, since her feet are smaller than mine—rest at the south quadrant. *Shoes to guide a rearward journey.* The full-moon wildflowers, spiderwebs, the iron rose hematite. A handful of pebbles, the pillowcase I cried on when I found out about Riley's death, a small mirror snapped off a foundation compact facedown in the dirt.

The big jar that normally holds change in the living room now contains moths beating their dusty wings against the glass. Nora truly earned her Pua doll. The moths are huge and have been successfully kept alive for days. I set them down carefully next to creek water.

The sound of my phone's alarm makes me jump.

Midnight. The witching hour.

I light the candles, calling down the four corners as I walk the circle. "I light this flame in the name of the North, grant me the blessings of the Earth. I light this flame in the name of the East, grant me the blessings of the Air . . ."

This I know. This is day-one stuff. Calling the corners, thanking the Goddess for her time, making my intentions clear. It's the same whether casting a spell for luck on a math test or resurrecting the dead.

I take out the velvet bag that, a couple of days ago, held Toby's mourning charm. Now it's full of herbs I need for the gardening portion of tonight. I sprinkle them inside the circle, reciting a chant I found in one of the books at Yarrow. "Let the soil be loosened, let the roots spring free, deliver what's underground unto me."

The dirt looks the same to me, but I can't waste time worrying about it. I squint at the pages of the grimoire, reading the spell as slowly as I dare and changing the pronouns as I go.

"I ask the Earth to return the unjustly dead. Infinite Mother, return her soul to the body in this soil. Set her heart to beating, as the wings of the crows fly. Balance her humors to resting." I kneel in the dirt and reach for the jar of creek water. I pour it carefully, making a wobbly power sigil inside the honeysuckle-branch circle.

"Take back the steel that stole her breath. Take back the tears I shed. Take back the time we have been parted. Bind her to her body with this dancing flame and midnight air, wishing breath and reflecting light." I dig my index finger into the dirt, making seven hash marks. The creek water makes them smear.

"Seven beating hearts to her one," I say, and it's hard not to recoil as I twist open the lid of the moth jar. I have to catch a fluttering fugitive in my hand and smack it down into the first tiny grave. I smash another to the ground, turning away from its writing body as I bury its wings. "Enough life to strike a spark." I crush each moth to the ground and scoop the crumbly soil over them. Not enough to smother them. They have to breathe until their lives trade for Riley's. "One for each day she will walk."

"Give back what was unjustly took," I say, and I'm not asking anymore. I'm telling. I'm telling the dripping beeswax candles and the moths dying in the dirt. I'm telling the stars watching over me and the wind pushing ice over my cheeks. "Hear me and heed me. This murdered girl will no longer lie. Set her feet to walking. Send her back to me."

And now the dangerous part. I lift the North candle and tip its flame into the nest of hair, then again onto my eyeliner-stained pillowcase. The flames shoot up, hot and high. The air stinks from scorched hair and melting plastic. Sparks fizz up into the breeze. I stand up straight, holding my arms over my head.

"So mote it be!" I scream at the moon, imagining every cell of power in my body as a blue lightning blaze surging downward, through the dirt and the roots and the casket. For a moment, I'm not stretch-marked skin or wet socks or girl-shaped. I am wielding the will of the Goddess herself.

Except.

There's nothing!

The twin fires in the circle die down to embers. There's no more hair. There's no more pillowcase. The lip gloss tube is melted to mush except for the thick plastic applicator. Even the wind has died down. There's nothing but the cavernous echo of failure inside me.

I crumple to the ground. Distantly, I wonder about the cops. Whether anyone driving by can see the flickering light of the candles. If I even give a shit. I'll tell them the same thing I've told everyone else—my parents, Dr. Miller, the not-going-to-help-me Goddess: My friend is dead. My friend was murdered. And I'm alone. I'll be alone whether I'm in a graveyard or the back of a cop car or at home in my room minus one Pua doll.

I beat my fist into the circle. "How could you leave me alone here? Why were you even at the creek that night? And why the fuck would anyone kill you?"

The question that needs answering. Guess I solved the riddle after all.

I hear the earthquake starting. It's like a semitruck hitting full speed, coming right at you, rumbling the ground miles below all the way up to the surface. I know I need to blow out the candles so that the quake doesn't knock them over and set the whole cemetery on fire, but nausea slams into me before the quake does. My spit goes hot and thin and clear all at once.

The ground trembles beneath me. It shakes the bile out of my throat. I roll to the side, clawing at the grass. The sounds of my heaves are buried under the roar of the plates shifting underground. I close my eyes to keep from watching my dinner fountain out. I can't seem to stop. I gasp for breath, and it only serves to refresh my body for another round. Everything is sour and hot and burning.

When the quake stops, my limbs are trembling and weak. Still shuddering, I'm curled into the fetal position with my cheek pressed into the cold ground. I hear myself whimper. I want water to rinse the bitterness out of my cheeks, but the water I brought with me is to tamp down the soil, to make sure that I don't leave any sparks behind.

Maybe I always expected the spell to fail. Riley was right. My confirmation bias is a hindrance to my magic. Or I never had any magic to begin with. The only people who ever believed that I do are Toby—a batshit biker granny—and Riley—the friend I failed to save.

The smell of cotton candy permeates the night air. It's an unmistakable scent—spun sugar swirled over flowers and baby powder. The bottle it sprays out of is round and obnoxiously pink. I saw it the day before yesterday in the bathroom above the Greenway Funeral Home. It was next to Riley's toothbrush.

"Mila?" The voice is right. Rasping and a little asthmatic.

I force myself to roll onto my back.

Riley Marie Greenway is standing in a short white party dress that's way too fancy for our surroundings and in flip-flops that are slightly too small for her feet. Her toenails have chipped black polish. I guess Mr. Greenway didn't think anyone would ever see them again. Her hair is loose around her shoulders, the bleachy yellow washed to white in the moonlight. Her dark eyebrows pinch together over her nose in a concerned slash.

"Were you puking?" she asks. Her eyelashes flutter, and she staggers forward a step, staring up at the sky. "Fuck a duck, it's cold. Why are we in the graveyard?"

I launch myself to my feet. My arms are around her shoulders, bracing her into a tight, probably smelly hug. The sweetness of her perfume isn't on her skin. It's set into the fabric of her dress. Her skin has the plastic stink of dollar-store toys—formaldehyde.

"Uh, hey, friend," she says, patting my back almost sarcastically. "Did we do a bunch of drugs I forgot about?"

I end the hug but grab on to her forearm, not ready to be separated. What if she disappears? "What's the last thing you remember? The funeral? The creek?"

"Which funeral?" She cocks her head at me. Her movements are robotic, halting, and slow. "I live in a funeral home, dude. You'll have to be way more specific." She squints at my chest. "Is that my necklace?"

I ignore the question for now. One death at a time.

"June and Dayton's service," I say slowly. Did I fuck up the spell and bring her back wrong? I try to remember any herbs for memory charms, but my mind is racing. Magic is real. Riley is real. Magic and Riley are here with me! "We went to their service on Monday, and then you—"

"June's dead?" Her eyes bug. "Holy shit! Is Xander okay? Why can't I remember any of this? Are you fucking with me?"

I did not anticipate having to break this news. I kind of thought the whole crawling-out-of-her-grave thing would be a giveaway. Although, from what I can tell, the grave seems undisturbed. While I was puking, the earthquake spit out Riley and swallowed everything inside the circle. There's no sign of the ritual left. The dirt is as smooth as if it had just been leveled with the side of a shovel. Thankfully my jacket and the grimoire are safely off to the side.

I squeeze her arm gently. "Ry, you died. You've been dead for almost an entire week."

She rears back, out of my grasp and away from me. The heel of her flip-flop stabs into the dirt, flicking soil onto her foot. She looks down and sways. When she turns back, the color has drained from her face.

"That's my grave?" she asks, but it sounds like she already knows the answer. "You brought me back?"

Briefly, says my brain, throwing a guilty look at the grimoire broadcasting that this is a seven-day deal.

"Yeah." I nod. "I did."

She lets out a long exhale, her eyes fixed on the grave dirt. "Wow. That's incredible, Blister. Really, that's beyond anything I could have ever guessed. I never would have believed that anyone could actually raise the dead. But you really did it—"

"What do you mean you wouldn't believe it?" I say, half laughing. I never thought I'd get to hear her call me "Blister" again. "The spell was in your new grimoire. The red one? Super old, giant fairy tale lettering?"

She reaches up, pressing the heel of her hand to her eye like she's dizzy. "I don't remember a new grimoire. I don't remember anything."

"It's okay!" I say quickly, grabbing her shoulder to steady her. I can feel the roughness of goose bumps on her 98.6 degree skin.

There's a zit starting to break the surface of her right temple. She's really here, too exact to be a memory. Tears splatter on my cheeks as I choke out, "You're here. It doesn't matter how."

"Actually, it really does matter how," says someone behind us.

My stomach lurches. Two figures emerge from the darkness, one taller and thin with brown bangs and impossibly long legs, the other shorter with the kewpie-doll face of a Disney Channel star.

June Phelan-Park and Dayton Nesseth. Risen from the dead.

June folds her arms over her chest, her eyes dark under blunt-cut bangs. "What the fuck did you do, Camila Flores?"

EIGHT

THE TEARS ON my face dry to a crust as June and Dayton stop at the edge of Riley's now-empty grave. I never would have guessed that raising the dead could make the cemetery look so much like homecoming. June is wearing a mustard yellow cardigan over a poofy blue dress. Dayton is covered in pink lace. Both of their necks look fine, but it's pretty dark outside since the grave stole my candles.

"You told me they were dead," Riley says, her voice edged with annoyance. I try not to be offended by her tone. I'm sure that the shock of returning to the land of the living is rough. Still, it would be comforting if Riley could smile or acknowledge how bonkers all of this is. I'm suddenly feeling very alone despite all my company.

"They *were* dead," I say, keeping one eye on June and Dayton. Like Riley, they appear unruffled by their trip topside, despite the fact that neither of them is wearing shoes and their feet are caked with mud and bits of grass.

"Oh, hi," Dayton says, batting her eyelashes and slapping on a bright, fake smile. There's a small diamond clip in her short brown hair. "What are you guys doing here? Something witchy?"

"Something freaky, more like," June says. Her lips stick out like a duck bill. "What are we doing here? What did you guys do to us?"

Riley shoots me a sidelong glance that is super familiar. She may not remember everything that's happened, but it's definitely her. The look means, *Should I cuss out these dummies, or would you like the pleasure?* I have never liked June or Dayton, but I should explain why they were accidentally ripped out of their afterlife.

"Well," I say. "I was here to work a spell—"

June rolls her eyes so hard it's almost audible.

"That seems to have brought you all back from the dead," I finish sharply. This is why I never talk to anyone about magic. Even when it literally jolts someone out of their grave, they can't help but be shitty and holier-than-thou. "I didn't mean to. I'm really sorry if you were in heaven with harps and halos and I ruined it."

Dayton's upper lip twitches. Mirroring June, she crosses her arms. "Ha. Yeah, okay. That's not even funny. It's just odd."

"Of course it is. These two are always odd," June says with a huff. She tips her head at me. She's not much taller than I am, but she manages to talk a long way down. "This whole fake-witch thing is so tired. I used to feel bad for you when people would make fun of you, but you're bringing it on yourselves now. Grow up. We're going to be seniors next year."

"*I* will be," I say, my patience starting to unravel at the edges. "You? Not so much. Because, again, you're dead. Gone. Donezo."

"Cool it before you start doing the Monty Python bird sketch," Riley says to me. She looks at June. "What's the last thing you remember? How did you get to the graveyard? Where are your shoes?"

June opens her mouth, but her eyes flash with confusion followed by a gust of anger. "If we were dead," she huffs, "then why weren't we buried?"

I rub my arms. The cold is starting to settle into my skin, but that could also be shock. I shuffle over to my jacket and tug it out from under the grimoire. The night air has chilled the denim, but I slide it on anyway. "If you weren't buried, then why are you wearing formal wear at midnight on a Sunday?"

Dayton shifts her weight from foot to foot. There is gold glitter polish on her toenails. I kind of hate how cute it looks with her dress. "So, how long have we been dead?" she asks. She's trying hard to keep her nose up, but she's not committing as hard as she was before. It could be the grass starting to make her feet itch.

"You two?" I incline my head to her and June as I button up my jacket. "Since last Saturday. Buried on Monday." I look at Riley. Even though she's right in front of me, all hale and hearty, it's hard to force the words out. "Y-you died after their service. We buried you on Wednesday morning."

"I feel weird," Dayton says, wriggling and writhing like she is trying to loosen a wedgie. She turns her head away from me and

Riley, whispering to June, "Like I'm wearing two super tampons?"

"It's gauze," Riley says. "It prevents corpse leakage."

Dayton turns back, gasping. Her giant brown eyes bulge under her eyebrows. "What would I be leaking?"

Riley takes a threatening step forward. "Whatever was left in you after embalming."

Dayton covers her mouth with a terrified squeak.

Riley smirks. I've seen her spout corpse facts to scare people before. It seems in poor taste to say it to the faces of actual corpses.

"Look," I say, "I told you I'm sorry. I brought Riley back so that we could figure out who killed her, and I guess I put more power behind the spell than I meant to. So I'll find a way to put you two back"—*in the ground? To death?*—"where you came from. Then Riley and I can get back to our business and you can get back to yours."

"You don't know who killed me?" Riley asks.

I dig my fingernails into my heart line. "You drowned in the creek. That's all we know."

Riley shivers. "Fuck a duck. I've lived here my whole life. I've never been in the creek before. It smells like sewage even up on the bridges."

"Excuse me." June snaps her fingers four times in quick succession like she's trying to get the attention of a dog. "Who the hell killed *us*?"

"Um," I say, stuffing my hands into my pockets. God, this is so awkward. "You did? You hanged yourselves."

"No, we didn't," June says, almost laughing. She plants a hand on her hip and looks to Dayton, who shakes her head in agreement.

"How the hell would you know?" I ask. "You don't even remember crawling out of your fucking graves. I went to your funeral. I read the newspaper article about it. You hanged yourselves in Aldridge Park on Saturday night. Dayton swung so hard, she lost a shoe. You had some kind of suicide pact. Sorry about it."

"No," June says again, and it's even more annoying this time because she adds a single finger wag to it that makes her look like Ms. Chu. "We wouldn't do that."

"No way," Dayton agrees. "Suicides go to hell."

"Also, why would we want to die?" June asks. "Our lives are sweet. We're pretty, popular, and it's only junior year. Plus, we haven't even been to the Rausch awards gala yet."

"And the alumni association is talking about having it catered by Olive Garden this year," Dayton adds.

"Why would someone kill Riley?" June asks, waving her hand in the air in thought. "And not us? It's nonsensical."

"You've got us there," Riley says. "You are much more murderable than I am."

"Rude," June says with a contemptuous click of her tongue. "So rude. I bet Sky Moony killed me. She was so jealous of me. Oh! Or Dawn. She copied my bangs."

"I can't believe I was murdered," Dayton says, sitting down in the dirt. She lifts her legs to her chest, carefully smoothing her skirt over them before placing her chin on her knees with a pout. It seems way too scrunched to be comfortable. Then again, my boobs would never allow for me to get my legs that close to my stomach. Dayton is exactly as delicate as I am not. "Do you have any idea how hurtful that is?"

"Being murdered?" I ask.

"It depends on how quickly your necks broke after the hanging," Riley notes. "If you suffocated, it would be long and painful."

"How could you say something like that?" June gasps, taking an affronted step back. "We just found out we were *murdered*, Riley Greenway. Have some respect."

"We were all murdered, June. Your death is not that special," Riley says.

Now that I think about it, hanging is a pretty brutal way to go. How would they have even done it themselves? Jumped off the tree branches with their nooses attached? I cringe at the thought and can't help but touch my own neck in sympathy. The girls are right; something about the suicide story definitely seems off. If Riley was murdered, maybe June and Dayton were, too.

Dayton lets out a sob. Have I mentioned how tired I am of watching people cry this week? I'm seriously over it. "I can't believe someone hated me enough to kill me." Dayton cries in tiny kitten mewls. "And now I have to live my life as a-a-a—" She starts to hiccup as tears shoot out of her eyes. I'm relieved to see that they're clear and not, like, blood or moth dust. I'm less relieved when she throws her head back and wails at the sky. "I'm a zombie!"

"Will you shut up?" I say, lowering my voice to a whisper. Not that it'll help if someone was driving by and heard the word *zombie* echoing through the night.

"Why?" June asks. "It's not like we can get in trouble."

"You might not be able to, but I sure as hell can." I look down at Dayton. "And you're not a zombie. You're *temporarily* not dead. The spell is only good for seven days."

She sniffles, her lips wobbly under her nose. "And then what?"

"And then you go back to wherever you were." I shrug. "But if you even think about eating a brain, I will plant you back in the ground myself."

This does not stop her crying.

June shows no inclination to console her friend. They are in the same boat, I guess. Everyone grieves differently—see: me screaming into my pillows for a week—and I imagine it's a lot worse when you realize that you're the one who's dead.

That far-off look is back in Riley's eyes. Under different circumstances, I might have teased her or poked her in the arm to get her attention, but I don't think it will be so easy for her to bounce back this time. And while she doesn't seem mad at me, I can't help but wish she were more excited to be here. I've spent a week desperate to have her back. I pictured her crawling out of her grave, ready to make up for lost time with revenge and sleepovers. Instead, she's cold and sharp, like she's already outgrown me in just a week of being away.

Sensing my interest, her head gradually turns to face me. Her eyes have a weighted sleepiness to them.

As someone who was woken up and told that her friend was dead—*thanks, Mom*—I understand that I need to give her some time to adjust. But if we really have only seven days together, what if she spends all of them distancing herself from me? Won't that hurt as much as if she weren't here at all?

"What now?" she asks me.

I swallow and attempt not to seem terrified. This isn't how it works. Riley never asks first. She's the planner.

But it was my decision to bring her back, and I can't back down now. I'm head witch in charge.

"I have to go back to school tomorrow, I think," I say. I scrape my lower lip with my front teeth, tearing off a slice of dead skin. "If all of you were killed by the same person, it has to be someone who goes to Fairmont. I can look for clues there."

I try to sound like I know what I'm doing, like I wasn't expecting Riley to come back to life with her killer's name on her lips.

"Excuse me." June's voice slices into my thoughts. "But what are we supposed to do while you're at school? Hang out in the graveyard? Have a picnic?"

I wonder if she was this nonstop sarcastic when she was with Xander. I could never understand how he was such good friends with her, even when they weren't dating.

"You could go home," I suggest, although it seems pretty obvious to me. "Spend time with your families. Say goodbye. They must miss you a lot. And you could tell them that you didn't kill yourselves—"

"That's a horrible idea!" Dayton says, getting to her feet and thrusting her hands on her hips. "They've already started grieving. It's been a whole week! What are we going to do, march in, freak them out, and then die again in seven days? That's not right."

Riley massages her temple like the sound of Dayton's voice might be giving her a headache. Can the undead get headaches? "She has a point. Best-case scenario, they have to say goodbye to us all over again. Worst case, they think they're going insane."

I wonder if she knows that people have been calling me crazy since she died. Was she actively watching me from the afterlife or just sending along hints and hoping they stuck?

"Then what do you suggest?" I ask.

Everyone's attention swings to Riley. Even June and Dayton aren't immune to the Greenway magnetism. There's something about Riley that feels like a leader.

She presses her lips together and closes her eyes before she says, "We'll go to Yarrow House. We can come up with a plan from there."

"Yes. Okay," I say. Pinpricks of guilt taint the relief I feel at having a real Riley-certified plan. "I can be there tomorrow after school. There's a mandatory memorial service during sixth period, but I can skip it. It's not like I'm mourning you guys anymore. And I can't handle listening to the show choir for a third time this week."

"Wait," Dayton says, taking two hopping steps to stand right in front of me. Up close, it's easier to see the thick postmortem makeup she's wearing. The foundation is like spackling paste spread over her cheeks. "It's *our* service? Like, the whole school is going to be honoring us?"

I take a step away from her. There's a hungry glint in her eye.

"That's the plan. Everyone got an email about it, parents included. But don't get it twisted. It's probably going to be a show-choir concert posing as—"

"We're going," June says.

"Uh, no. You're not," I say firmly. "If you think seeing you would freak out your families, why wouldn't it emotionally scar the entire school?"

June over-enunciates, her mouth stretching and contracting around each letter. "We are going."

In the distance, I can hear a motorcycle engine revving. I have to get the girls settled at Yarrow House and then get back across town with no car, and it's almost one A.M. already. I'll have to move quickly or else be prepared to dole out whatever I own to my sisters if they catch me sneaking back in.

Tomorrow, I have to look at my classmates and figure out who had the motive and means to kill three people in a week. At some point, I'll have to really wrap my mind around the fact that *holy fucking shit, magic is actually real and I brought back the dead.*

Dayton bobs her head in agreement and jabs a finger toward me. "Don't fuck with us, Mila. We're zombies."

"No. You aren't," I say. "You're visiting life."

She grants me one of her sunny smiles. "And tomorrow we're visiting school. Let's go to Walmart and get some black clothes!"

"You and what money?" I ask.

I look to Riley for help, but she shrugs one shoulder and tugs at the hem of her dress. "I would like a change of clothes. Any chance my parents did my roots before they buried me?" I shake my head at her, and she frowns. "Fuck. I need a hat."

I reach under the sleeve of my jacket and free the black elastic band. I snap it as I follow the undead girls down the hill of the cemetery, leaving their empty graves behind us.

NINE

THE TWENTY-FOUR-HOUR Walmart is only a couple of blocks away from the back entrance to the graveyard. Even so, as we pass through the automatic doors and into the stark lights of the warehouse store, I can feel sweat beading in my baby hairs and sliding down the backs of my ears.

The store is eerily empty, the wide aisles seemingly waiting for a tumbleweed to blow through. I've never seen the checkout lanes without lines of people backed up all the way to the jewelry display case. But I guess Cross Creek isn't really an up-all-night kind of town. Even our restaurants close by nine.

June, Dayton, and Riley make a beeline for the clothes department, looking laughably out of place in their fancy dresses.

I can't help but feel responsible for them—it is my fault that they're back from the dead—but they don't need me to help them steal clothes. I can't stay with them every second of the next seven days. No one likes a helicopter witch.

I make my way over to Riley, who is poking at her roots while looking in a mirror next to a display of knit hats. She scowls at her reflection, wrapping a piece of her long hair around her index finger. "Do you think bleach would take? I mean, my hair was always dead, right?"

"It couldn't hurt to try," I say. I have no idea if it'll work, but then again, the little I do know about hair dye is from Riley anyway. She taught me how to do her hair because her arms get tired when she has to reach the back of her head and she gets punchy when the bleach starts to sizzle her scalp.

She tugs at the skin under her eyes, exposing the pink curve of blood vessels in her lower lid. As she moves on to checking her gums, I can see a corner of myself in the mirror, too. My hair is frizzy and windblown. My makeup is smeared from sweat and tears. There's dirt on my neck. I look more like a zombie than she does.

"What is the last thing you remember, Ry?" I ask.

She frowns at me in the mirror and reaches for a gray beanie. She tugs it down over her ears. There's a bouncing bauble on the top of it that makes her head look pointy.

"I don't know," she says. "It's not how my brain is used to working. I never think, 'What's the last thing I can remember?' I just remember or I don't. Like, I remember eating roasted potatoes for dinner, but I don't know *when*. I've been dead for almost an entire week. What if I'm remembering a dinner from months ago?"

She has a point. I comb my fingers through my hair until my reflection is less ghoulish.

"You don't remember June and Dayton's service?" I prompt.

She tries on a slouchy green hat. "No."

"Do you remember finding out that they were dead?"

I had been over at the Greenways' studying when Xander got a phone call from June's parents asking if he'd seen her that night. Even though they were broken up, it wasn't unusual for the two of them to study together or be at the same parties—honor society kids tend to stick together. Hours later—after I had run home for family dinner and gone to sleep—Riley called, sounding shell-shocked. Her dad had been summoned to Aldridge Park to retrieve June and Dayton's bodies. He brought Mrs. Greenway with him because Xander was too bereft to help acquire his dead friends. Riley hadn't been able to stay on the phone with me for long because she needed to hold her brother while he cried.

"Neither of you could sleep after the call came in," I tell her now.

"No," she says, her voice on the edge of growling. "I don't remember any of that. I get that you're trying to help, Mila, but please stop. I don't like that you know things about me that I don't. And even if I got all my memories back, I'm going to die again soon, so what does it matter?"

Her words hit like a punch to the gut, and my breath catches. I want to shake her by the shoulders and scream in her face. *You helped me bring you back*, I think to myself. *You sent me the book. You lit the way. I did this for you! Oh, and by the way? I did actual magic, so cheer up, because maybe fairies or unicorns are real, too!*

Instead, I manage to grind out an "I'm sorry. I'll, um, leave you alone, I guess."

I stumble away from her, leaving her to her hats and misery. She doesn't stop me.

It's not that Riley has always been the easiest to be around. She's the only person I know whose surliness can equal mine. Her dad used to call us the Frowny Girls until Riley schooled him on how telling women to smile is sexist trash. But I've never felt her crabbiness aimed at me, at least not like this. Normally our foul moods combine together and aim outward. Now, though, there's this black cloud hanging over us, edging out the relief our reunion brought me.

It's like she doesn't want to be here.

It's like she's mad that I brought her back.

I can hear June and Dayton debating something a couple aisles over. The rising and falling of their voices sets my teeth on edge. I can't help but feel like prey when they're around. It's not like I value their opinion of me, but it's exhausting to have to counter every insult and be on the defensive at every turn, especially without Riley to help me out.

Acid burns up my esophagus. It wasn't that long ago that I was puking my guts up, and I realize I should probably throw down a couple of bucks for a bottle of antacid. One of us should actually *pay* for something. The other girls are planning on wearing their new black clothes right out of the store. Even if they're caught on camera, it's not like anything bad could happen to them. Or, at least, nothing worse. Getting murdered has really shifted everyone's threshold of what counts as shitty.

The aisles in front of the shuttered pharmacy are packed tight with vitamins, protein shakes, and the faint smell of ammonia. I pick up a bottle of generic Pepto-Bismol. The plastic safety wrap around the rim bites into the skin at my thumb as I drag my nail along the easy-tear perforation. The cap twists off without any child-safety tricks. Chalky mint floods my senses as I throw back a shot of the pink sludge.

Holding the open bottle to my chest while I will myself to choke down another swig, I walk out of the aisle and make my way deeper into the store. Everything looks so mundane. I brought the dead back to life and yet there's an empty McDonalds cup hidden on the shelves of the kitchen section. There are literal walking corpses here and yet there aren't any scented candles that smell like real apples. I did big, real magic using a bunch of flowers and an old-ass book, and I feel just as lonely now as I did when my best friend was dead.

I turn toward the home-goods section. I don't know how much a pillowcase costs on its own, but I would pay a lot of money to keep anyone in my family from asking why mine is missing. Mom would never stop lecturing me about taking good care of my possessions—read: *her* possessions that she lets me use—and Izzy and Nora would never back off if they thought I'd used it for magic. Which I did. So a replacement, even a mismatched replacement, is better than sleeping on a naked pillow. I won't even begin to imagine how totally fucking bonkers Mom would be if she saw eyeliner stains on a bare pillow.

Before I can turn into the bedding section, a tremor runs up my arms and legs. For a second, I think it's another wave of nausea, but I immediately realize it's something else. A deep thorniness—the hollowed-out bone marrow feeling of not sleeping mixed with the spine-scraping of trying to chug something carbonated. My neck cracks to the side of its own volition, the joints popping.

That's when the screams get to me. The bottle of Pepto explodes pink goo all over the floor and the toes of my boots. I kick it out of my way, picturing Dayton's fine-boned hands cracking into a blue-vested employee's skull. Why didn't I take her seriously when she said she was a zombie?

My boots skid on the cement floor as I whip myself around the corner to the accessories department, where I left Riley. June and Dayton are with her, all of them staring at a shattered mirror. Suddenly, real fear digs its claws into me, holding me back from them. Standing in front of me aren't the dewy faced, fancy-clothes-wearing girls I walked in with. They are transformed or, I guess, reverted to their former states of decomposition.

June's yellow cardigan is on the floor. With a choking sound that might have started as a scream, her hands scrabble against the skin around her neck, which is mottled with a livid purple-and-black bruise in a V shape that angles up to her ear.

Dayton's neck has similar markings, although hers are fainter. Her veins are bright against her pale skin, a thousand spiderwebs the same color and texture as a crumbling block of blue cheese.

Riley turns to face me, a nightmare revealing itself in slow motion. A deep gash bisects her forehead. Inside her bloated, bruised face, her eyes are sightless white. Grayish lips crack as they open, weeping blood in the corners of her mouth and letting loose the sulfuric smell of a chemistry lesson gone wrong.

I reach for her. She gasps as my fingertips graze hers. In an instant, color floods back to her face, and a blink literally brings the hazel back to her eyes. She wets her mended lips and looks at the others as they transform back into their neat and pretty state, makeup and all. Riley tears June's hand away from the hanging bruise that is no longer visible.

"We're okay," Riley says hoarsely. "It's okay. We're back to normal."

Dayton keeps her attention on the broken mirror at her feet, which are still bare. Her lips quiver as she whimpers, peering into the shards. She presses her fingertips to her bare neck.

"That's what they did to us?" she whispers. "That's how much they hated us?"

June hugs herself, arms wrapped tightly around her own waist. "When we find them, I'm going to rip their eyes out of their head."

Riley narrows her eyes at me. She hasn't picked a hat yet, but there's a pile of them on the counter next to where the mirror was before it fell to the ground. Or was thrown.

"Where were you?" she asks.

"Getting Pepto," I say defensively. I hold back the urge to remind her that she basically sent me away.

"No," she stresses, taking a step toward me. Glass crunches

under her flip-flop. "Exactly how far were you? We were fine one second, and the next—poof! We were full-on *Walking Dead*. Is this what it's going to be like, Mila? What did you do to us?"

"I don't know!" I say. I hate that *us* means her and June and Dayton. She's supposed to be on my team. I whip my backpack around and drag out the grimoire. The heavy book rattles the jewelry display case as I toss it down and rip past pages to get to the Lazarus spell. I plant a finger on the ingredients list. "Here. Your spell book. Your resurrection spell. All I did was follow the instructions."

The girls crowd around me, reading over the spell. I've memorized every word of it, and there's nothing about the living dead randomly rotting. Riley doesn't seem to believe that, though. She slaps the pages aside, reading through spells for poisoning and lust and a curse that makes sheep molt all their wool.

"There's nothing else in there about being undead," I say with a huff. "We're all in this together, equally lost."

"I don't accept that," June chimes in. "Just because it happened once doesn't mean that we're going to go all gross every time you walk away. We can't have a perma-babysitter."

"No," I say. "You can't. I need to sneak back home, like, an hour ago."

"You should have thought about that before casting midnight spells," Dayton says primly.

I start to remind her that bringing *her* into the world was an accident, but June cuts me off with a sweep of her hand.

"We're in a Super Walmart. We have room to experiment. Plus," she says, looking down at her dirty toes and wiggling them, "I want shoes."

With June, Dayton, and Riley in matching black knockoff Keds, we stand in front of the entertainment department like we're squaring off for a duel. I hook my thumbs into the straps of my backpack. June is at my side. She volunteered to be the control in the experiment. I think she doesn't want to feel the big bruise on her neck again, which I can't say I blame her for. I really don't want to see it again myself.

"We'll start toe to toe, like this," June says. She moves to stand directly in front of Dayton, motioning for Riley and me to follow suit. She seems to settle into her skin with each mandate. I forgot that she was on the Leadership Committee—bossing people around is her element. "And then we'll all move backward, count-ing our steps. Ready?"

We step back once in unison. I already feel ridiculous.

"Two," June says, examining Dayton's and Riley's faces.

"Two?" Dayton asks. "We only took one step."

"But we all took one step," June says with a sigh. She points to her own chest then Dayton's. "One, two. We count in twos."

"Oh," Dayton says. "But what if the problem happens on an odd number?"

"Shut up and walk," Riley says.

We step back again.

"Four. No change," says June. I really feel like she should have a clipboard with her to make hash marks on, but if I say this to her as a joke, she might actually track one down. We're only, like, twenty paces away from office supplies.

"Are you guys hungry?" I ask.

"Why?" Dayton asks. She wiggles her fingers next to her face in a way that makes me think of Nora teasing me at the dinner table. "Afraid we're going to want some brains?"

Sort of.

"No," I say aloud. "I was wondering if I should get you guys some cereal or something for Yarrow House."

"We're capable of getting our own food," Riley says, taking another step backward.

"Six," says June. Then, "We *might* be capable of getting our own food. That's what the experiment's results will show."

"Among other, grosser things," Riley murmurs.

"Eight," says June.

We all lurch back again. June and I pass the movies section and get closer to toys. For years, it was my job to keep Izzy and Nora away from this side of the store. They would dig their heels in, hugging boxes of Legos and Lalaloopsy, their faces covetously pinched. In the event of a tantrum, the three of us would be sent to sit in the garden department to wait for Mom and Dad. Because there is nothing fun about the garden department.

If it *is* my fault that June and Dayton and Riley went all horror show, will I have to put myself in outdoor timeout? It's been a pretty long time since I sat on a bag of fertilizer.

"I'm kind of thirsty," Dayton says. "Crying always makes me thirsty. Is that because I'm losing, like, eye water?"

"Kind of," June says patiently. "It is dehydrating. Ten."

"Sorry, Riley," Dayton says, patting Riley's shoulder. "Is water a sore subject for you? I could have a Gatorade. That's good for dehydration."

"It's fine," Riley says tightly, glaring at the hand touching her. "I'm not mad at all water. Just the creeks."

"Twelve," says June. "Fourteen."

"That's fair," says Dayton to Riley. "When I find out which tree I was hung from, I'm going to burn it down."

"Hanged from," June corrects. "Sixteen."

"Or not," I say, having to raise my voice a little now to be heard by everyone. "Because you'd burn down all of Aldridge Park?"

"You wouldn't understand," Dayton says pityingly. "It's a dead-girl thing."

Oh great. Another clique I'm not cool enough to join. Possibly literally. I wonder if their body temperature drops the farther away that I walk. Or can my magic keep them warm but not pretty? Would it be rude to ask?

Conversation peters out around step thirty. June keeps counting beside me, the soles of her new shoes squeaking against the floor with each step. At a hundred paces, we're backed into the camping section. Shelves of lanterns and portable stoves tower high over our heads. My body involuntarily swings toward a box of cookware as my organs try to turn themselves inside out in that same agonizing wave that kept me from making it to the pillowcases earlier. Queasiness twists everything inside me.

In the distance, I hear my name being called in a screech. June and I pause in unison. Searching the distance, I can see two bobbing figures running in our direction. They have a long way to go to close the gap between us.

"Mila?" Dayton's voice squeaks from somewhere near the exercise-equipment aisle. "Come back please!"

I rush forward, as eager to be less sick as they are to be less dead-looking. June scrambles to keep up with me. I can hear her counting down under her breath between pants. Riley and Dayton are corpsified again, although it doesn't seem to hinder their running ability at all. Which is another knock against the zombie theory. Their opaque eyes, on the other hand, are maximum zombie. They bounce back to normal faster this time, but it takes until I'm directly in front of them to stick.

"A hundred steps," June says definitively. "That's how far we can go from our witch before we start getting disgusting again."

"I have a name," I say.

"A magical choke chain," Riley mutters, biting the inside of her cheek. "Fuck a duck."

"At least a hundred steps is easy to remember," June says.

"Yeah, thank God," Riley sneers. "How else would we remember except for actually turning back into fucking corpses?"

"We really can't see our families again," Dayton says softly. "Unless Mila comes with us."

June sniffs. "Like a spinster aunt in a Victorian novel."

"Hey," I bite off.

"What's the point of a spell that won't let you leave your witch?" Dayton asks. "Wouldn't people want to go back to living their lives?"

"No," Riley says, lifting her chin. I know that face. There's determination in the set of her jaw. "You come back to kill the fucker who offed you."

TEN

COMING BACK TO school feels different this time. Instead of being jittery and jumping at every shadow, my shoulders are squared with purpose. I'm confident that someone in these halls killed Riley, June, and Dayton. And that nagging voice—a cross between my mom and Dr. Miller—that says I'm crazy is gone. I'm not crazy. I brought back the dead, and I have the power to get justice for them.

Caleb Treadwell is absent from chem, saving me the trouble of having to pretend to apologize for knocking him over last week. With the whole counter to myself, I decide to ignore Mr. Cavanagh's lecture and open my notebook to the last page. I start a Venn diagram of the three not-so-dead girls. All three were juniors, but that's where the comparisons end. June and Dayton were in a totally different social hemisphere than Riley, only ever occasionally crossing paths through Xander.

I gnaw on the end of my pencil. Xander was at June's wake when Riley died. I wonder if the Nouns were there, too. June and Dayton were Nouns themselves, but they were Proper Nouns and, thus, in a higher social sphere. The lower-caste Nouns are most of the Fairmont Academy speech and debate team, but thanks to some crossover with the honor society—and some strategic dating—they have a prime real estate lunch table. Their desperation to be top-tier popular makes them all the most vicious. The Nouns are bootlickers, brownnosers, and—when the situation warrants—shameless tattletales. Could they be killers, too?

June said she wouldn't have been surprised if Sky Moony or Dawn Mathy had killed her. Although her "Dawn copied my bangs" theory doesn't explain killing Riley or Dayton.

But maybe it wasn't a personal killing at all. Maybe it was tactical. The only thing that all of Fairmont Academy cares about is the Rausch Scholarship. It's not even that much money—the alumni association scrapes together a couple grand for the scholarship itself and then drops three times as much on the awards gala. But it's prestigious, and prestige goes a long way in Cross Creek.

June said herself that she and Dayton wouldn't have killed themselves because they hadn't been to the Rausch awards gala yet this year. She assumed that both of them would be invited. Before two weeks ago, everyone knew that our class's scholarship was June's for the taking.

But Riley was right behind her in grade point average. Then Dayton, who, despite being dumb as an empty sack, always managed to be on the honor roll and in a thousand clubs.

Would someone really kill for the honor of a big party and a page in the yearbook?

I look around at my classmates. There's Cain Gonzales, the only other junior Latinx at Fairmont, who spends 80 percent of his day screaming, "*I don't know anyone named Abel!*" And then there's Dawn, who might want to be the breakout star of the Nouns instead of always being lumped in with Sky, Angel, and Diamond.

But mostly I see people whose names I don't know. Anonymous faces—like mine—who don't fit into any clique or club even after three years at this school. Winning the Rausch Scholarship could make senior year different for someone on the fringes of Fairmont Academy. People would eat lunch with them and say hello in the halls. I think plenty of people would kill for a more pleasant high school experience.

Which means the real question here isn't who would kill for the notoriety of the Rausch Scholarship—but who *wouldn't*?

My internal undead-girl alarm goes off at the same time as the sixth-period bell. It feels the same as it did in Walmart—an instant of my entire body feeling like a ripped-open scab, followed by cold sweat that leaves me reaching shakily for the Pepto in my backpack. The girls are nearby. *Where* they are, exactly, isn't immediately clear, thanks to the student body dutifully filing into the courtyard behind the cafeteria.

Aniyah Dorsey has trapped Principal Chu near the back entrance to the cafeteria. She's holding an iPhone threateningly toward the older woman's mouth. Does she know that she looks like a cartoon of a reporter right now?

"Ms. Chu," she's saying as I move past them, "how would you respond to people who say that on-campus memorials, especially mandatory ones like this, sensationalize and even promote teen suicide?"

The principal's face dents into a deep glower. "Who says that?"

Aniyah doesn't blink. "The Society for the Prevention of Teen Suicide."

"Oh." Ms. Chu's face falls. "No comment, Aniyah. Please just enjoy the free period."

Aniyah catches sight of me. Her face brightens—not the reaction I usually elicit. "Mila! Can I talk to you about your reaction to today's event—"

I breeze by her. "Nope. Busy."

The dark green metal picnic tables where the cool kids usually eat lunch are covered in white display boards and butcher paper signs with clumps of students sitting beside them, staring hungrily at the gathering crowd, trying to trick someone into eye contact. A banner has been hung across the cafeteria's back wall that reads: *Fairmont Academy Celebration of Life!* There's an empty podium underneath with a microphone being set up.

At first glance, it looks like we've all accidentally wandered into an outdoor science fair. Or a prolife rally. But, in order to avoid being stepped on by a passing horde of girls in matching fleece vests, I pass too close to one of the picnic tables and realize it's a bake sale. There are plates of lumpy homemade cookies and obviously store-bought pies being sliced to slivers. I hate to admit it, but I kind of get why Aniyah wanted to quote me on how I would react to this. I could probably write most of her article with swearing alone.

This is massively and breathtakingly fucked up. In sixteen years, I have never seen anything try so hard and fail so spectacularly in equal measure.

"Cookies are a dollar!" chirps the girl nearest the cash box. I think I recognize her as one of the show-choir goons. She has the glassy-eyed perma-smile of someone desperate for attention. Although I guess she could also be one of the theater kids.

I arch an eyebrow at her. She must not know me either if she's peddling at me.

"I have to pay to celebrate life?" I ask, inclining my head to the giant sign looming over us.

The guy cutting pie with a cafeteria butter knife stops and turns his head to me. He is also wearing an enormous smile. I raised the actual dead last night, but these kids are giving me the heebie-jeebies like whoa.

"We're raising money for the Dayton Nesseth memorial fund," he says, pointing down at their butcher paper tablecloth, which I have avoided reading. It's covered in drawings of rainbows and trees and hearts like a shitty yearbook collage. It says: *Bake Sale for Dayton's Memory Tree! Help us plant a magnolia tree that will keep Dayton Nesseth's memory alive forever!!!*

"A tree," I say to the smiling bake sellers. I suck my teeth in thought. Residual Pepto makes them grainy. "Doesn't that seem kind of, I don't know . . . fucked up? Considering that Dayton literally died hanging from a tree?"

Smiling Girl's smile fades from cheery to pleasant as she considers my question. "No," she decides. "It wasn't a *magnolia* tree. This one will have beautiful flowers that Dayton would have loved."

I can't help but look out, hoping to catch a glimpse of Dayton to gauge her reaction. Last I heard, she was pretty pissed at trees.

"What about the other girls?" I ask, not looking at the smiles directly anymore. These two are less terrifying if I watch their eyebrows instead.

Smiling Guy's eyebrows pull together. "They weren't in show choir."

"Yeah," says Smiling Girl. "Maybe their clubs did something nice for them?"

Just brought them back from the dead and paid for a week's worth of snacks, I think, walking away without buying a cookie. Before we split up in the Walmart parking lot last night—well, super early this morning—the girls hadn't yet decided what they could or wanted to eat, so I'd sent them on their way to Yarrow House with a bag full of peanut butter, crackers, and Gatorade.

Now I'm worried that if Dayton has any kind of sugar craving, she'll reveal her corpse face to the smiling kids and demand a free cookie. Not that I think the show-choir kids don't deserve to be terrorized—they are a plague on our school and, really, society at large—but Dayton would definitely blab that I was the one who brought her back from the dead. She wasn't the brightest star in the sky before she was murdered—she once asked our freshman science teachers when unicorns went extinct—so a full week of being actually brain dead can't have helped.

The other booths are equally—or more—offensive. The swim team is asking people to sign Dayton's framed swim cap so it can be hung in the locker room. People are collecting money for a yearbook tribute that they are calling *Gone but First Let Me Take a Selfie*. There's a raffle for a Starbucks card if you can correctly guess all of June's favorite things. And, inexplicably, there's a face-painting booth where a group of sophomores is being transformed into sophomores with My Little Pony cutie marks on their cheeks.

"This is actually worse than I pictured it," Riley says, appearing at my shoulder. She's wearing a black Giants cap, the brim pulled down to her nose, obscuring all but her downturned lips.

I can't stop the rush of relief I feel at seeing her. I know that my dead-girl radar has already buzzed, but it's extra comforting to feel her disdain for the event radiating. It's an inch away from being totally normal. She falls into step beside me, keeping her shoulders up to her neck so no one passing by us will be able to see her face.

"Were you gonna mention this?" She reaches into her back

pocket and pulls out a folded paper with a piece of tape flapping on the top. Her last bathroom selfie stares up at me. The program from her funeral. She must have found it on display somewhere. It wouldn't be hard—it seems like they're on every bulletin board. "Aniyah wrote a poem about me?"

I snort. "Oh my God, isn't it the worst?"

She flips the program over and reads, "*Riley: she looked at the stars so shyly.* I think I looked at the stars pretty forwardly. Like 'Fuck you, stars, I'm staring right at you!'"

"Maybe she just admired you. Thought of you *highly*."

Her lips slant up. "Then she should have lied and called me *smiley*."

After endless lectures from Toby on the dangers of rhyming incantations, Riley and I loved making up the worst couplets. Most of the time, I liked it even more than real spellwork.

"Did you sleep okay?" I ask. "I mean, *do* you sleep now?"

She flinches a shrug and stuffs the program back into her pocket. "I slept as much as I could with June and Dayton talking all night. It was like crashing a sleepover that no one wanted me at."

I stub the heel of my boot into the pavement. "I can't believe I brought them back, too."

"Toby always said the magic you work would come back times three. I didn't think it'd be so literal."

"Me either."

"And I could think of better ways to spend my afterlife than in an abandoned house with two people I've hated since kindergarten. Also, when you're not with us, we're, you know, disgusting monsters. Yarrow doesn't have running water, so I can't get the formaldehyde stink off my skin." She watches as a pair of face-painted girls giggle and run past us. "I guess I don't really want to be alone in water anyway. Drowning kind of ruins the charm of a hot bath."

"Right. Sorry. Fuck." Without thinking, I reach for the elastic band at my wrist and snap it. I sense Riley's question without having to look at her. You can't hide new developments from your best friend. Not that I'm trying to hide it.

"It keeps the screaming to a minimum," I explain.

"Fair enough," she says in that way that means that she won't press for more information if I don't want to give it. And I don't. There's no way to explain the rubber band snapping without going into detail about how not okay I was without her. I don't want it to seem like I'm guilting her. It's not her fault she's dead, and I'm not going to fish for a thank-you for bringing her back. Especially because I'm not sure that I'd get one.

We skirt around the edges of the courtyard. I spot Dayton in giant black sunglasses and one of the beanies Riley stole. She gives me a covert wave before unscrewing the lid on a bottle of Gatorade and taking a long drink. I really never thought I would see the day that Dayton Nesseth waved to me from across the courtyard. Who knew necromancy could make you so popular?

Dr. Miller is sitting alone at a card table with an assortment of pastel pamphlets spread over it. She doesn't smile at me, but she makes a lot of intense eye contact. "Camila. How are you?"

"Fine," I grumble. I throw a shoulder into Riley's arm to push her along, but she doesn't budge. She pulls her hat down even lower and sneaks a glimpse of Dr. Miller.

"You've already replaced me with a woman in a red blazer?" she says under her breath.

"Shut up," I whisper back.

Dr. Miller seems oblivious to the fact that she is the subject of our private chat. She makes a theatrical scooping motion at Riley. "Are you one of Camila's friends?" She stresses the word *friend* as though actually physically throwing it in my face. I know what she wants to say is *See, Mila, and you said your only friend was dead.* And what I want to say in return is *Yes, she's back for a little vacation unless I can figure out a way to sacrifice more moths to keep her alive past Sunday.*

Dr. Miller gives a genuine smile as her line of sight travels beyond me and Riley and into the distance. She picks up her hand and gives an almost adorable finger wave.

"Xander!" she calls.

Riley nearly jumps out of her skin. Cursing a mile a minute, she stumbles and spins away, disappearing into the crowd just before Xander appears next to me.

His face is shadowed and grayish with exhaustion, but he manages some of his sparkle when he sees me. He opens his arms, and my brain takes a second to say, *This is a weird wave*, before I realize that it's a hug. I'm enveloped in warm Xander smell—eucalyptus deodorant, ocean salty sweat, and a tinge of cumin earthiness. I don't think we've ever hugged before.

Who am I kidding? I know for a fact that we've never hugged. We did high-five once, and the memory of it kept me warm for many, many winter nights.

His arms are shockingly solid around my shoulders, squeezing tight without a hint of self-consciousness. I can't help but notice how his hips latch perfectly inside mine like a key slipping into a lock. The realization makes my knees buckle. How do skinny girls fit with their dudes? Do they just rest up against each other? I could keep Xander Greenway's sharp hipbones bolted in my softness forever.

Except he lets me go because he's grieving and probably not thinking about boning down at the Fairmont Academy Celebration of Life.

"You're back," I say stupidly.

Yeah, duh, Mila. He's back because he's here in front of you, formerly very close to your front.

Has the voice in my head always sounded like June making fun of me?

"I'm back," he says. "My parents finally let me out."

His eyes follow the back of Riley's Giants cap. Fear spikes like thumbtacks in my veins. I reach out and grasp his forearm. Now that I'm touching him—again! Twice in one day!—I have his attention, but I have no idea what to do with it to make sure he doesn't spot Riley. She didn't want him to see her. The girls agreed that seeing family was not okay. Do I cry? Or make a joke? Do I even know any jokes? Nora was pretty obsessed with knock-knock jokes a few years ago. I can't remember the punch lines to any of them, though.

But Xander doesn't seem to mind that I'm touching him. His head dips, turning the bright light of his attention solely onto me. Tired as he is, his face warms to fleecy softness. I can feel Dr. Miller watching us, waiting for a chance to leap into our conversation, so I use my gripping hand to lead Xander out of earshot of her and her pamphlets.

"Why is she so obsessed with me?" Xander asks as we come to a stop. He flicks a look over my shoulder at Dr. Miller, his face going shadowy and sneering. "I've only met her once. I don't want her help. Didn't anyone ever tell her that no means no?"

"Maybe you're irresistible. You're eighteen now, right? A woman has needs, Alexander."

That shocks a laugh out of him. It wipes the gloom away for a second. "God, that's sick."

Doubt makes my lips itch to keep the words locked inside. I want to keep his laugh floating in the air around us, not wipe it away. "You're a tragedy gold mine. I only lost one friend this week. You lost two and a sister."

"It's not a contest."

"Of course not. You have me beat three to one."

My smile must not be that convincing because his voice goes serious and his focus clasps on to my face. "Are you doing okay?"

I raised the dead, I think as I gaze into his arctic ice eyes. *I raised the dead, and I let them crash their own funeral, and I should probably know where they are, but I definitely don't.*

I can't tell him any of that, so instead I say, "Yeah, I'm fine. Eating, sleeping, functioning." I gesture around us with the hand still branded with his arm warmth, the fuzz of his sweater trapped in the sweaty crease that is my heart line. "Celebrating life. Have you tried a Dayton cookie yet? There are rumors of a June sno-cone somewhere."

"I haven't had the pleasure," he says. I wish I could replay the word *pleasure* in his voice over and over again until I wore all the meaning out of it. "I heard some people talking shit, and I had to get away from them. Something awful happened, you know? Three people are dead. They should show a little respect. At least pretend to be sad. I don't want to hear my classmates talk about people I cared about. People I loved."

I would love to press pause on the conversation here and make him dissect that last statement like a biology frog, examined and labeled within an inch of its death. Xander and June dated for most of last year, but they broke up over summer vacation without warning. Riley had almost no insight into what happened except, "*I don't know. The hell beast just isn't around as much anymore.*" The breakup hadn't even changed them that much. June dated some other guys, but she and Xander had stayed friends. They stayed in the same clubs, kept the same company, shared study tables at the downtown Starbucks.

So, while it is possible that he loved her as a pal, it's equally likely that his loins still burn for a girl whose neck is only kind of attached to her body when she's more than a hundred steps away from me. Figures.

"People are assholes," I say.

He laughs quietly. "That should be your catchphrase."

"Isn't it?"

"Maybe. It always seems to apply."

"Who were the shit talkers?" I ask, looking around the packed courtyard. "Was it Dan Calalang? He seems like a real dickhead. He dented my passenger side door when he parked his giant-ass SUV too close, then he refused to pay for it."

Xander nods. "He was one of them. Him and—what did you and Riley used to call them? The Nouns?"

"Everyone calls them that, Xander. Their names are, in fact, all nouns."

"Technically, everyone's name is a noun." He chuckles. "But their friends tend to just call them Angel, Sky, Diamond, and Dawn."

"Everyone says Dawn's name last. Do you think she's noticed?" *Would that be motive enough for murder?* "They must have been at June's wake with you, right? They were friends."

"Funeral reception," he corrects. "They were there, yeah."

Huh. The Nouns have an alibi. The killing spree couldn't have been bangs-related. Which lends more credence to my Rausch theory.

"But I don't know if I would call them June's friends," Xander continues, his shoulders slumping. "Friends shouldn't spend your memorial spreading rumors about you."

"What kind of rumors?" I ask.

His mouth turns into a scolding quirk, but his eyes laugh with me. "If I told you, I'd be helping to spread them."

"Come on." I nudge him with my elbow and give him my

cheekiest smile. "Give me a ballpark. Are the rumors regular catty or wholly unbelievable?"

But I'll never know because my knees go weak, and this time, it has nothing to do with Xander's hips. I can feel each of the three girls passing out of the hundred steps. It makes the magic-induced nausea double, then triple. Pepto leaps up my throat, splashing my back molars in acidic mint. I force myself to swallow it and shove myself away from Xander without explanation—not that he'll need much of one past the nasty gargling sound I just made. I'll be humiliated when I have time to be.

Now I run toward the cafeteria, using my own sickness as a compass toward June, Riley, and Dayton.

Holy hell, I hope no one's brains are being eaten.

ELEVEN

THE NOUNS ARE on the other side of the cafeteria, stuck between the line of metal dumpsters and the chain-link fence that cuts the parking lot off from the courtyard. June looms over her friends in full zombie mode. She has pulled her hair into a topknot to showcase the horrific bruising at her throat. In direct sunlight, I can see how blue her skin is, especially against the vivid red of the burst blood vessels in her eyes—eyes that are focused on the four quivering, weeping Nouns.

"I made you popular! I told people that speech and debate wasn't for losers. I *lied* for you." June's voice is a menacing croak. You can almost hear the rattle of her collapsed windpipe. "And this is how you repay me? You come to *my* party and spread rumors about me? I will haunt the shit out of you! You'll never win another competition or take a test or go to a dance without me there, being dead and reminding you what assholes you are."

I start to run toward them, but someone grabs my elbow, yanking me around the corner. The rose quartz necklace bounces painfully off my collarbone as I am pulled to a stop, facing the parking lot. I turn and am greeted by a black-and-orange baseball cap, along with gray lips that turn pink as they say my name.

"Mila, hold up," Riley says, giving my elbow another tug. "You can't barge over there. If people see her change back near you, they're going to figure out you're a witch."

I scoff and pull my arm back. "It's way too late for that. Did you forget that you outed us as witches freshman year? You told Ms. Chu that keeping *The Crucible* on the required reading list would inspire witch-related hate crimes on campus."

She lifts the brim of her hat so I can see her roll her eyes. "I told everyone we were Wiccan. You brought three dead people back to life with some candles and an old-ass book that probably came from eBay. You did real, live magic. Like rewrite-the-universe-to-your-will *magic*. That's not the same as making charm bags."

"You said it was!" I say. I can't believe what I'm hearing. This time last week, Riley would have literally punched me for even implying that there was a difference between our little spells and true magic. She would have screamed blasphemy and stormed off. She would have given me a silent treatment that would turn my stomach inside out. Riley Greenway *knew* that magic was real, and she would never, ever let anyone second-guess it. "You have always, always, *always* said that what we were doing was real magic. And you got pissed if I treated it like a game or said we were killing time."

"Yeah, I also pretended to believe in Santa for an extra year because I found out the truth before Xander. Sometimes people need to believe in magic, Mila. That doesn't make it real! Religion is supposed to make you feel good. Make you less scared and more present. That's all. Wicca made you less angry and me less lonely, and it pissed off our parents. That was enough for me. I didn't need the spells to work. They never worked! Spells are just prayers with more steps and a name that scares people."

Toby's voice floats through my head. *Any book that purports to have the answer to death isn't Wicca, I'll tell you that much. This is some dark shit.*

Why did magic work for the first time when I cracked open that grimoire? Was it the book? Or me truly believing that it could work?

"Fine," I say to Riley. "Then we were both wrong. Because magic is real as shit, and June is going to give all the Nouns PTSD."

"So what?" She laughs, and the sound is burlap rough. "Since when do you care about the Nouns? They're trash people! Or did you make friends with them while I was dead?"

"No! But I'm responsible for this. And, as someone in the middle of curating my own traumatic stress one zombie at a time, I'm gonna go ahead and try to save some other people."

"Ugh. We're not zombies. Also, you're friends with my brother now?"

"Yeah, someone we loved *died*, so we've had all of two conversations." I don't have time to argue about this. I don't know what June is planning on doing to the Nouns or how much she'll spill if she's left alone with them for too long.

"Go find Dayton," I tell Riley. I flex my shoulder blades. Having someone out of range of my magic is like an itch I can't reach. "She's more than a hundred steps away."

Riley adjusts her baseball cap and slips her hands into the pocket of her hoodie. "Okay, but later we're going to have to talk about this Frankenstein's monsters situation we're in."

"Can't wait," I say with a level of sarcasm I usually save for my sisters. I'm starting to think that death has corroded some of Riley's personality along with her memories. A week ago, I don't think she would have let the Nouns be terrorized by a reanimated corpse.

Or maybe she would have and I would have gone along with it because it was her plan?

While Riley slips back inside the cafeteria, I sneak forward. The Nouns are still being lectured by a monster and also probably collectively pooping themselves, so they don't notice as I duck behind the dumpsters. Even though it's not that warm out, the smell of hot garbage is baked into the rusting metal, and I have to hold my breath as I step over puddles of who knows what.

"So, which one of you was it?" June's voice is starting to lighten back to its usual flutter as she continues to rage at her friends. "Which one of you tacky bitches killed me?"

There's a nervous wheezing of four voices all trying to communicate the word *no* without being able to fully formulate it.

"None of you are going to admit to it?" June snarls.

"W-we had a competition that night," says one of the Nouns.

There's a sucking and sputtering of snot before someone else adds, "Honor society isn't the same without you. Caleb doesn't even want us to meet at Starbucks anymore."

"Don't say that name to me!" June screeches. "Don't you ever talk about him and me in the same breath again!"

In the distance, there's the wheezing sound of a pitch pipe and the choral hum of the show choir warming up. Oh no. They're going to sing "I'm Always Chasing Rainbows" again, and I'm not at a safe distance away from them. Why couldn't June have chased the Nouns to the other side of the school?

"Even if you didn't kill me, I have some things to say before I go," June says. I can see the toe of a black sneaker tapping on the other side of the dumpster. "Angel, I cannot believe you're wearing earrings you stole from me right now. But you've always been super fake. Everyone talks about it. And Diamond, I never liked spending the night at your house. Your carpeting is tacky and smells like dog butt."

I clear my throat. Using the gremlin voice I used to use to terrorize my sisters through our shared wall, I screech, "Run away, debate nerds! Run away and never return!"

Apparently, they don't need coercing. I can hear the patter of stumbling steps and panting breath. I walk around the dumpsters and find June, her face returned to pretty disdain. Her lips puff petulantly.

"Did you really just quote *The Lion King*?" she asks.

"Did you really just threaten to haunt your friends?"

She watches the empty corner the Nouns disappeared around—toward the cafeteria or their cars, I'm not sure which. "They are not my friends. Friends wouldn't talk smack about you at your own funeral."

"Celebration of Life," I correct.

"Same difference." She sniffs. "I thought they'd have nice things to say. We were friends for two years. Two years of study groups and bake sales and parties. They couldn't muster one nice thing to say about me? 'June had good hair.' 'June really was a good listener.' 'Great taste in jewelry.'"

"Angel must have thought so if she was wearing your earrings," I say, interrupting her reverie. It's weird hearing her compliment herself in the third person. Weirder that she thinks of herself as a good listener with multiple nice qualities.

"And telling everyone that I slept with Caleb Treadwell." She shakes her head until her top knot loosens. Her hair spills back to her shoulder in a ripple of brown silk. "How disgusting is that? Me and that loser?"

I haven't figured out how the girls' memories work yet. I haven't heard any rumors about June and Caleb, but without Riley to pass gossip from Xander's strata to ours, I'm pretty far on the outskirts of Fairmont society. What if June already knew about the rumors and forgot? What if she stopped being friends with the Nouns weeks ago and woke up from her dirt nap thinking everything was cool between them? How many other important memories could the girls have forgotten?

My face must be betraying my confusion, because June takes a threatening step toward me.

"What?" she growls.

I lift a shoulder in a lazy shrug. "I mean, you don't really remember, though. You don't remember anything from the last two weeks, right? So it might not be a lie."

She crosses her arms and sighs. "Can we just go? I stole a box of cookies from Walmart, and I want to eat them in my nasty new room in that disgusting abandoned house before the raccoons wake up. Where are the others?"

"Um." I close my eyes and search myself for the signs I'm coming to think of as my magic boundary lines. "Somewhere at least a hundred steps in any direction?"

She groans. "God. Do you think my parents canceled my cell phone already? It sucks not being able to get in contact with you guys when I need to find you."

"Cell phones can be tracked," I say. "But I think my sisters have walkie-talkies I could borrow?"

"Even that sounds better than nothing."

"I'll see what I can do."

The show choir is continuing its performance in the courtyard, but I can feel that Dayton and Riley are too far away to watch.

June and I make a circuit of the school, and I have to agree with her about the walkie-talkies. Having to intuit everyone's locations rather than being able to send a text sucks, especially while traveling with the pouting corpse of the former most popular girl in school, who keeps pointing out landmarks like I've never been on campus before.

"There's the bench where Xander asked me out for the first time," she says, flicking her hand toward a metal bench identical to every other metal bench on campus.

My hackles rise. I shove my fists into the pockets of my jacket. This is one of my worst nightmares, being regaled with stories of Xander and June with nowhere to run.

Well, there's everywhere to run. Campus is large, and the outdoor hallways are deserted. But it would be rude to abandon one's zombie. Even if it is just *one* of one's zombies.

"It was a Tuesday," she says wistfully, pressing her hands delicately on her stomach as though keeping butterflies at bay. "He asked if I wanted to get a Frappuccino after school, and I was like, 'Uh, yeah, we always get Fraps on Tuesday,' because that's when we have honor society meetings at Starbucks, and he was like, 'No, do you want to go *with* me.' It was really sweet."

"Yes, Frappuccinos have a lot of sugar," I say tersely, taking a sharp turn toward the gym. Dayton was on the swim team, so I figure she might be visiting the pool.

"And this was before he was really popular. He was cute, but he didn't play a sport or perform with anyone. He was a hot nobody."

"Why are you telling me this?" I ask.

"You were talking about how I don't remember anything. But look at me go! Remembering stuff."

"No," I clarify. "I was saying that you don't remember the last two weeks. You started dating Xander a year ago. Plus you broke up, so it's not like it's a super-fond memory for you."

Her eyes bug in annoyance. It looks eerily like her corpse form. "Assume much? Xander and I agreed to break up because we both needed to spend more time studying. And I got so bored. He was always working, and it's not like I could visit him at funerals—"

I can't stop the noise of dissent that comes scraping out of my throat. I have spent hours and hours of my life at funerals, helping Riley fold programs and dust the urns and pointing inconsolable mourners toward the bathroom. I've vacuumed the parlor, and once I assisted Xander in loading a casket into the hearse when Mr. Greenway threw his back out.

June didn't stay away from the funeral parlor because Xander was too busy to see her. She stayed away for the same reason everyone in Cross Creek did: She was too skeeved out by the idea to face it. No one else knew that it was worth braving death itself to get to have Riley and Xander in your life.

Without thinking, I reach up and touch the rose quartz necklace. My brain replays the moment Xander hooked it around my neck, the sensation of having him close to me. The cool breeze reminds me of how his breath curled behind my ear.

"Xander was never a nobody," I mutter. He has always been Xander, who hates onions and loves the sound of acoustic guitar. Who cares so deeply that he cried when he lost the science fair two years ago. He left his experiment in the parking lot afterward, where the rain beat the poster board back to wood pulp.

Suddenly, June claps. The sound echoes off the buildings that surround us. "Oh my God! You have a crush on your best friend's brother? You're such a little cliché!"

My stomach sinks, and for the first time in twenty-four hours, it has nothing to do with magic. Just a mocking laugh and a reminder of my place in the world—the absolute bottom with no hope for getting any higher. It makes me want to dump June back in her grave and never look back.

"Having a crush on the most popular guy in school is cliché, no matter whose brother he is," I grumble. "So let's drop it."

"I mean, I get it, obviously," she says, definitely not dropping it. The opposite of dropping it. Picking it up and spinning it around on her finger. "The eyes alone, right? But also the abs and the hands and the teeth and—"

"Yeah, I'm sure you can list all his better parts, but let's not and say we did, okay?"

She gasps loudly. Why didn't she ever do any plays? She's got the same disingenuous glint in her eye as the theater kids. "Get your mind out of the gutter, Camila Flores. I would never tell you about Xander's better parts. Unless you really wanted to know . . ." She looks at me sidelong and bursts out into giggles that build on each other like soap bubbles. "Oh my God, you're blushing so much. How is the scariest girl in school a virgin?"

"I'm not scary," I snap. I am a virgin. There's no reason to deny it. Even if I tried, I'd fail the pop quiz that would certainly follow.

"Yeah, okay." She snorts. "The ever-present Doc Martens and your jacket with the pentagram drawn on the pocket? I'm sure you dress like that because it's *so* comfortable. It doesn't make you feel like a badass? You don't get dressed trying to look like a punk-rock witch?"

I do get dressed thinking that I look like a badass. Like being Mila Flores is something dangerous and sharp. But right now, I'm all soft meat in a costume that isn't fooling anyone but me.

"I dress like this because I found the jacket and the boots at Goodwill. Like most of my clothes. *Anyway*"—I stress the last word, hoping to steer us away from the topic—"don't tell the others about Xander. My thing for him, not his . . . thing."

"This is actually the most embarrassed I've ever been for another human being," June says, grinning at me. Even though we're walking, she puts her hand on my shoulder in mock protection, the way I do with my sisters when I want to be an asshole and make fun of them. "Mila, you are a junior in high school. At the very, very least, please say *penis*."

I swat her hand away. "What if I don't and say that I did?"

The hairs on my arms rise. I have to fight to keep walking as all my organs lurch forward. Saved by the nausea.

I spit a thin stream of hot saliva onto the concrete, and June jumps back, even though there's no chance of her getting hit. Not that she wouldn't deserve it.

"They're close," I say, panting.

I have to swing in a couple different directions before the queasiness abates, pointing us toward the theater. I don't know why

Dayton and Riley would be here. The entire school is in the court-yard, so we're just walking into a big empty building with a bunch of seats. But I know we're on the right path because as June and I make our way through the doors, I feel the shudder of crossing the boundary line. The lobby is decorated with pictures of old plays and choir competitions and talent shows. There isn't a performing arts school anywhere nearby, so Fairmont enrolls a lot of kids who want to study theater or dance but don't have any better options.

There's a piano tinkling on the other side of the lobby doors. Hazy overhead lights wash the blue padded seats in warmth. Dayton is standing center stage, her eyes closed. I wonder if she's imagining an audience. Her hands flutter near her cheeks as she sings.

"Some fellows look and find the sunshine. I always look and find the rain."

My sigh is covered by the tinkling of the piano tucked into the back corner of the stage. I can see the black-and-orange Giants hat bobbing over the keys as Riley plunks out a vague accompani-ment to "I'm Always Chasing Rainbows."

I shouldn't be surprised that she knows how to play it. When we first met, she would constantly complain about her piano les-sons. Mrs. Greenway thought that playing an instrument would help Riley make friends. It didn't work. As Riley pointed out many times, piano was a solitary instrument. Besides, once she was finally allowed to quit lessons, Riley and I could just hang out after school. Friendship achieved.

The song finishes with a clink of high notes and a whispery

vibrato from Dayton. She opens her eyes and looks down at her hands. With a guilty jolt, I realize that she wasn't closing her eyes because she was enjoying herself so much but because she hadn't wanted to look at her own dead body. She sends a glance over her shoulder at Riley.

"Thanks," she says.

Riley stands up and shrugs instead of saying, "You're welcome." She sees me and June watching from the aisle and leans her back against the piano, folding her arms across her chest. "I knew you had to be close. It got easier to play once my left wrist unbroke itself."

I can't tell if she wants me to be apologetic or not, so I choose not. I didn't kill her. I just brought her back. And I'm not sorry for it. We all have to make do with this fucked-up spell. If I can spend alone time with June Phelan-Park, then Riley can deal with her own broken bits when I'm not around.

June climbs the stairs onto the stage, glaring daggers at Dayton. "We looked everywhere for you. You can't just run off, Dayton. It's rude."

"*You* ran off," Riley says. "To threaten your friends."

"Not my friends," June snaps. "Not anymore. I don't forgive. I'm a Taurus."

Dayton wrings her hands against her stomach. Her nails are torn to shreds. The black jeans she stole from Walmart are slightly too big and bunch around her knees. "I'm sorry. I was watching the show choir warm up, and I realized that I'll never get to sing with them again."

"That's not a huge tragedy, right?" I ask, coming farther down the aisle to lean on the lip of the stage. I crane my neck to look up at the girls. "They kind of suck. Trust me, I've listened to them perform that depressing song three times in the last week, and it was shitty every time. You sounded really good."

Dayton sends me a grateful smile, but I can tell she doesn't mean it. Her eyes are sadder than I've ever seen them. "But that's the problem. I never got to be a soloist. All the show choir competitions are in spring when I have swim team. The director was afraid that I'd miss too many shows for swim meets. Which isn't even true." She sits down hard on the stage and puts her face in her hands. Her thin shoulders shiver. When she speaks again, her voice is mousy and wet. "And now I'm dead, and I'll never get to solo. I'll never sing in public or swim or do anything ever again. I'm a dead loser with nothing to look forward to. Coming back feels terrible."

I don't know if she means coming back to Fairmont or coming back to life.

TWELVE

THE DAY AFTER the Celebration of Life, I tiptoe up the rickety stairs to the porch of Yarrow House, my arms laden with bags of McDonalds, a tray of sodas, and a duffel bag full of supplies. Unable to knock, I kick the kitchen door twice. There's a shuffling of feet, something crashing to the floor, and a muffled curse before the door swings open. June snatches the food and the sodas without saying hello. Ice clicks against the paper cups as she spins away.

"Lunch is here," she calls to the others.

"You're welcome," I say to her as I toe the door closed behind me.

The kitchen has been ransacked. The shelves where Riley once meticulously cataloged all our magic supplies are now a mess of tangled herbs and loose stones toppled into one another.

All the candles that we'd been saving to use in spells are lit around the dark living room—on top of stacks of books and wedged onto the wilted mantelpiece and on chunks of broken bricks that must have been collected outside from the crumbling chimney. Unfortunately, none of the candles are scented—the essential oils can counteract spell ingredients—so there's nothing to cover up the house's ever-present perfume of mildew and mouse fur.

The flames send flickering shadows against the boards on the windows. The girls lounge on the sagging, dirty floor under the sagging, dirty ceiling. A white cat weaves around the room, its sharp ears twitching at sounds too quiet for me to hear.

"Is that Binx?" I ask Riley.

She doesn't look up from rummaging inside one of the fast food bags, hunting for her nuggets. "Dayton's scared of mice, so I went home and grabbed him. He's a good hunter."

"Yeah," June says, sitting down in front of the fireplace with a large order of fries. "Except Dayton is also scared of dead mice."

Dayton makes a yelp of indignation into a Filet-O-Fish. "They're gross!"

I open the duffel bag and pull out the blankets and sheets I pillaged from my linen closet. I sit down on top of the pile and accept a bag of food from Riley. "Won't your parents wonder where he is?"

"That's the whole point of having an outdoor cat," she says. She makes a line of sauce containers in front of her. The plastic cuts clean lines in the dust. "They come and go. He'll be here for a couple of days. By the time my parents worry that he's not eating the food they put out, he'll be back."

I can't argue with that. I bite into my double cheeseburger, effectively spoiling my dinner. Which is in less than an hour. I'll have to be home to help set the table the second the sun sets, not that I can see the sun from Yarrow. With the blacked-out windows, time sort of stops in Yarrow House. It's unsettling, but I suck it up since the girls have to endure it.

"So, I've been thinking about why someone would want to kill you guys," I say, hiding the food in my mouth behind a flimsy napkin. "I think it might have something to do with the Rausch Scholarship. You were all top contenders for it this year."

June rolls her eyes. "*I* was the top contender. My essay was about how important my work on the charter school board was." She arcs a hand through the air, imagining a headline. "'Guiding the Flow of Communication' by June Phelan-Park. I was so gonna win."

"Mine was about staying positive in the face of adversity," Dayton chirps. "My whole family went on a mission trip last summer. It was life-changing."

"It was in San Diego," June says. "You could find poorer people if you'd stayed in Cross Creek."

"Joke's on you," Dayton says. "We were helping farm animals. I brushed an alpaca."

Riley cuts her eyes at me. "What does this have to do with us being murdered?"

"It's kind of the only thing you guys have in common," I say. "And, for whatever reason, basically everyone at Fairmont wants to win the Rausch."

"We want the party, duh," Dayton says. "It's like your own private prom."

"Xander's scholarship gala was so awesome," June says. She shakes out a ketchup packet between her thumb and forefinger and tears off the edge with her teeth. "It was even better than prom. Someone snuck in a flask of vodka—"

"I did," Riley interrupts.

"You did?" I ask. "You never told me that."

Riley swings her head to look at me. "I didn't want you to be jealous. It was when I was dating Myles." She seems cautiously hopeful that she's remembered something from her continued blackout period. "When was that?"

"The end of May."

Her face falls, and she turns back to her line of nugget sauces. "Anyway, Myles found a handle of Seagram's—"

I gag. "You drank *found* vodka? Why would I be jealous of *found* vodka?"

"Because," Riley says heavily, "it was at the Rausch dinner with popular people."

"And I'd be hella jealous of you getting drunk with who? The Future Zombies of America here?"

"Excuse you," June says. "Riley was only there because she's Xander's sister. No one thought she was cool."

"And you were only there because you were Xander's girlfriend, and you puked all over the dashboard of his brand-new car on the way home," Riley says.

"People are already talking about how you guys dying means

that the scholarship is up for grabs now," I say. "All we have to do is figure out who would want it enough to kill you."

Dayton takes a pull from her soda and wrinkles her nose. "And then what?"

"And then we get them to confess or take them to the police. Justice, revenge. You know, the whole reason I brought you back to life?"

"You brought us back by accident," June corrects. "You just wanted your friend back."

Irritation makes my lips crackle. I rub them together to keep the first ten things I think to say in reply from shooting across the room like bullets. "Okay, sure. But don't you *want* someone to go to jail for killing you guys?"

The room goes quiet except for the sound of Binx's rolling purr as he rubs his head into Riley's side.

June takes a loud slurp from her soda. "Whatever. It's not like they could kill us again."

"The affairs of the living aren't really our business anymore," Dayton says with a world-weary flounce of her wrist.

"What?" I gape at them. "You're not serious, are you? Someone murdered all of you in one week. It was a fucking rampage. Why would they stop murdering people now that it's working out for them? They'll probably try to kill me when they realize that I'm searching for them."

Riley pops a nugget into her mouth. A drop of honey mustard splashes onto her lower lip. "Then stop searching."

"I can't!" I yell. The sound makes Binx dart across the room and leap up the stairs. "If anyone else dies, it'll be my fault for not stopping it. And have any of you considered that what you do while you're here might have an effect on what happens Sunday night?"

"Sunday night we die again," June says. "Kind of no matter what, according to your old book."

"And what happens after that?" I snap. "Do you think you'll get to go to your 'eternal reward' if all you did with your second chance was yell at the Nouns and steal from Walmart? Assholes don't get to go to heaven."

June slams down her soda. "We didn't ask to come back to life! *You* brought us here."

"No one asks to be born either," I counter. Barbed anger curbs my hunger. I toss aside my burger, letting it skid and fall apart on the floor, beef rolling over pickles. "You still get judged based on what you do with your time on earth. And, guess what? You have been a total dick for sixteen years, so maybe spending a couple of days doing something for someone other than yourself would help your chances of a decent afterlife."

"I'm not a dick," Dayton says, masticating fish sandwich angrily at me.

Riley snorts. "Yes, you are."

Dayton gasps, her eyes saucer-wide. "I was always nice to you! Name one mean thing I ever did to you."

Riley grips her own knees until her knuckles angrily jut, bone white, from her hands. "You made fun of me for years. You convinced everyone not to come to my birthday parties. You ruined any chance of me having any kind of social life. You labeled me a freak, and everyone believed you."

Over the years, I have heard many stories about Riley's lonely childhood. The solo piano lessons and Bible study and birthday parties alone with Xander and a cake. But she never mentioned how it all started.

"You never told me Dayton was the one who told people not to go to your birthday parties," I say.

"Well, she was," Riley snaps. "I didn't want to dwell on it or anything. It seemed pathetic to stay mad about things that happened in elementary school. And I guess I thought I would live long enough that it wouldn't have ruined my *whole* life. But that didn't happen. So thanks, Dayton. You're the reason I had literally one friend before I died. You scared everyone else away from me."

"You live in a funeral home," Dayton says shrilly. "It's a scary place!"

"It's really not," I say. "Unless you're scared of carpeting, it's just an apartment over a showroom.

"A showroom for death!"

"Caskets," Riley corrects. "Empty caskets. They're fancy boxes with different kinds of fabric inside. It's like being scared of jewelry boxes."

"Jewelry boxes of death!"

"It *is* pretty creepy," June says, twirling a fry.

Riley narrows her eyes at her. "Don't even get me started on you. I can't believe my brother dated someone as stuck up as you. You wouldn't even come to dinner with my family."

"Okay, but you guys were always eating somewhere bizarre. I don't want to eat food from Thailand or India or wherever. Who even knows what's in there? Why couldn't you eat something normal?"

"We can't all subsist on buttered noodles and self-righteousness," Riley growls.

"And, for fuck's sake, stop using *normal* as code for *white*," I snap. "Your life isn't the ruler that the rest of the world gets measured against."

"I never said that it was," June says stiffly.

My face goes hot as I think of all the reasons June has ever made fun of me. I'm brown and she's not. I'm fat and she's not. I'm Wiccan, shorter than her, live on a different side of town, drive an older car, prefer Coke over Pepsi. And on any given day when she was alive, she found a way to make me feel ashamed of that. I think about the wave of shameful relief I felt sitting in the pews at her funeral, listening to Xander eulogize her. As his eyes filled with tears, a euphoric calm settled over me knowing that June Phelan-Park would never torment anyone ever again. That there would never be new June insults to make me doubt myself or anyone else.

"Yes, you did. Every single day, all you did was point out how people weren't like you and how that made them weird or shitty or just less than you. You tried to make everyone fit into a June-shaped box, and you cut them down until they understood that they never would. How many people have cried in your face after you said something to them? Because, let me tell you, that's a super-easy number for me to figure out, personally. The only people I have ever made cry are my sisters. So what about you? Yesterday, you hurt all the Nouns enough to make them cry."

"They were saying shitty things about me first!" she shouts. Her cheeks are flushed with anger.

"Yeah, but they thought you were dead, so they weren't doing it just to hurt you. You went for blood. So that's four people you've made cry in the forty-eight hours since you've been back. What about before that? Who else did you eviscerate with your words? Can you even remember all of them? Or did you not care enough to keep count?"

Her mouth stays clamped shut, but her eyes shimmer with hatred. Given enough time, she will be able to craft my own personal nuclear-destruct codes. But I'm not interested in breaking down today. There's a murderer on the loose.

"If you guys don't want to help me find your killer, then fine. Sit here until Sunday and then walk yourselves back to the graveyard, for all I care. I'll find a way to get justice without you. But I promise, if anyone else dies this week, it will be your fault for sitting back and doing nothing."

"I don't care what she said about their debate competition," June muses. "I still think it was Sky. She used to love listening to *Serial*. That's so creepy."

"Sky has an alibi," I say. "She was with the other Nouns and Xander at your wake when Riley died."

"What about Dan Calalang?" June asks. "He's always had a crush on me."

"He's a senior. He isn't eligible for the scholarship."

"God damn it," Riley groans. She stands up and blows out the nearest candle. As it gutters tendrils of smoke into the air, she kicks the stack of books it was resting on so that they all slide across the floor. *Wicca in the Kitchen. The Witch's Encyclopedia. Herb Magick. Spells for the Teen Witch.* "Are you a witch or aren't you?"

THIRTEEN

I SHOW UP to Yarrow House with another load of fast food—
Chipotle today—and a pad of paper. We need to game-plan the
spells we'll need to find the killer and coerce a confession out of
them. The girls promised to spend the school day digging through
our magical library.

I don't think it's been long enough to hazard a visit to Lucky
Thirteen. The way Toby freaked out on me—was that only a week
ago?—makes me uneasy to go back and try again. What if she
sniffs out what I've done or what I'm planning to do next? I'd
rather face her when I have fewer secrets.

June and Riley are sprawled out on opposite ends of the living
room, faces buried in books. In the stretch of floor between them,
rune stones and tarot cards are spread out in various piles. I set
the bag of burritos next to a cross of Goddess tarot, and I have to
balance carefully to keep from crushing polished quartz.

"I tried to teach them divination," Riley says, rolling her eyes. One of her eyebrows twitches, and she kicks aside the red grimoire that brought her back. "Turns out trying to read the future isn't that fun when you don't have one."

"You should have seen that coming," June says. She's on her stomach, her feet almost inside the fireplace. She licks her finger and turns the page in *The Teen Witch's Book of Shadows*. "Mila, did you bring the highlighter I asked for?"

I pull a single yellow highlighter out of my jacket pocket. It's Izzy's. I'm not a highlighter person. June snatches it from me without looking up from her book.

I nudge a Ten of Swords card out of my way and sit down on the bottom stair. The candlelight doesn't reach the top of the staircase, but if I squint, I can see where the light goes pale near the broken window in one of the upstairs bedrooms, letting in just a hint of sun.

"Where's Dayton?" I ask, aiming the question at Riley.

She scowls at me. "Out somewhere. I'm not her babysitter."

"She can't just go wandering!" I say, imagining zombie Dayton skipping around, scarring children and causing accidents with her blue-cheese-veined face. "What if someone sees her?"

Riley combs her hair over one shoulder, her fingers deftly braiding it as her face stays unruffled. "They'll gain a new appreciation for how connected their heads are to their necks?"

"I can hear you," June says.

Riley tips her head closer to her shoulder, so that her joints pop as she continues to braid. "Like you aren't jealous of my neck."

The back door bangs open. The dusty floor is audibly scuffed by Dayton's skipping step. At least, I think it's Dayton. She's bundled up like the Invisible Man in Riley's Giants hat and a super-thick black scarf that she unwinds with one arm, the other clutching a large bottle of blue Gatorade to her chest.

"Is that new Gatorade?" I ask.

Dayton examines the bottle, giving the contents a swirl like it's a fine wine. "Yes! I went to the gas station. But no one even questioned my monster face."

"I doubt that," June says. "You look ridiculous."

"Ridiculously hydrated!" Dayton says with undeterred cheeriness.

I can't stop myself from smiling back at her. There's something infectious about Dayton's unrelenting positivity.

"We haven't found much in these spells," June says, uncapping the highlighter with her teeth. I forgot how intense she gets about studying.

"We haven't found dick," Riley says.

"That's not true," Dayton says. She plops down on a tarot spread and unscrews the top from the bottle of blue Gatorade. When she smiles again, her teeth are tinged the same color her skin turns when she zombies out. She bends in half with a stream of frenetic giggles. "We found out that there are spells for orgasms. Bibbidi-bobbidi-*ooh*! Isn't that hilarious?"

June makes an uncomfortable amount of eye contact with me, the corners of her mouth twisting up like there's an Allen wrench ratcheting up her maliciousness. "Only if you aren't the one in need of magical assistance with your sex life."

I glare at her in return, wishing I had enough magic to burn her with the heat of my annoyance. If she tells Riley about my crush on Xander, I swear that I will have to hurt her. Maybe I'll stay one hundred and one steps away from her until Sunday night so that she has to spend the rest of her time on Earth with her neck all lopsided.

"Riley came up with the bibbidi-bobbidi part," Dayton admits, wiping happy tears from the corners of her eyes. "Has she always been this funny?"

I cast a glance at Riley, who stays sheepishly focused on finishing her braid. I don't know how comfortable I would be taking compliments from my childhood bully either.

"Yeah," I say. "She has been. You've been missing out."

"We haven't found any spells for revealing foul deeds," June says with a note of seriousness. Studying is not a joke to her. "We could make someone fall in love, have better luck with money, or have boundless and plentiful orgasms—"

Dayton bursts into giggles again.

"But," June says, raising her voice, "there's nothing about revealing a murderer. There are some small truth spells that we might be able to fashion together into one giant spell, though. But Riley says there's a chance that could kill them."

"I'm willing to risk it," Riley says. "They killed us first."

"Mila, can I use your phone?" Dayton asks pertly. "I can't remember the last time I was on the internet. Think of how many Snapchat filters I've missed!"

I frown at her. "I don't have Snapchat. And you can't take pictures of yourself or talk to anyone."

"But I could read all the posts people have been writing about how much they miss me," she says, batting her lashes. "What if I promise to leave only footprints and take only memories?"

With a sigh, I take my phone out of my pocket and pass it to Dayton. She rubs it against her face the same way a cat rubs itself on plants it likes. She opens the web browser and types rapidly with both hands.

"That's the stuff," she says with a sigh of relief.

"You're such a weirdo," June says with a snort.

Dayton ignores her and holds her free hand out to me. "Headphones?"

I hesitate, unsure of what exactly is lurking in Dayton's ears. Sure, she looks pink and clean right now, but I know that a couple of minutes ago she was literally rotting. But it's rude to discriminate, even against the sort-of dead.

I unwind the headphones from their perma-ball in my pocket. Dayton pops them into her ears and hunkers down. Binx trots down the stairs, squeezing past me to sniff the Chipotle bag before wandering into the kitchen, presumably to find something more alive to eat.

"She always ends up on her phone instead of studying," June says, inclining her head at Dayton. "She's better at study breaks. I had to ask her to stop coming to our meetings at Starbucks. She was too distracting."

I frown at her. "You kicked your best friend out of your club?"

June highlights a line in her book with one long swipe. "I don't rank my friends, Camila Flores. I have a lot of them. None are better than the others."

"The *best* in *best friends* isn't a quality judgment," I say. Leave it to June to make everything a race to be first in her heart. "The *best* is for the closest. The person you trust the most. The person who"—I can't help but look at Riley—"who you'd bring back from the dead."

Riley glances over at me, her face expressionless but pinker around the edges. "Don't expect June to understand loyalty. She was born an ice queen and will die an ice queen. Twice. The night she died, no one even knew where she was. Not one of her friends. She was sneaking around, and no one will ever know why." Her eyebrows shoot up, almost knocking into her brown roots. She touches her lips like they're infused with magic. "Mila, I—"

I gasp. "You remembered something! Something recent!"

"Oh, spare me," June snaps. "You could have just made that up. Why would you know where I was the night I died?"

Riley scrubs her hand over her cheeks, jaw slack with astonishment. "My brother got a phone call from your parents. We were watching TV—something stupid about aliens. The house phone rang, and we thought it was a business call—a pickup for Dad. That's what the house phone is for. But Xander answered it, and it was your mom. She said you weren't answering your phone and no one knew where you were. But Dayton wasn't with you." She swings her head to look at Dayton's oblivious face, intensely watching my phone. "Because Xander texted her and the Nouns, and none of them had seen you either. And then your body and Dayton's were found by an old man walking his dogs before sunrise. My parents went to collect you, and Xander cried so hard that he threw up. And I called Mila while he cleaned himself up." She swallows. "Right?"

"Yes," I say in a whisper. "That's exactly what happened."

She presses her hands into her temples as though trying to squeeze her brain. "After that, it goes dark again. I don't remember my dad preparing the bodies or the families coming to pick out caskets or—"

"Stop!" June shouts, a tremor running through the word. "That's me you're talking about. Not some random dead body."

Binx trots back into the room, chasing a skittering spider. His tail knocks through a pile of rune stones, and I move my leg out of the way so that both of them can pass by me.

"June," I say delicately, "the more you guys can remember, the better. It could help us catch your killer if we knew exactly—"

"I don't want to remember 'exactly,'" she interrupts. She tosses aside her highlighter and scoops Binx up before he can kill the spider. He goes limp in her hands with a face that implies that some great indignity has fallen upon him. "I don't want to know how they got us alone or what kind of rope they used or how they managed to lift us up in the tree. I don't want to remember the last thing they said to me or if I had to watch Dayton die or if it was the other way around. It doesn't matter. Because we're still dead, and turning a killer over to the police won't change that, so just stop it! Stop digging around for why. As the murdered party, I don't care! I can't have my life back!"

Dayton pops out one of her headphones, her thumb on the screen of the phone to pause it. "Hey, June? Sorry to interrupt, but could you come here for a sec?"

June drops Binx onto the ground. He mews lightly and pads over to Riley.

"Traitor," Riley whispers to the cat as he head-butts her knee.

Dayton turns the phone around so that the rest of us can see it. She has paused a video on Facebook. The image is grainy and dark, but I easily recognize my lab partner's face. Caleb is frozen onscreen, his mouth open and his hair mussed under a bulky video game headset. He's wearing a black T-shirt with a picture of a red-and-white umbrella on it. Dayton points one of her bitten nails at his neck. It's hard to see since the video is so small on my phone screen, but I can just barely make out a silver chain peeking out of the collar of his shirt. On the end there's a tiny charm, a heart-shaped lock.

"Oh my God," June breathes. "Is that my monogram necklace on Caleb Treadwell?"

"How many Tiffany J necklaces do you think there are in Cross Creek?" Dayton asks.

"Isn't that a serial killer thing?" I ask, winding the rubber band around my wrist as my heart speeds up. "Keeping a trophy from the victim?"

Caleb has never been secretive about how much he wants

the Rausch Scholarship. As the principal's kid, Caleb must have attended a dozen of the awards galas, watching other people getting lauded while he got hungrier and hungrier for the spotlight.

Why did Caleb know so much about what happens to a body after a hanging? Did he stand under June and Dayton as they tried to kick their way down to solid ground again? Did he hold Riley underwater?

He said that the road was clear for him now. Did he clear his own way?

"What is this video?" June asks. "What's he doing? Did he say anything about me?"

"He's playing video games," Dayton says. "It was a livestream. It started autoplaying, and I saw the necklace—oh my gosh, were *sweatpants* the last thing we saw?"

"No," June says, staggering backward away from the phone. The heel of her off-brand Keds crushes the corner of a loose sheet of paper containing a luck spell that Toby handwrote. June shakes her bangs and squeezes her eyes shut. "Just because he has my necklace doesn't mean that he killed us. Look at Mila! She's been wearing Riley's little pink necklace. That doesn't mean she killed her."

Riley settles Binx into her lap. Loose white fur spreads over her black jeans instantly. "She *is* holding it hostage."

I reach up and wrap my thumb and forefinger around the spike of rose quartz. The stone is the same temperature as my skin.

"I'm not holding it hostage," I say. With every ounce of magic and determination in my body, I will my cheeks not to burn.

"Xander gave it to me. Your parents threw it out before your embalming. He saved it for me."

"Oh, how sweet," June says, her eyes vibrating with barely contained mania. "You've been saving something for him, too, huh?"

"What?" Riley asks.

"Shut up, June," I snap. "Dayton, what's the date on that video?"

Dayton swipes and magnifies and checks the calendar built into my phone with a few pinches of the screen. "Sunday, October eighth."

I rub my hand over my lips, feeling the same sense of divine intervention that I had when the grimoire showed up on the porch. Except Riley is here, watching me through narrowed eyes rather than on the other side, giving me hints.

"That's the day after you two were found. I'm sorry, June, but how else would he have your necklace? It's not like you were friends."

"This is exactly what I didn't want," June says, her voice quivering. "I don't want to think about him taking things off my body. I don't want to know what he did to us before we were dead."

"But this could be why the Nouns thought you guys were sleeping together," I say calmly. "You die, and then he starts going around with your signature piece of jewelry? It's not like he'd say, 'Oh yeah, I pulled it off her corpse.'"

"That was just a rumor!" June squeaks. "And why would it just be my necklace, huh? Why nothing of Dayton's or Riley's? If he killed me, then he had to kill all of us!"

"Oh," says Dayton, "I don't normally wear jewelry. We can't

wear anything in the water during swim practice, so I just fell out of the habit. I wonder what he took off of me?"

"How intact does your hymen feel?" Riley asks darkly.

The color drains out of Dayton's face. "Oh God. I don't know. Could I feel it before?"

"Riley!" I say as disgust and fear march over my skin. "For fuck's sake. No, Dayton, you can't feel your hymen. According to the news, your body was missing a shoe."

"Riley is being a textbook Scorpio," June says. "They always want to push your buttons. Don't listen to her, Dayton."

Riley shoves Binx out of her lap. Tears rise in the corners of her eyes, but she drags them away with the back of her wrist. "That's not true! We literally don't know what happened to us. We don't know anything except now there are trophies and serial killers and we're running out of time to get revenge. You might not want to know what happened to you, June, but I promise you it's so much worse than you're imagining."

"Shut up, shut up, shut up!" June screams, covering her ears.

"No!" Tears leak down the sides of Riley's face, but her voice is steady. "You can try to hide from it, but he loved killing you so much that he is walking around openly wearing something he stole from your corpse." She reaches out, shoving June's shoulder. "So what are you going to do about it? Stop sitting back and waiting for everyone else to do the dirty work for you. You aren't a princess. You're a walking, talking dead girl. And the sooner you get angry about that, the sooner you can do something other than read through spells you don't even fucking believe in!"

"Fine!" June whirls into action, moving in a blur across the room. She grabs the red grimoire off the floor and slaps the pages aside. With the candlelight coming from the mantel beside her, her face looks like a demented mask. Her whole body is shivering, even though the air is thick and unmoving.

"This," she announces, swinging the book around. Her fingertips are bleached white where they dig into the brown pages.

The spell she's holding up to us is almost as long as the resurrection spell. The heavy-handed calligraphy across the top reads: *Draw the Rot Out of the Heart of Your Enemies.*

"I saw it when we looked through the book on our first night back." She is having a hard time keeping her voice steady as her jaw continues to tremble. "We can do a truth spell to force the confession we need to call the cops. But this"—she taps the book four times in quick succession—"this is what I want. This is the revenge I need."

"Okay," I say. The bloodlust in the room is as palpable as the candle smoke and Binx's dander. Revenge has hovered over all of us since the girls came back, but suddenly it has direction and a name. We will draw the rot out of Caleb Treadwell. We will stop him before he kills anyone else. I squint at the list of ingredients. "Let's figure out where to get a calf's heart, then."

Dayton claps her hands together. "From a baby cow!"

FOURTEEN

DUST KICKS UP under all four wheels of my car until it looks like I'm dragging a dingy fog with me down the driveway to Yarrow House. Thankfully, the paint on the car is already beige, so it won't be any more noticeably dirty when I get home than when I left for school this morning. Not that I think either of my parents would actually ask me where I've been. That would require them making eye contact and speaking to me.

I jam my elbow into the horn. I know there isn't a clock in the abandoned house, but the girls haven't had anything to do today except gather acorns for the truth spell we patched together yesterday. I had to fight after-school traffic all the way through town, and I still managed to be on time.

I roll down my car window and stick my head out.

"Let's go!" I shout. I toot the horn again.

There's a glimpse of short hair and visibly veined skin around the side of the house. Spotting me, Dayton rounds the corner of the porch, waving her swollen fingers wildly. Her corpse form is truly horrifying in the daylight—one of her opaque eyes looks ready to fall onto her cheek, the bruising on her neck is a rainbow of gruesome colors—but I force myself to smile at her as widely as my inner cringe will allow.

She turns and shouts to the others before dashing down the broken stairs of the porch. Riley and June appear behind her, moving as quickly as their wounds will allow. I can see a bone jutting out of Riley's broken left wrist that snaps back into place as she hits the dead grass at the end of the driveway. June's neck wobbles as she jumps off the porch but straightens out once she lands.

Dayton whips open the passenger door behind me and slides in. Her skin smooths out to peachy cream, and her eyes realign into brown irises and pinpoint pupils under long lashes. She beams at me in the rearview mirror.

The other doors open and close hard enough to rock my little Toyota back and forth. Riley settles herself into the front seat as June buckles in behind her.

"Where are we going?" Dayton asks, clapping her hands against her knees.

"Somewhere no one will recognize you guys," I say. "Buckle up!"

Riley's eyebrows pull together sardonically under the folded brim of her gray beanie. "Why? We're already dead. We don't feel pain anymore."

"Yeah," Dayton agrees eagerly. "I had a nail go all the way through my foot this morning, and I didn't even notice!"

"Um. Cool, I guess?" I say, holding back a shudder. "But if you fly through my windshield, my parents will be super pissed."

"Fair point." Riley straps the seat belt across her chest. The second I hear the buckle click into place, I throw the car into reverse and speed back down the driveway.

We take the back roads out of Cross Creek, following the border of woods as it curves around the edge of town. The trees have started to turn colors, flagging the route of our escape in golds and reds. No one talks, so I turn the radio on low. It's still set to the pop station that Izzy insists on listening to when I have to take her somewhere. June hums along softly in the backseat. Riley's fingers keep time against the curved armrest built into her door.

Dayton has her face pressed to the window like a giant puppy. I hold my breath as we pass other cars. They last thing we need is to be seen by anyone's parents or Aniyah Dorsey, kid reporter. I take a couple of detours so that we don't drive past any of the bridges over the creek or Aldridge Park. I don't want to ruin a perfectly good outing with reminders of where the girls died.

We pass over the county line and drive alongside the train tracks. It's not as scenic here as it is in Cross Creek, but no one from Cross Creek would bother driving half an hour to run their errands, so this is our safest bet. Unless they, like us, needed to stop into Mercado del Valle, which is unlikely since Cross Creek is one of the whitest places on earth. I don't think most people in town even know that we live within driving distance of a Mexican grocery store.

"What do we need from here?" Riley asks as we climb out of the car.

"Candy!" Dayton says, bouncing around to the front of the car. "And more Gatorade."

"A cow's heart," I say. "And some charcoal."

"Then can we draw the rot out of Caleb's heart?" June asks, folding her arms over her chest. Of the three girls, she's the only one who seems determined to turn her limited wardrobe into multiple outfits. Today, she's wearing her black leggings with the mustard cardigan she was buried in. It's cute and effortless in a way that makes me think about strangling her before I remember that Caleb Treadwell already did.

The grimoire is pretty vague about what drawing the rot out of a person actually does. Personally, I hope that it'll take the shitty murderous part and leave behind the sliver of good in Caleb. That way he can march down to the police station and turn himself in. Otherwise, we'll have to move on to phase two of the plan: luring him into the basement and force-feeding him the truth spell that, for some reason, is made mostly of acorns.

"Yes," I say to her, leading the way through the parking lot. "We can draw the rot out of his heart when we have a heart to start with."

"Magic is so stupidly literal sometimes," Riley says.

We pass through the automatic sliding doors. Inside, hospital-bright lights hover over our heads, and the sound system blares as Selena sings "Bidi Bidi Bom Bom." Unlike the grocery stores in Cross Creek, everything smells delicious, thanks to the taquería housed at the other side of the building.

"You guys can look around, if you want," I say to Dayton, June, and Riley. "I have to go to the meat counter. There's a bakery against the back wall if you want to grab anything to take back to the house."

Dayton's face lights up. I can almost see the cookies dancing in her eyes. She immediately darts toward the bakery.

"Try to stay within a hundred steps!" I call after her.

"I'll go track down the charcoal," Riley says. "And maybe some matches? The spell will move faster if we have more than one way to light shit on fire."

"Sounds like a plan," I say.

I look at June, waiting for her to come up with her own reason to wander freely, but she sticks by my side. Lucky me.

The meat counter wraps around most of the right wall of the store. Beef takes up most of the middle of the counter. Ground, steak, sides, flanks, tongues, all marked with small yellow signs. I read Spanish much better than I speak it, although the mercado's signage is all in Spanish and English, so it's not really a true test of my skills.

"¿Cómo puedo ayudarle?" asks the man behind the counter.

I swallow. I get so nervous speaking Spanish to non–family members. I only ever really use it to talk to my grandparents or eavesdrop on my parents' phone calls.

"Un corazón de res, por favor," I say, quiet and uncertain.

The man nods, not showing any sign that he thinks the order is weird or that my conversational skills are about as refined as a three-year-old native speaker's. I wipe my sweating palms on my hips.

The man behind the counter peels what is unmistakably a heart out of the display case and slaps it onto the scale. June and I both flinch.

"Was Caleb wearing my necklace today?" June asks.

I nod. "It was tucked into his shirt, but I could make out the outline of the lock."

It's pretty ballsy—if actively psychotic—to wear a token of the girl you murdered to school. But seeing the heart-shaped lump under the collar of Caleb's shirt made me more resolved to cast today's spell.

The man behind the counter hands me the heart neatly wrapped in brown paper and asks if I need anything else. I shake my head.

"¡Muchas gracias por su ayuda!" June says to him brightly. I must look shocked, because she rolls her eyes at me and says, "I'm in AP Spanish."

Of course she is. Was. Whatever. Even racist white girls speak Spanish more naturally than I do.

"Any news on you and Xander?" June asks as we walk past the fish counter. Even the dead cod packed in ice look more comfortable than I feel right now.

"There is no me and Xander," I say.

"Why not?" She blinks at me like this is a rational question. "I'm dead. There's nothing standing in your way now."

"Gee, thanks," I say. "Except he's still Xander and I'm still me."

I don't tell her that he sent me a text message after the Celebration of Life on Monday to see if I was feeling better. You know, since I almost puked on him. It was the sweetest thing that has ever embarrassed me to my very core. I told him that I must have been poisoned by a Dayton Nesseth Memorial Tree Fund cookie.

"Look, Mila," June says with an obnoxiously forced maturity. "You're not doing yourself any favors by secretly pining. You can either want people who want you, too, or you can move on. You're wasting your life with all this unrequited love. Why would you like someone who doesn't like you back?"

"That's not how crushes work," I snap. I'm holding the heart package too tightly. The paper crinkles loudly. I loosen my grip so that I don't damage the meat. "It's all hormones and feelings and illogical shit. I can't stop liking Xander because he doesn't like me."

"You don't *know* if he likes you. If you really knew that he didn't, if he looked you in the face and was like, 'Ew, no thanks,' you'd be too ashamed to keep lusting after him."

"What the hell, June? Are you trying to make me cry?"

"No! I'm trying to help! Because he hasn't said that. And I don't remember him ever saying anything like that in front of me. Not that he would have told me if he was into someone else. He's way too polite. You should ask him if he's into you. You never know!"

I sigh. It's not like June and I are two different species. It is possible that Xander could like us both.

"Maybe I don't want to know the answer," I say tightly.

"No. You don't want to know if the answer is no. Of course you'd want to know if it was yes."

I would. But I won't give June the satisfaction of saying so. She's already too high on her own assumptions.

We find Dayton and Riley in the party-supplies aisle. The top shelf is lined with piñatas of famous cartoon characters—SpongeBob, Dora, Elsa from *Frozen*—along with the more traditional star and donkey shapes.

Dayton's arms are laden with a container of assorted pan dulce and more bottles of Gatorade. Riley hugs a small bag of charcoal briquettes, a box of matches, and a new container of salt, which she shakes at me.

"Can never have too much salt on hand," she says.

"Can't you?" June asks.

"It's a witch thing," Riley says. I'm almost ashamed at how happy it makes me to hear her say it. "Please tell Dayton we don't need a piñata or confetti."

"I know we don't *need* them," Dayton says, juggling the items in her arms. The pan dulce rattle against their plastic container. "But I think it would liven up the house. It's so gloomy in there."

"I'm not paying for a piñata," I say. "You guys are bleeding me dry as it is. And you can't fit a piñata in your pockets, so I'm gonna guess you can't steal one either."

"Fine," Dayton says, her lips stuck out in a pout. She pushes the pan dulce into my arms. "Here."

"While I check out, you can go to the taquería and pick out whatever you want for dinner."

"We had burritos yesterday," June says.

"Chipotle is burrito-like," I say. "This is the real deal. Trust me."

Riley hands me the bag of charcoal. "Do you want me to order you some pupusas? That's your order here, isn't it?"

"It is," I nod, incredulity making my heart—the one in my chest, not in my hands—weightless.

She grins at me, showing all her teeth. "Coming right up."

We return to Yarrow House with our stomachs filled to bursting. Even June couldn't find anything shitty to say about our dinner at Mercado del Valle. The drive home was full of satisfied sighs and June playing DJ with the music downloaded to my phone. Apparently everyone likes pupusas and Bruno Mars.

It turns out that the basement under Yarrow House is actually the most well-preserved room. The stairs creak under my weight, but no more so than the front porch does, and the handrail is in place and doesn't even wobble, although the wood is rough and splintery. The walls are made of unpainted cinder blocks, and the floor is cracked cement. Only one corner has any mold, so the smell is negligible. Mostly, the room smells like the sagebrush Riley burned to cleanse the space for spellwork.

Last night, one of the girls pulled the board off the single small window that faces the woods. Now that there's real live daylight slanting in through the unbroken glass, we don't need as many candles as we expected.

The sheets and blankets I brought from home earlier in the week are spread out like sleeping bags at a slumber party. Dayton said that the girls moved down here because it was less likely that the floor would cave in under them, unlike the top floor, where the boards are all rotted and water damaged.

The room is colder since we're underground, but I seem to be the only one in need of a jacket. The others busy themselves with gathering supplies, scurrying up and down the stairs to grab everything. I can tell that they worked all night after I left them yesterday: Riley has already patched together a few truth spells in the notebook I gave her, the ingredients we had on hand are stacked on one side of the room, and the red grimoire is propped on a rickety wooden chair, open to the page with the *Draw the Rot* instructions.

With a ringing clang of cast iron on cement, June drops a Dutch oven full of wood scraps in front of the chair. The spell requires a lot of setting different things on fire, and she's in charge of making sure we don't burn the house down around us.

"I mean, only one of us can actually die," she said in a mocking singsong as I delegated fire duty to her on the drive back to Cross Creek. "So, you really want me to protect you?"

"Yes, June. Please don't kill me. Also, if you burn down the house, you'll have to camp in the woods until Sunday night."

"Ew," she said. "Camping is gross."

Pretty strong words coming from someone currently sharing her house with two other dead girls, a dozen raccoons, one surly cat named after an obscure Disney character, and an increasing number of dead mice and spiders, but whatever. At least she agreed not to actively participate in my death.

Dayton reads from the grimoire, double-checking the ingredients June placed inside the Dutch oven.

"Why doesn't this rhyme?" she asks. "Aren't magic spells supposed to rhyme?"

The stairs groan as Riley marches down them, carrying Binx in her arms. I've noticed that she's been holding on to him more and more, like she's afraid he's going to run away or end up liking one of the other girls more than her. As a former outdoor cat, Binx doesn't relish the attention. His purrs have been replaced with a low-pitched whining sound that makes me think of a distressed cow.

"Spells are for visualization, not poetry," Riley says, parroting words that Toby has said to us a thousand times. "The clearer the image in your mind, the more effective the spell. Rhyming spells are fine if they're well written, but most people sacrifice image clarity for a strong rhyme."

"Right," I say, dragging my nails through my hair. "Like we could rhyme *rot* with *pot*, but what if we just got Caleb stoned? Or turned him into an actual cooking pot?"

"Or we could accidentally make him hella hot," Riley says with a single flick of her eyebrows. She doesn't smile, but I can feel her delight as June clenches.

"He could get lost on a yacht?" I add.

"Oh, then it would be all for naught."

I almost forgot how goofy Riley could be. That we could be goofy together. Images of gummy bears thrown into each other's mouths and leaf fights in the woods flash through my mind, and I feel a pang in my chest. Riley and I used to do fun, silly things—we didn't stay up until sunrise every weekend having serious discussions about revenge or spells gone wrong.

"Stop," June demands, cutting off our rhyming.

Riley tips her head. Binx wiggles in her arms, his unhappy noise rising like a siren. "I apologize a lot."

"Okay, I get it," Dayton says. "Rhyming is stupid and doesn't belong in magic."

Riley drops Binx to the floor. He makes a loop around the room, sniffing and nudging things, his green eyes wary as ever.

Dayton turns and leans against the cinder-block wall, her hands pressed behind her. She bounces on her toes, her tongue wedged into her cheek. "So, is that how you brought us back, Mila? Did you *visualize* the wrong thing?"

"I don't think so?" I frown. The resurrection spell is a blur of big emotions, meaningless words, and the earthquake that shook the puke out of me. "I don't know. I mean, I could have visualized it wrong. The whole school was talking about you guys dying, and the last time I saw Riley was at your funeral. I guess you could have popped into my mind at the wrong time. Maybe it's because I asked to help get justice against Riley's murderer and he's the same guy who killed you?"

"Maybe the universe sensed how good you two would be at gathering spell ingredients," Riley says, sweeping a hand around the room. She smiles at me again. "You know, in Haiti, zombies are actually slaves that someone feeds a bunch of drugs to? They supposedly make a hallucinogen out of puffer fish toxins and human remains."

"That is disgusting." June shivers.

"Yeah, we really got off easy being brutally murdered and then resurrected by vague and shady means."

"We have everything the book says we need," Dayton says, raising her voice over Riley's. "Do we need to chant or something?"

"I don't know what you think witchcraft is," I say slowly. "But it's a lot less rhyming and chanting and a lot more lighting candles and hoping something happens."

"Like most religions," Riley says brightly.

I don't know what has cheered her up so much today—remembering stuff? Getting out of the house? Belly full of quality food?—but I love it. It feels like I really have my blister back.

"Okay," I say. I square my shoulders. I am a leader. "Let's get to work."

I have cast many spells in the daytime, but this one seems strange. The grimoire doesn't say anything about what time or moon cycle is best, so I have no choice but to use my family dinner as the stopwatch on it. The hazy sunlight coming in from the basement window and illuminating the paper-wrapped heart does feel sort of ridiculous. Not that I'm going to say this out loud. I'm supposed to be The Witch, using all my mystical powers to draw the rot out of Caleb's heart regardless of time of day or atmosphere.

Still, casting the resurrection spell at midnight in a graveyard felt cooler. Witchier.

Riley takes a piece of white chalk from the ingredients pile and draws the circle in the middle of the floor. I direct June and Dayton to place the white candles at the north, south, east, and west corners of the room.

I unwrap the heart and ball up the paper. The meat is wet and slick in my hands. And heart-shaped. Not like a valentine, but like a page of a biology textbook come to life. It has ventricles, for fuck's sake.

I don't have a knife with me, and I don't want to slow down to hunt for the ceremonial dagger. I dig my nails into the heart and tear an opening in the middle. It's not as pliant as a cut of steak. The heart is a muscle, and this one was well used before it ended up at Mercado del Valle. But I rip it with the same sort of jagged mark that a broken-heart emoji has. I set it on top of the wood in the Dutch oven. My fingers are tacky with blood. The whole basement smells like iron.

Riley lights the candles, whispering in a familiar rise and fall as she invites the Goddess into the circle. June picks up Binx and sits on the bottom stair, watching as I pack the heart with salt and charcoal and a chunk of tiger's-eye stone. The rest of the cast-iron pot is filled to the brim with dried herbs and spices. I find the big box of fireplace matches. It sticks to the blood on my hands.

"Open the window," I say to Riley.

Setting the grimoire on the ground, she drags the wooden chair under the window and balances on the seat. Teeth digging into her lip with concentration, she pushes open the small window. Cold air whooshes inside, and the stink of blood lifts.

I make a shooing motion with my hand, and the girls all back up against various parts of the wall.

I take a deep breath, strike a match, and light the kindling under the heart. Smoke pools lazily in the bottom of the pot. Sparks crackle. The herbs light. And then it's a fire. A roaring, snapping fire that swallows the heart and everything inside it. I need to talk fast.

"Enemy of mine," I say, pitching my voice low for effect. Magic is real, and the Goddess provides, and blah blah blah, but I also want it to look as impressive as it is. "The evil inside of you rots you. For the deeds you have paid no penitence, let that which rots you mark you. For the hurt you have brought others, let that which rots you mark you. For the acts you have committed in defiance of the Goddess's will, let that which rots you mark you. For the lives you have taken and those left behind, let that which rots you mark you."

I pour another handful of salt into my palm.

"So mote it be." I throw the salt at the pot. The flames lick higher, almost touching the ceiling in a huge orange column, a hundred times wider and stronger than it was a second ago.

The girls jump. I do, too, when Riley looks at me through the flames. Her eyes are white. Then the giant flame shrinks as quickly as it started and burns down to embers. The only thing left in the pot is a smoking nub of tiger's-eye stone. Riley blinks at me, and her eyes are hazel again.

Did I imagine they were otherwise?

There's silence except for the susurration of the candles at the corners of the room eating through increments of wick.

"What happens now?" June asks nervously.

As cold as I was a minute ago, there's sweat building at the nape of my neck now. "We hope that it did something."

Dayton reaches into her pocket and lets a handful of confetti fly over our heads. "We did magic!"

"Fuck a duck, Dayton," Riley says, plucking a piece of confetti off her own cheek. "Did you steal this much when you were alive?"

Dayton blinks at her. "Yeah. Duh. How did you get stuff?"

FIFTEEN

IN THE REVERB of the third-period bell, backpacks swish against bodies, feet pound against the cement, and classroom doors slam shut. In an instant, I am standing alone in the middle of the hallway behind the main office.

I follow the long line of cream-colored lockers down the wall, watching the numbers grow. All the hallways at Fairmont are like cement tunnels, making my footsteps echo. I catch myself tiptoeing and force my feet to act normal, my spine to straighten.

It's hard not to look sneaky when you're sneaking.

I've never really bothered with my locker. It's all the way across campus, near the gym. If I get tired of carrying my books in my backpack, it's easier to get them out of my car than to try to run from one end of Fairmont and back between periods.

But June's locker is prime real estate—a stone's throw from the student parking lot, halfway between the main building and the cafeteria. She stole it from a freshman the first week of school by putting her own combination lock on it and then convincing that kid he was crazy for thinking it was his to begin with.

I know this because she told the story in painstaking detail yesterday before I left Yarrow House. She was delighted with her own "ingenuity." I told her it sounded sociopathic.

"You don't have to pathologize everything, Camila." She sighed at me heavily. "Now, do you want my combination or not?"

I check my phone for the number again. I could probably pathologize how impersonal it is. It's nothing symbolic in June's life, like a birthday or an anniversary. Just the number the lock came with.

This is as much a favor to June as it is a fact-finding mission. She convinced me to get hit with a tardy slip so that I could dig through her stuff for clues and also see if anyone left her any post-mortem presents.

Dayton couldn't remember her locker combination, and Riley never even bothered to keep a lock on hers since she never used it. So June is our only chance.

Luckily, June was also the most popular of the three of them. Not that I would ever give her the satisfaction of pointing that out.

Even before I'm in front of the locker, I can see paper sticking out of the vents cut into the door. I hold my breath and spin the lock to the appropriate, randomly assigned numbers. As the door swings open, I have to catch falling notebook paper that says, *I hope you found peace* in tearstained cursive. It's from Angel. I wonder if it was written before or after June accosted her by the dumpsters.

In front of a neat line of textbooks, there's a heap of Post-its and old Starbucks Treat Receipts and a tiny folded piece of lined paper. A mini-memorial.

I unfold one of the receipts. On the back, in block letters, it says, *Why did you take Dayton with you, you selfish bitch?*

Well. Not all memorials have to be complimentary, right?

With one last check over my shoulder, I scoop up all the notes and stuff them into my backpack. We can sort through them later to see if anyone left anything that will jog June's memory about the last couple of weeks of her life. I shake out her textbooks to make sure there's nothing hidden inside and grab a solitary spiral notebook.

I try not to look too guilty when I slip into chemistry. Mr. Cavanagh doesn't even pause writing on the whiteboard. He just says, "Tardy."

"Sorry," I say, probably not sounding sorry at all.

I collapse onto my stool next to Caleb, who tsks his tongue and shakes his head like he's disappointed in my lack of dedication to punctuality. His sandy hair is rumpled in a way that says "just woke up" rather than "trying to look like I just woke up." The delicate sterling silver chain of June's necklace barely peeks out from under the jacket he's wearing.

I remember Dayton wondering what Caleb could have taken off her corpse. If he's wearing June's necklace, it would stand to reason that he's got less visible trophies on him, too. Maybe not Dayton's shoe, but he could have something recognizably Riley's.

His pencil lead snaps, and he turns his back to me, hunching over to rummage through his backpack. All I can see inside are various notebooks—color coordinated, labeled in black marker—and a zippered pencil pouch. No earrings or baggies full of toenails or anything super weird. Maybe his backpack isn't close enough for his liking. The necklace is on his person. The other stuff could be in his pockets or something.

"Hey," I whisper as he straightens with a freshly sharpened pencil. "Do you have any gum?"

"Mila." He draws the *uh* sound out in avuncular disapproval. He bares his teeth at me. "You can't have gum on campus. You trying to get me detention? Cavanagh doesn't care who my stepmom is."

"Nope," I say, making my eyes wide and innocent, Dayton-style. It probably doesn't work on me, since Dayton doesn't wear three layers of eyeliner. Nothing says *fuck off* like eyeliner as dark and heavy as my soul. "Just hoping to freshen my breath is all."

He relaxes a fraction and reaches into the pocket of his sweats. Before I have a chance to get grossed out, he's pulled out a slim tin of mints. He holds them out to me. As his thumb flicks open the lid, I notice that, inside his sleeve, his forearm is mottled red and shredding. Like a snake shedding its skin.

I smile as I set the mint between my teeth. *That which rots you marks you, motherfucker.*

☠ ☠ ☠

Maybe I'm imagining it, but my stomach heaves as I walk into the parking lot after school. I stop and look around at the people swarming off campus, the line of parent-driven cars parked in the loading zone. I hold my keys a little tighter and move a little more stiffly, listening too closely to the crunch of wheels on pavement.

There's no reason for my magic sensor to go off at school. My stomach does have other things to do—like process the cafeteria food I ate earlier or tell me when I'm about to look stupid in front of large groups of people.

"Mila, are you okay?"

Aniyah Dorsey stops beside me, her face scrunched in the sunlight. She squints at me from behind her glasses.

"You look sick," she says. "Do you have, like, food poisoning or something? Is that why you were late to third period today?"

"What? Are you spying on me?" I snap.

She cocks her head at me. "Jesus. I'm trying to be nice."

"People aren't nice to me," I say, walking away from her. I want to get to my car. I want to find the bottle of Pepto floating at the bottom of my backpack. I want to know that this feeling isn't magic.

"But you're such a peach!" Aniyah calls sarcastically to my back.

I get in my car in a hurry, throwing my backpack at the passenger seat before I buckle up. I take a second before I turn the ignition to sigh at my own paranoia. It must be leftover guilt at breaking into June's locker. Even with her permission, it is sort of a breach of trust with my peers. If anyone saw me do it— especially if that someone was Aniyah—I'd be stuck in meetings with Dr. Miller until the end of time, talking about why I don't respect other people's grieving.

There's a blur of movement outside. My heart leaps into my throat and I scream as two black-clad figures press their hands against the passenger window.

The figures stop moving. Riley lifts the bill of her Giants hat and frowns at me.

"Really?" she says, her voice muffled through the glass. "We look normal right now."

They do look normal in that they aren't zombied out. They do not look normal in that every single person on campus thinks that they are currently buried across town.

Swallowing embarrassment and panic, I unlock the doors. Riley tosses my backpack off her seat, and it lands next to June.

"Did you get my cards?" she asks.

She doesn't wait for me to say yes before she rips open the zipper and starts digging around inside.

"What the fuck are you guys doing?" I ask, twisting around in my seat and looking out the back window as people walk past us. "What if someone sees you? What if someone saw you before I got within a hundred steps of you?"

"If they see us now, we're just three people in a car," Riley says, pulling her seat belt over her chest.

June nods, pulling one of the loose Post-its out of my bag. "And if they saw us before, we would have told them not to tell anyone under pain of eternal haunting. We had a plan."

I grip the steering wheel until my palms burn. "Why are you even here? This is, like, the number one place you could get recognized."

"Dayton's gone," June says, flicking aside a note.

"What do you mean she's gone?" I ask.

"Obviously you heard me," June says, holding a piece of lined paper in front of her face. "Aww. Dan Calalang left me a note. It says, *Wish we'd fucked*. Ew."

I yank the paper out of her hand, wad it up, and throw it at her shoulder. She gasps, and Riley rolls her eyes.

"What kind of gone is she?" I snap. "Did she poof? Did she die again? Did her head fall off and you guys lost it?"

"She's been going out for Gatorade every morning," June says, rubbing the spot where the paper hit her, even though we both know she can't feel pain. "And today she didn't come back."

Riley scrapes the heels of her hands over her knees. I can tell that she's worried but she doesn't want to show it. "I tried to do a spell to find her, but nothing worked. I tried dowsing over one of her scarves, and I did, like, thirty tarot spreads, but they were all dead ends."

"Probably because she *is* dead. There's no energy to follow or whatever," June says. "We don't need magic. We need to put a bell on her. Like a cat."

I look back at Riley. "Did you try a natural spell? Something more connected to the earth?"

She narrows her eyes at me, making the same face her mom

does when she thinks she can smell incense. "Well, normally I would use my necklace for dowsing, since it's been properly charged and acclimated to me, but since *you* have it, I had to settle for the big clear quartz pendulum."

I try not to rise to the bait. I fist my hand to keep from touching the necklace. "I'm just saying that I've been more successful not using store-bought supplies. Organic matter gets better results."

She scoffs. "You do one big spell and suddenly you're the expert?"

"Riley." I gape at her. "I brought back the dead."

"Mostly by accident! And you must have fucked it up because you brought me back without my magic."

"How do you know you had any magic before you were dead?" June asks.

"We don't have, like, proof," I say. There have been a lot of coincidences that could have been magic—boys who liked her back and tests aced without studying and finding keys lost between the couch cushions. But that was like saying that wishing hard enough made you a witch.

"You had enough proof to go and try to use a spell out of a book I bought! And it's not like you did it perfectly since you brought *them* back!" She hooks her thumb at June. "Unless your organic ingredients included eye of newt and toe of bitch!"

"Excuse me, don't drag me into your witch fight," June says. "I'm here because I want to find Dayton. She's never been gone this long."

"Did you guys look anywhere else before you came here?"

I ask. "Dayton wouldn't come back here. She hated the Celebration of Life."

"We all hated that stupid memorial," June says. "We didn't need to search the school. We needed *you* so that we could be people again. We're still on a magical leash. It's not easy walking around town with a broken neck, you know."

"Dayton seems to be managing!" I say.

Riley huffs, watching someone walk behind the car through the side mirror. They don't seem to notice us at all. "No one has formed an angry mob with pitchforks and torches, so I don't think she's been spotted yet."

I try not to imagine Dayton with her broken neck and veiny face, holding on to a bottle of blue Gatorade like a teddy bear while the villagers of Cross Creek encircle her, ready to bash her brains in.

"Where would she go?" I ask, glaring over my shoulder as June digs back into my bag for a fresh round of memorial notes. "Is there a special gas station she goes to? Who has the best Gatorade selection?"

Riley bangs her head against the headrest. "She's never told us where she goes. She leaves and comes back with food she stole. It usually doesn't take more than a couple of hours, but she's been gone all day. It's not like she could get lost here. She's lived in Cross Creek her whole life."

"If she's not lost, then why would she be gone for this long?" I ask. "June, you're her best friend. Is there anyone she would reveal herself to? Other friends she'd want to see before she died again?"

"She wouldn't want anyone to see her zombie face," she says, looking at me over the edge of her note. "It freaks her out just seeing her reflection."

"If she didn't want to see people, what if she wanted to see a place?" Riley asks. She rubs her hands together, digging her thumb into her life line. "What if she went home?"

SIXTEEN

JUNE IS A shitty copilot. Despite remembering her locker combination and every slight she's ever experienced, she claims not to know a single street name in Cross Creek. She shouts directions moments before I need them, so it takes me a few minutes to realize that Riley's shoulders are creeping up to her ears because we're turning the corner onto Laurel Street.

"Did you know that she lived near you?" I ask Riley.

Riley turns and looks out the window, her bloodless lips pressed together. The lawn of the Greenway Funeral Home is a bright green beacon coming closer and closer to us. Xander isn't home yet, and there aren't enough cars around for a service. I can picture Mr. and Mrs. Greenway inside, listening to the emptiness echoing throughout their home. I wonder if we'll even find Dayton in the neighborhood or if Riley just wanted to glimpse her own house.

"We're here!" June suddenly blurts out.

I slam on the brakes. Dayton's house is across the street and four doors down from the funeral home, but it's still too close for comfort. I can see the sun glinting off the hearse's trim. Riley hesitates for a second before unbuckling herself.

June, however, pops out of the car and tips her face up to the sunlight like she's photosynthesizing. I get out and run to her side.

"Can you attempt to be less conspicuous, please?" I whisper loudly, grabbing her arm and dragging her back over to the car. "If you get recognized, it will be really fucking bad for all of us. And for whoever recognizes you."

Riley hugs herself, her spine so stiff that I'm positive she's actively restraining herself from looking back at her house. Or running to it. "Aren't we about to get recognized by Dayton's whole family? How are we supposed to search for her without being noticed?"

June flicks her wrist at the empty driveway. "There's no one here. No minivan, no Nesseths. They can't use the garage because they converted it into a playroom. We'll go around."

She strides past the garage, disappearing around the corner. Riley cuts her eyes at me, and I give her a half shrug. Breaking into the Nesseths' backyard is pretty low on the scale of weird shit we've done this week. I let her go ahead of me. I want to believe that she wouldn't bail and run home to see her parents, but I'm honestly not sure.

The side gate opens with a pull of a cord, which seems pretty trusting of Dayton's family. I hold my breath, waiting for an alarm or even a barking dog, but I hear nothing except the sound of June's shoes on the gritty stone path.

The backyard is huge. Against the back fence is a long pool that's still mouthwash blue and leafless, even though it's autumn. There are toys everywhere—a tiny bicycle with training wheels next to the gas barbecue, plastic dolls and Frisbees partially hidden in the grass, bottles of bubbles and tubs of sidewalk chalk nestled next to the sliding glass door.

I never thought about how many siblings Dayton had. I remember seeing some little kids at her and June's memorial service, but I hadn't paid any attention to them. Seeing the lone little bike makes my stomach clench in a way that I know is unrelated to magic.

June presses her face to the door, but the glass is obscured by white lace curtains. Behind them is the faint shape of a dining room table, but there's no movement.

Riley stands next to me, eerily still. Her elbow knocks into mine, and I turn to see her deep frown, her hat hiding almost all the misery in her eyes.

Almost.

June gives up on the door and whirls on us. "Can't you . . . you know? Sense her? Isn't that one of your powers?"

I scowl at her. I really don't like the word *powers*. It makes me sound like I'm pretending to be a Monster High doll. Otherwise, she's right. I should be able to feel if Dayton's nearby. The terror of being caught trespassing is just getting in the way.

"Or do you need to have something more *organic* to help you out?" Riley adds tightly.

"I'm sorry you can't do magic anymore," I say, louder than I mean to. "But can you not be an asshole right now? I didn't do anything to you."

"Sorry," she says. She bites her bottom lip and turns toward the pool. "I didn't think it would be this hard to be back but not— Holy shit!"

Her arms drop to her sides, and she takes three long strides toward the pool. She gets so close to the edge that I'm terrified she's going to dive in and recreate her death. Instead, she kneels down and points toward the deep end.

At the back corner of the pool and eight feet down is Dayton. Her body is coiled into the fetal position, her hair floating around her head in wisps.

"Jesus Christ," June says, running to Riley's side. "Why isn't she floating? Shouldn't she be floating? Dead bodies float."

Dayton's head pops up, and all three of us jump back. Bubbles come out of her mouth as she smiles up at us. Feet fluttering, she propels herself upward in a fluid sea otter twist. Her head breaks the surface, and she blinks water out of her eyes.

"Oh, hi," she says, bobbing slightly as she treads water. Across the chest of her high-necked bathing suit are the letters *FACS*— Fairmont Academy Charter School.

"That's all you have to say?" June says, putting her hands on her hips. "I thought you were dead! Again. Or more. You know what I mean!"

"Nope," Dayton says with a sunny smile that doesn't crease her cheeks quite as deeply as it usually does. "I'm the normal amount of dead. Well, I'm a little prunier than normal." Her body dips down lower into the water as she holds up a hand. The tips of her fingers look like brains.

"Why the fuck are you hiding at the bottom of a swimming pool?" Riley asks.

The smile slips off Dayton's face. She gives a sad dog paddle toward us. "I'm really sorry, Riley. I know you're still mad at water. I didn't want you to have to get this close to it ever again."

Riley growls and splashes her hand into the water. "I don't care about the water! What are you doing here? You've been gone for hours."

"And where are your clothes?" I ask.

"I hid them in the hose pot," she says, pointing one of her painfully wrinkled fingers at a stone pot under the kitchen window. "I just wanted to be close to my family again. I know we all agreed that it wouldn't be right to talk to them, so I've been coming here for a little bit every day after my brothers and sisters go to school. At first, I missed the smell of home, so I found a spare key and walked around, saying goodbye to stuff. But then I found my swimsuit, and I couldn't resist . . . I mean, I don't have to breathe! My muscles don't get tired! I was beating all my old competition records!"

"Wait," I say, looking from her to June to Riley. "You don't breathe?"

Riley shrugs. "We won't die if we don't."

"It's a hard habit to break," June adds. "You just kind of keep doing it without thinking."

"I could just swim and swim and—" Dayton pirouettes in the water, her eyes closed, the same way they were when she sang in the theater. "But today the gardener came to mow the lawn, and I was too far away from Mila to pass for alive, so I hid. And then I hid for too long because I heard my brothers and sisters get home from school. I would have come back to our house later, I promise. I wasn't running away or anything—I was just waiting for my family to go to the farmers' market." She presses her lips together in a sad smile, her eyes distant. "I could hear my mom promising to get my sister one of the vegan cupcakes she likes. We help run our church's booth at the farmers' market on Thursdays, so we eat dinner there and then go listen to the band." Dayton pauses and looks back at us. "Thank you for coming to look for me."

"Of course we came to look for you," June says sharply. "We're your friends. We were worried."

I bite the inside of my cheek. Two weeks ago, the thought of being called Dayton's friend would have made me laugh for five straight minutes. Today, it wears like a scratchy sweater. Uncomfortable, but functional.

Dayton swims over to the ladder and heaves herself out of the water. Her movements seem clunky aboveground. Water splashes onto the pavement as she combs her fingers through her hair.

"Did the spell work on Caleb?" she asks me as her wet feet slap toward us.

"I think so," I say, relieved to have good news. "One of his arms is turning scaly, and the skin is sort of falling off? I only caught a glimpse of it up his sleeve, but it looked like it was rotting pretty good."

"Hm," June says, wrinkling her nose. "I thought the rotten-heart thing would look more like bread mold or like bugs coming out of his mouth."

"I was hoping he'd drop dead," Riley says. "Murderous asshole."

"There's still time for any of those things to happen, too," Dayton says cheerfully, clasping her hands to her stomach. "Mila could totally do more magic if the first spell isn't big enough."

I can feel Riley's glare, but I don't look at it directly.

"Besides," Dayton adds with a hop of excitement. "Mila only saw Caleb's *arm*. He could have fish scales all over him now. His butt could be falling off because there's so much evil in it."

"You think all the evil in Caleb Treadwell is located in his ass?" I ask.

Dayton throws her hands over her mouth as she erupts into giggles. Her body bends in half, and tears leak out the corners of her eyes as she sputters, "Think about his flaky, evil butt!"

I really don't want to find this funny, but June lets out a pig snort and turns away quickly, like we won't notice. And that makes Riley smile. So I let myself laugh along with Dayton as she mimes scratching her butt and finding clumps of it falling off in her hands.

"I guess I should get dressed," Dayton says, finally, after we all get winded. "June, would you mind getting me a Gatorade out of the garage? The side door should be unlocked."

"That's where you've been getting Gatorade?" Riley asks.

"There's a flat of it from Costco," Dayton says with a shrug. "I didn't want it to go to waste. I'm the only one of my brothers and sisters who likes blue."

"They buy everything in bulk," June says. "Chips, cookies, cereal."

"Fuck a duck," Riley says. "I'm coming with you. We need snacks."

The two of them go around the other side of the house. I watch them, wondering if I should follow, wondering if they even really need me here at all.

"When people talk about ghosts, they always mention their unfinished business," Dayton says, pulling her wad of black clothes out of the hose pot. She stands awkwardly, her eyebrows high on her forehead until I realize she's waiting for privacy. I turn around and stare at the pool. "Like you get stuck here because there's one thing that you need to do. When you brought us back, I thought that getting revenge on Caleb was our unfinished business. But it's more complicated than that. Everything is unfinished. Our whole lives. There's no amount of catching up we could do in seven days to make that better. Today I heard my mom's voice, and it wasn't enough to last me forever. Everything we ever did together was the last time." There's the wet suction and slap of spandex stretching and snapping. "I'm not going to stop missing them."

"I'm sorry," I say, watching the surface of the water rippling in the slight breeze.

"I know you didn't bring me back on purpose," she says. I can hear her feet hopping against the cement. "But I am glad I'm back, you know? I'm learning new things and having new adventures.

But coming here was the only familiar thing I've been able to do this week."

"Dayton," I say with a wince, "I don't think you should come back here again. It's too much of a risk. What if your parents come home early from work? What if a neighbor sees you? Or one of your brothers or sisters? What do you think it would do to them if they saw you . . ." *As a fucking monster.* "With your wounds?"

"I know," she says in a small voice. "That's why I didn't tell you guys. I knew you'd make me be smart about it. It was nice while it lasted. That's sort of what being back for a week is—nice while it lasts."

I close my eyes and clench my fists too tight, imagining the girls back in the graveyard, trapped under new headstones. My chest gets tight with future loneliness. I swallow hard.

"I'm gonna go wait in the car. Tell the others to hurry up," I say. I walk back up the paving-stone path before she can stop me.

I lean against the side of my car, pressing the heels of my hands against my eyes. Guilt and grief turn my stomach. I know that I brought Dayton and June back by accident, but that doesn't mean it's not my fault. Maybe if I were a better witch, they wouldn't need to stay within a hundred steps of me. Maybe they'd be able to spend the week with their families. Maybe Riley would be able to cast spells, too, and she'd have one less reason to be mad at me.

But in a couple of days, I'll even miss her glares and shitty comments, because they're hers.

A car slows to a stop. I hear the whir of the window rolling down and then, "Mila?"

My hands fall away from my eyes, eyeliner smeared into my palm. "Xander?"

I say it louder than I want to, but also—hopefully—loudly enough for the girls to hear.

Xander's elbow is propped in the window of his little silver car. He's in a midnight blue sweater that makes his eyes even more starkly, defiantly bright with worry. Because he's caught me almost crying outside of Dayton Nesseth's house. Great.

"Are you okay?" he asks, glancing over his shoulder for any oncoming traffic.

I wave him off. "Yeah, I'm fine. I was just . . . thinking about Riley."

It's not really a lie, even though it feels like one when he lets his own sadness wash over his face. It makes his forehead line and his jaw tense.

"What are you doing over here?" he asks.

"I . . ." I wonder if he thinks that I just park near his house to feel close to his dead sister. Or—humiliatingly—to him. Is it worse to seem pathetic or like a stalker? Are they equally bad? What would a normal person be doing on Laurel Street in the midafternoon?

"I was going to the farmers' market," I blurt. "There was no parking downtown."

"Are you going by yourself?" he asks.

My mouth goes dry. This is becoming more and more humiliating. I'm sure June is going to have a field day. "Who else would I go with?"

It takes every ounce of willpower not to look over my shoulder at the garage where Riley is raiding Dayton's family's snacks.

"I'll go with you, if you're up for company," he says. "It's cool if you're not."

I know I must look shocked because I feel almost numb. Did I step outside of reality at some point? "You want to hang out with me?"

"Yeah," he says with a laugh. "We used to hang out all the time."

With Riley. We've never hung out just the two of us. There was always Riley in the front seat of the car or between us on the couch or to keep the conversation going while we worked in the showroom at the funeral home.

"Okay," I say. "That sounds cool."

"Awesome. Meet me down at my house. Unless you want a ride?"

"No. I think I can manage to cross the street on foot."

He smiles at me as he drives away, and I brace my back harder against my car to keep from fainting. I glance over my shoulder at the fence. Between the slats, I see short, pruney fingers waving goodbye to me and then reaching up high to give me a thumbs-up.

Walking up the street with Xander, I notice that I'm actually much shorter in relation to him than I thought, eye level with the stitching on the shoulder of his sweater.

"How's being back at school?" he asks. "You haven't been kicked out again, have you?"

"Surprisingly not," I say, scuffing my heels through clumps of dead leaves on the sidewalk. "It's been as good as it can be.

Everyone has always avoided me, so at least now I can blame it on pity instead of fear."

He snorts. "Why would people avoid you?"

"People are scared of me. My face naturally spells out *fuck you*."

"No, it doesn't." He looks down at me, eyes wide. "It says, *Hi, I'm Camila Flores, don't waste my time with your indecisive bullshit*."

My laugh catches me off guard, and I almost let out a June-snort. "I mean, who wants their time wasted?"

"I think most people spend their entire lives wasting time and waiting for something better," he says softly. "You always seem like you know what you want. I've missed that about you."

Sweat is pooling in my palms. I rub them as discreetly as I can against the sides of my legs. "You saw me a couple of days ago."

"For a second," he says, rolling his eyes. "It's not the same."

"Nothing's the same," I choke out. "Riley's dead."

Nodding, he rubs his hand over the back of his neck, keeping his focus trained on the ground. "Since everything happened," he says slowly, and I know that he's talking about June and Dayton and Riley, although I don't know what order he's putting them in, "I feel like I've been betraying them every time I'm not miserable. And I know that's not how grief works. One second of being happy doesn't erase all the other moments of mourning. I know that I can't stay sad all day, every day. But I can't help but feel like people are looking at me and judging me for not being sad enough. Or for being too sad. I can't figure out what the normal amount is."

I remember not being able to cry at Riley's funeral and how I ached to look normal and squeeze out tears even though I wouldn't have been able to feel them.

"I know exactly what you mean."

"Right," he stresses. He reaches out and touches my elbow, light as a feather settling in the crook of my arm and gone just as fast. "I don't feel that way with you. I don't feel trapped. I know you understand. You don't need me to pretend to be something else."

"Why would I want you to be anything except you?" I ask.

He smiles, his face shining with that spark that draws me in like a sucker moth. "Do you know how many people have told me to cheer up this week? Or changed the subject when Riley or June or Dayton comes up? It's like living in a glass box. Everyone's afraid that if I breathe wrong, the whole thing will break. Or they want me to break down so they can watch."

"You feel like you're removed from everyone," I say, thinking of my family eating meals without me, my parents sending messages to me through text or my sisters. "Like they think your sadness is contagious."

"Yes," he says on a sigh. "But if you smile through it, they think you're not processing it enough."

"Like Dr. Miller."

"Exactly like Dr. Miller. She's still stalking me. She came and observed me at lunch yesterday."

"Are you sure she isn't just into you?" I ask.

"God, I hope not. I don't want to be anyone's sad-guy fetish."

I have bad news for you, Alexander . . .

We cross the street and round the corner where the Cross Creek Cinema is. The noise rises to a chaotic level. Laughing. Haggling. Shouting. A game of tag. I'm shocked at how crowded it is. It feels like everyone in town—minus the Flores family—is here, clamoring for some hella fresh produce.

I'm hit with the smell of a hundred different foods—overripe persimmons and roasting meats and cupcakes and herbs. I actually didn't think it was possible to be more overwhelmed tonight. Three different people brush me as they walk by with overflowing official Cross Creek Farmers' Market tote bags. The kids playing tag squeeze between Xander and me to run, full speed, toward the stage erected in the park.

Fuck. Downtown dead-ends at Aldridge Park. Where June and Dayton died. Why didn't I think of that before? What if Xander freaks out when he realizes where we are?

"This is way busier than I imagined," I say.

"You've never been here?" he asks. Lies spin through my head, but he interrupts my thoughts. "I guess you wouldn't have. I can't really picture my sister volunteering to hang out in a giant crowd like this."

Up ahead, I see Aniyah Dorsey at a booth. She has that too-interested look on her face that makes it seem like she's memorizing everything to write down later. A little kid with white-blond hair is handing her a pamphlet and pointing up at the sign on their canopy, which reads *Creekside Community Church*. There are a couple of other kids passing out pamphlets near the booth, none as blond as the one talking to Aniyah. They all have round elfin faces with easy smiles.

Why is Aniyah talking to the Nesseths? Does she have a sudden interest in evangelism, or is she sniffing out information on their dead sister?

Xander stops and turns, snagging something from the stall closest to us. He flourishes it to me, and I see that it's a chunk of apple on a toothpick.

"Are you still doing magic?" he asks.

"Are you asking because of the apple?" I ask, popping the piece into my mouth. "Because I'm really not a poison-apple, heart-in-a-box kind of witch."

"Trust me, I know," he says as we walk away from the apple seller. "I've sat through a lot of Wiccan rants. No poison apples, no flying monkeys, no pointy hats, no crystal balls."

"But you know that crystal balls exist? I just don't own one. Riley was more of the crystals-and-essential-oils one. Big stuff for big results."

Riley never had the patience for minute details. She wanted to string every bead at once, slap on a coat of paint, and call it done. I had the patience to gather and dry herbs for brushes. She could pull flowers, I could press them in wax paper. She preferred to buy spell ingredients, but I was always poorer and happier to hunt for them in the woods or neighbors' gardens.

Except now that job has been outsourced to June and Dayton.

"So, you don't care if you get big results?" he asks, shoving his hands in his pockets. "How will you know if it works?"

"It depends on the spell," I say carefully. "Not everything can have a definitive result. Most of witchcraft is just being present."

"And grateful?" he asks. "Riley said it was about being grateful for everything."

"Right," I say. I love that he gets it. That he already knows. "Present and grateful."

He leans over and bumps our elbows together, his face alight with mischief. "Do you think you could do some magic for me sometime?"

"It depends on what kind of magic you need," I say. My whole arm tingles where he touched it, and I have to actively restrain myself from pressing against him again. "I'm better at the crafty parts. Like making flower crowns or pentagrams out of sticks."

He smooths the hair out of his face, his lips pursed in momentary seriousness. I wonder if he was thinking of big magic—easing his grief or pulling lottery numbers out of thin air or even trying to bring Riley back. But instead he twitches a shrug. "Anything. Dumb stuff. Riley never wanted me around when she was doing spells. Do you think you could remove a zit with magic?"

I laugh. "Your skin is basically perfect. I'd have to find a spell to give you a zit before I could try to get rid of it."

"Okay, then whatever kind of magic you want. Just let me know if you need someone to hold a sage brush for you. It's the only thing Riley ever taught me to do."

"I'll consider it," I say, knowing that it'll be a while before I have a spell to do that isn't life or death.

We wind through the crowd, Xander occasionally stopping

to say hi to someone from school. Most of them I don't know by name. None of them would know me as anything except the fat witch of the junior class. Yearbooks will be opened. Facebook stalked. People will tell the story with confusion and shock: *Camila Flores, a Fairmont Academy junior, member of zero clubs, haver of no superlatives, was at the farmers' market with her dead best friend's brother, Xander Greenway. They were seen sniffing vegan soaps and guiltily taking business cards from shopkeepers.*

Or maybe the only person who will tell the story is me, to myself every night before I go to sleep, because it might as well be a dream.

"Look," Xander says, pointing ahead of us. "Isn't that . . ."

I flinch as he trails off, terrified that he's pointing to the reanimated corpse of his sister or his friends, even though I'd know if they were close. But instead I see a table draped in black velvet with no fancy tent over it like the other booths. Toby is sitting behind a collection of charm bags and cheap stone necklaces. Her motorcycle is parked behind her, shining as silver as a razor blade. She sees me and smiles with her teeth but not her eyes.

"Mila, good to see you," she says as Xander pulls me toward the table. She tilts her face toward Xander. The movement flexes a muscle in her chest, making the snake tattoo on her boob seem to slither against her burnt skin. "And Riley's brother. It's been a while."

"Yes, ma'am," Xander says. We may be Californians, but Xander was taught to be Retail Southern. There's something about courtly manners and a slight drawl that charms the mourners and makes them buy bigger caskets. "The girls stopped needing me to drive them around once Mila got her own car."

"I'm glad to see you two have found each other in this terrible time," Toby says, seemingly unswayed by Xander's *ma'am*. She gestures at her wares with a sweeping motion. "See anything you need? I'll give you the student discount. Luck bags for that next big test? A money charm? I have a beautiful iron rose hematite. They form themselves, you know, under high pressure . . ."

The muscles in my back turn to stone. The iron rose isn't on the table. It's in Riley's grave with the rest of the ingredients for the Lazarus spell.

Oh fuck. She knows I stole it.

"We're fine," I say, already starting to pull Xander away. "Thanks, Toby! See you later."

"Don't forget to come in for Samhain," she calls after me. "'Tis the season to reap what you sow! Blessed be!"

"Blessed be!" I call back, now pulling Xander's hand in earnest. He opens his mouth, possibly to ask questions that I really don't want to answer. Flop sweat is starting to gather in my baby hairs. Toby knows that I stole the iron rose. She might even know *why*. "Do you want to dance? I love this song."

I don't know what song is playing. We aren't close enough to hear the words. I scurry through the crowd, Xander keeping pace with me easily.

There aren't a lot of people dancing in the grass in front of the stage erected at the entrance to Aldridge Park, but there are enough that I don't feel totally ridiculous when I join them. I've never considered whether or not public dancing is something I would be comfortable doing. Riley and I avoided every single Fairmont event that could even accidentally lead to dancing— homecoming, Sadie Hawkins, marching band concerts, speech and debate competitions where our team won—but I already asked Xander to dance with me, so I can't back out now.

The band—a tsunami wave of white dudes, all of whom look like they might work with my mom at the bank—plays Daft Punk's "Get Lucky" with a full horn section. It kind of rules, actually.

The music isn't loud enough to drown out all my fears, so I try to dance them out instead. I throw my shoulders into figure eights. Toss tangles into my hair. Flick my hips like I'm trying to catch a flint. And Xander keeps up.

Trust that I know too much about Alexander Greenway. I know which great uncle he was named after and that he prefers crimson to primary red and that he eats an unhealthy amount of Lucky Charms because he does, on some level, believe that they are lucky. I know that the color of his eyes is the same color that I think shivers would be if you could see them. The best Christmas present he ever got was tickets to a Giants game in San Francisco, but he got super carsick on the drive there. I know that he is one of the only people on the planet who likes Jar Jar Binks and that he's afraid of being upside down on roller coasters.

But I had absolutely no idea that this boy could dance.

And yet.

This is no awkward middle school shuffle he's doing. He moves like he knows his body, which is enough to make the sweat on my forehead start to slide down the backs of my ears. He puts his hands on my hips, letting my rhythm direct his. I set my hand on the back of his neck because I've always wondered what it would feel like to hold him this way. It's wonderful. His skin is feverishly hot and dewy, and I can even feel a zit under the wool of his sweater.

Back acne isn't a turn-on or anything, but it humanizes him in a way that I really need right now.

We dance hard and fast for two more songs—a song about a jitterbug and "Uptown Funk," because only monsters walk away from "Uptown Funk"—before I need to take a breather and a cold shower. We move away from the makeshift grass dance floor, stepping onto the sidewalk that winds through Aldridge Park. Without discussion, we follow the path into the orange haze of the park and sit on a cold metal bench.

"This was nice," Xander says. He wets his lips and smiles over at me. "Thank you for letting me have fun."

"Thanks for coming with me." I reach for the rose quartz. My thumb rubs one of the edges on the stone. "I've been kind of in hiding since Riley died."

"I noticed," he says. He blows out a sigh. Sweat makes his hair shine as he rakes his nails through it. I recognize this as his "thinking unpleasant thoughts" motion. Like he assumes that being upset will muss his hair. "I'd hate it if we stopped being friends because Riley's gone. I've always really liked hanging out with you, but I never wanted my sister to think I was trying to get between you two. Do you know how hard it was for her to make friends before you came to Cross Creek?"

I nod, too aware of my pulse and the drops of sweat collecting behind my ears. "Riley always said that no one would come play at your house. That you couldn't have birthday parties at home."

He draws his lower lip between his teeth and swings his head, looking away from me. "It wasn't just birthday parties. It was every day. Riley had zero friends before you moved here. No one wanted to be anywhere near her. She couldn't even take ballet lessons with the other kids in her kindergarten class because the parents were scared she'd tell them about corpses and give them nightmares. Kids tortured her."

"Dayton," I blurt, and then shrink back when he frowns. "She said Dayton started it."

"Dayton wasn't the only one. It was everyone. My parents put her in activities she could do by herself. Piano, Bible study. Things that she wouldn't need friends for. But they didn't care if she liked those things. They didn't care that she was so obviously lonely. And she was always so sad. Why couldn't they see what they were doing to her?" He squeezes his eyes closed, his whole face pinched in so much pain.

"They couldn't have known," I say, because the Greenways isolating Riley didn't make Caleb Treadwell target her. They messed up in a lot of ways, but they aren't the reason she died. "They wouldn't have hurt her on purpose. Your parents are good people. You know that."

He lifts his face to mine. Both sets of his eyelashes are wet. The splashes of red veins in his eyes makes his irises look like blue moonlight. "After this week, I don't know anything anymore."

I know magic is real, I think as I examine the sad lines of his face. *And maybe heaven, too. I know I've wanted to kiss you since I was eleven years old.*

We both know your sister would never have hurt herself, and I am going to punish the asshole who took her from us.

"That's okay," I say. Our knees bump together as I close the space between us. "You don't have to know anything right now. We'll just not know anything together. That's less shitty, right? We'll do the witch thing and be present."

His mouth flinches a smile. The movement shakes a tear out of his eye. "And grateful."

"Grateful as fuck," I agree. "Most people never had a Riley to begin with. Or friends like June and Dayton."

He huffs a laugh. "You never liked them."

My thumb rubs over the rubber band on my wrist as I think of Dayton making June, Riley, and me laugh until we cried in the Nesseths' backyard just a couple of hours ago. "Maybe I just never had the chance."

"I've missed you," he says softly. "I understand if you have to disappear again, but . . . I don't know. Don't? Please. After everything . . . I can't lose you, too."

"You won't. I promise," I whisper. "I'm right here. I've always been right here."

I wrap my arms around him, pulling his head down to my shoulder. His breath shudders hot against my neck. I rub my fingers through his hair, pushing against the grain, my nails scratching his scalp in soothing circles. I want to tell him that Riley didn't kill herself, that she's here, probably pissed that I left her alone in the Nesseths' garage. But I can't break a promise to Riley, and Xander wouldn't thank me for keeping the secret from him just long enough to lose her again.

So we sit wrapped up in each other, breathing in soft unison. In the distance, the band plays a new song. The trumpets are blaring, but they feel miles away.

SEVENTEEN

I HAVE TO find a way to lure Caleb to Yarrow House tonight. When we came up with the plan, I offered to bring the truth-spell potion to school since he has to drink it for it to take effect. But the girls reminded me that I shook them out of their graves and promised them revenge, so I can't rob them of it now. Besides, we're not sure how long the truth spell will last, so it'll be best to have Caleb close to the ingredients in case we need to whip up a second batch.

At lunch, I go behind the cafeteria to avoid the watchful eyes of teachers and campus security. My legs ache from dancing at the farmers' market last night, so I stretch them out across from the dumpsters where June emotionally scarred the Nouns. The wind is graciously pushing the trash stink into the parking lot rather than at my face.

There are texts from Xander waiting when I turn on my phone.

XANDER: *We've never had the same lunch period. Is this a Fairmont Academy conspiracy? Do you think Ms. Pine would flip my schedule if I asked?*

I'm glad that there's no one around to see me smiling like a dork. Xander and I have never had a text conversation that wasn't about Riley except for when he asked about my health after the Celebration of Life. He only has my phone number so that he could get ahold of his sister when her phone was dead. But maybe last night means that we're going to be real friends without Riley acting as a buffer.

ME: *I don't know if Ms. Pine would, but I bet you could talk Dr. Miller into it. Just bat all your pretty lashes at her.*

I almost jump when I see Xander's three dots pop up on the screen.

XANDER: *Flirting with the school psych is probably a one-way ticket to more counseling.*

ME: *How are you even texting me right now? They won't let you be valedictorian if you get caught with your phone on during class.*

XANDER: *I was never going to be valedictorian. Top ten, maybe. Peer counseling meets during homeroom hours. If you signed up for peer counseling, we could get your lunch hour switched. How well are you doing in math?*

Phone's out because I "forgot my calculator."

ME: *Oh, you're LYING to people to talk to me?*

XANDER: *Yep. Points for dedication to friendship?*

ME: *Are we keeping score?*

XANDER: *10 points for hanging out in public. Negative 100 points to me for crying on you.*

ME: *Obviously crying in front of each other is bonus 100 points. Only real-people friends grieve together, X.*

Shit. I'm supposed to be on a mission of revenge and righteousness, not blushing and texting. I open Facebook and log in, using June's phone number and password. The girl might not have many memories of her life in the weeks leading up to her death, but her Facebook password was locked and loaded. Priorities.

Hundreds of notifications blow up the screen. I forgot that her account has become an ongoing vigil for friends and family.

I open a chat window and type in Caleb's name. I also have to open the text draft that June made of what she wanted the message to Caleb to say.

> *Caleb,*
>
> *I'm not gone. Come to the abandoned green farmhouse*
> *on Knapp Road at nine P.M. tonight or prepare to have the*
> *shit haunted out of you for the rest of your miserable life.*
> *<3 June*
> *PS: Bring my necklace. I know you've been wearing it.*

I attach a video I shot of June standing outside of Yarrow House after we cast the rot spell. In it, she's waving and unsmiling, the wind slipping eerily through her hair. Our goal isn't to make Caleb totally believe that June is back from the dead. It just has to make him interested enough to show up. Presumably, no one else knows about the necklace, and the footage of June has never been online before—which pre-murdered June would never stand for—so hopefully this will kindle his interest. If not, then we have to kidnap him.

I really don't want to kidnap him. I'm almost positive that Ms. Chu would have me expelled if she caught me home-invading her.

A door closes around the front of the building, and I have only enough time to stash my phone in the pocket of my jacket before Aniyah Dorsey comes around the corner. Her hair is in big, fist-sized ringlets today, and she's wearing an EFF YOUR BEAUTY STANDARDS T-shirt. It's really cute. I hate how intense my clothes envy is.

"Mila, hi," she says breathlessly.

I wonder if she knows how often she uses people's names when she's talking to them. I feel like every time I see her, she's saying my name like I don't already know who I am. Or to prove that she does? Maybe it's a journalist tactic.

"Were you looking for me?" I ask. "Or did you need to look in the dumpsters for something?"

I pull my phone back out, closing out all my tabs to save on battery life and also to look busy.

"I just wanted to say hi," she says. She rocks back and forth, her ankles slightly bowed.

"Oh. Hi?"

A new text from Xander pops up on my screen, and I forget about Aniyah altogether.

XANDER: *Real-people friends? Is that a thing?*

ME: *It's the step between acquaintances and besties. Obviously.*

XANDER: *You know, I think we already had a word for that. It's FRIENDS.*

ME: *Anyone can be "friends." Real-people friends are people you can cry in front of or call in the middle of the night.*

XANDER: *Gotcha. Real-people friends. I look forward to your middle-of-the-night calls.*

Oh, fuck. Is this flirting? Am I swooning?

"So, you and Xander Greenway, huh?" Aniyah's voice cuts

through my private moment of textual flirting. Blood rushes to my cheeks, even though she's the one who should be embarrassed for being such an unabashed snoop.

I flip my phone upside down so that she can't continue her spying.

"I'm not going to answer any questions about my personal life for the *Fairmont* . . ." I empty every drawer in my brain, but the information just isn't there. "What's your 'newspaper' called?"

I struggle to make air quotes. I don't want to drop my phone.

She frowns so hard that her glasses slip down her nose. "It's the *Fairmont Informant*."

"That is the worst name I've ever heard. Why didn't they call it the *Fairmont Snitch* or the *Fairmont Narc*? It's like they want people to avoid you."

"People don't avoid me because of the name of the newspaper," she says, folding her arms over her chest and narrowing her eyes at me. "I'm fat and black in the middle of the whitest place on earth. And what makes you think that I even want people to talk to me?"

It's kind of cool to talk to someone who gets how absolutely tragically white this town is. And someone else who self-identifies as fat who isn't using *fat* as code for *ugly* or *ew-I-ate-a-big-meal*. Even Riley has only ever called me *curvy*, no matter how many times I correct her. But I have spells and texting to get back to, so I turn on some of the scary that everyone's always talking about.

"You are nonstop interviewing people," I say, keeping my voice and my face expressionless. "You pry into conversations, take notes on gossip you hear in bathrooms, and then you print it, praying that this will be the story that people actually read even though no one ever does."

"Yeah," she says slowly. "I don't write the newspaper for anyone in Cross Creek. There are hella journalism scholarships that no one wants because journalism is a dying industry, and they are going to be my way out of this town. Any other questions?"

"Why did you want to say hi to me? Are you writing an article about people hanging out with people above their social class?"

"No. I saw you and Xander out at the farmers' market yesterday—"

"Aw, and you didn't get a chance to say hi? Sorry we missed you. 'Kay, thanks, bye."

Her nostrils flare as she takes a steadying breath. She adjusts her glasses and tips her chin up regally.

"Look, you've lived in Cross Creek for only a couple of years. You moved here in middle school?" She doesn't wait for me to agree with her. She pushes ahead, waving her hands like the flow of conversation is motion-activated. "I know you were friends with Riley, and I'm really sorry that she killed herself—"

I get to my feet, sticking my phone safely in my pocket as I start to walk away from her. "Nope. We're done here."

"Mila, please!" Her fingers scramble for a hold on the sleeve of my coat, but it slides out of her grasp. "The Greenways are weird, okay? They always have been. Like, I don't think there is such a thing as a normal mortician. You're lucky that Riley's gone so that you don't have to get in any deeper with them—"

I don't know where the rage comes from, but I swing out without thinking about it. My forearm is braced against Aniyah's collarbone, pinning her to the wall of the cafeteria. Her eyes bug at me, surprised but not scared. Which sucks. I've never pinned anyone to a wall before. It should elicit a bigger response.

"Aniyah," I breathe. "I don't know you. You don't know me. You have no reason to believe me when I threaten you, so I'm gonna need you to listen to me very, very closely. I am a fucking witch, and if I hear you talking shit about my dead best friend or her family again, I will curse you into the ground."

She rolls her eyes. "Okay, that's not what Wicca is."

I shove her away and straighten my jacket. "It is the way I do it."

After sneaking out while Izzy washes tonight's dinner dishes, I park even farther away from Yarrow House than normal. I doubt that Caleb has any idea what my car looks like—mostly because my car looks like a thousand other cars in Cross Creek, and the sun has already set—but it doesn't hurt to be prepared. I've filled my backpack with supplies for tonight's horror show. Walkie-talkies bargained off my sisters complete with fresh batteries, the last herbs we need for the truth spell stolen from neighborhood bushes and my spice cabinet, pepper spray in case shit goes south, Gatorades for everyone to toast with in case shit goes our way.

The girls have obviously been hard at work. When I walk into the kitchen, there's a path of unlit candles marking the way to the basement steps. There are no signs of life in the living room except for Binx, who is chowing down on a very fat, wiggly field mouse. Blood stains the white fur around his mouth. It's a shame that the mouse will be long gone by the time Caleb gets here. It would be hella unnerving.

Riley stomps up the stairs from the basement. She gives me a smile before she notices the cat mid-murder in the living room.

"Thackery Binx. That is a shitty way to greet company."

"He's an outdoor cat," I say. "He's never needed manners."

"Fair point," she says, bobbing her head. "Where the hell did you go yesterday? You disappeared and left your car behind. Dayton said you were going to the farmers' market, but that sounded nuts—"

"No, she was right," I say. It's suddenly very hard to maintain eye contact. There's a strip of shiny white fabric wrapped around her wrist that I recognize as a piece of her burial dress. She sees me staring and cradles the arm and its makeshift bandage to her stomach.

"My broken wrist isn't bouncing back as fast when you come back," she says hurriedly. "Well, nothing is bouncing back as fast. The spell did say we were going to die again in a week. We're like ground meat slowly spoiling, and our best-by date is coming fast."

"You aren't meat, Ry. You're a person."

"A person being held together entirely by magic. When you aren't here we're all gross and goopy, but we still eat and talk and sleep like we're normal and alive. But we're *not* alive, and that's kind of becoming more clear." She pauses, then waves me off with her unbandaged wrist. "Don't worry about it, okay? It's really not a big deal. Just don't be surprised if June's neck flops around a little. Now, for real, why did you go to the farmers' market yesterday? Were you running low on shitty music and homemade apple butter?"

"I went with Xander," I say. And then quickly add, "I was standing out front waiting for you guys, and he drove by. I couldn't tell him why I was really there, so I said I was going to go to the farmers' market. He wanted to come with me." Her eyes are bulging so hard that I can see the whites all the way around. "What?"

"You went on a date with my brother?"

"What? No!" But I have to stop and think about it. "We just hung out. I mean, we danced but then also cried. It was friendly mourning."

"Who cried?" she asks. "Him? You?"

"Mostly him," I say. And then, quickly, "Not that I'm not sad that you died, but I get to see you still and he doesn't, plus he's pretty torn up about June and Dayton dying, too."

"Right," she says, biting the inside of her cheek and nodding. "He must miss his friends . . ." Her voice drifts off. "You and he never hung out before I died though, right? I've been remembering a lot lately, but this feels new."

"It's new," I say. "A lot of things have changed in the last two weeks. We had this nice moment when he gave me the rose quartz necklace—"

"*My* necklace," she interrupts. "Which you won't give back to me because you had a *moment* over it?"

The way she says it makes it sound like the stupidest reasoning ever, but that doesn't make it less true.

"He gave me his dead sister's most prized possession, Ry," I say. "He'd notice if I wasn't wearing it. What am I supposed to tell him? That you're back and pissed that I borrowed your jewelry?"

"You're right. It's a good thing, I guess," she says, a little distant. "I don't want him to be alone. He needs a good friend right now. Why not my blister? You can keep his crybaby butt in line." She flashes me a quick, tight smile. "How much time do we have? The sun went down forever ago, but we lost track of the minutes when Dayton got 'Monster Mash' stuck in her head."

Half pulling my phone from my pocket, I check its clock. "We have half an hour. If Caleb is perfectly on time."

She motions for me to follow her back downstairs.

The basement window has been boarded up again, and my eyes sting as they adjust to the darkness. The single wooden chair is in the center of the room, and candles burn in every corner, making June and Dayton's shadows huge and distorted on the walls. The spell ingredients are piled neatly on top of the grimoire, alongside the mason jar we need to mix everything in. It's more twee than a heavy, ancient chalice or something, but it's the only cup we had on hand.

"Mila!" Dayton says. "How was your date?"

"It wasn't a date," I say, handing her my backpack so she can sort through everything. "We just hung out."

"You and Xander are perfect for each other," June says. "His natural Gemini flow won't erode your Libra firmness."

"Um. Cool," I say, picking up the Mason Jar of Truth. "Thanks, June."

You have to take what you can get in the June Phelan-Park compliment department.

I pour honey and vinegar into the jar, then add dried herbs, dandelion fluff, and a slew of acorn caps. I twist the lid shut and shake the mixture hard enough to make my arms quiver, reading the chant out of the grimoire.

"Let the truth raze down the lies that bloom, let the truth raze down the lies that bloom."

Riley takes a piece of chalk and writes a series of sigils under the wooden chair. One for peacemaking. One for free-flowing speech. One for luck.

"Let's hope they work," she says, dusting off her hands.

Dayton hands me the empty backpack and one of the walkie-talkies.

"Okay, get out," she says, her face as smiling and pleasant as ever, even as she starts to push me toward the stairs.

"What?" I push back. "What the hell? Caleb is going to be here, like, any minute."

"Exactly," June says. I can't help but notice that her breath is not minty fresh. It's distinctly rank. Like rotting fish and old milk. It might the only thing I've ever smelled that is worse than wet cat food. Is this part of the not bouncing back that Riley mentioned? "We can't scare him with you around. You make us look normal. We've been practicing our zombie faces every night this week. Dayton, show her."

Dayton puts up her hands like she's a tiny attacking bear. Throwing herself into my face, she growls and waggles her tongue, groaning loudly.

"Oh," I say, hooking a thumb toward Dayton, who is standing in freeze-frame so I can admire her work. "I see the problem. This is adorable."

"But imagine it with her neck all broken," Riley says. "And the white eyes and the veins and all that shit. It's pretty gross."

"Yeah, we realized that we can see part of Riley's skull in the right light." Dayton beams. I choke down the urge to puke. This is definitely a dead-girl thing.

"You'll feel when you're far enough away, right?" June asks.

"Right," I say. I can't keep the touch of disappointment out of my voice. Not to sound like the Little Red Hen, but I made the potion, I found the murderer, and I don't even get to be part of the scream team? That's trash.

"We won't let you miss out on the truth spell," Riley promises. "We'll use the walkies to bring you back once he's thoroughly scared."

Feeling a bit like I'm being kicked out of the clubhouse, I run back upstairs. Binx is nowhere to be found, although the decapitated head of his mouse is staring at the wall. Gross. The house isn't big enough for me to get a hundred steps away, so I go out into the chill of the night and walk into the woods until I feel the snap of the thread connecting me to the girls. The air is cold enough to sting the inside of my nose. The waning gibbous moon is trapped on the other side of the branches over my head.

Bouncing up and down to keep warm, I watch as a bicycle kicks up dust all the way down the driveway. The dark outline of a person walks up the porch, scaring off a small raccoon. I assume he sees that the front door is boarded up, because he walks back toward his bike. I bite the inside of my cheek. I really wish I had Harry Potter–style magic, where I could point a wand and have the door magically open for him.

It seems to take an entire decade, but Caleb finally walks around the side of the house, whispering something I can't hear. He sees the back door and goes inside.

I snap the elastic band at my wrist. I don't know if I still need to wear it, but the snapping has become a habit. Tonight, it's helping me stay alert when all I want to do is text Xander or run to the basement to watch Caleb getting his comeuppance. I can't even hear his screams from this far away.

The walkie-talkie buzzes to life in my hand. There's so much static that I can barely make out Riley's voice calling me back.

I'm panting as I rush down the stairs to the basement again. This isn't the most menacing entrance for the Grand High Witch of Cross Creek, but I don't need to worry, because Caleb doesn't notice me. His sandy brown hair is in front of his face, and he's sobbing into his chest as Dayton ties his arms around the back of his chair with more of the white fabric torn from

Riley's burial dress. June is backed all the way against the wall, her hands splayed against the stones. Her face is ghostly white like she's been haunted herself. The bruise on her neck is slow to disappear.

Caleb pulls in a rattling, vacuum-like sob. This might be the first time I've ever seen him not smirking or looking for someone to high-five. He doesn't even seem to notice that his arms are being tied to a chair or that there are sigils under his feet. He only has eyes for June.

"I can't believe it," he says in between brays. "God, June, I've missed you so much."

EIGHTEEN

"YOU MISSED ME?" June repeats. Hearing the roughness in her voice, she lifts a self-conscious hand to the disappearing bruise on her throat. Blood oozes out of her nail beds. Her eyes narrow. "You don't miss me. Mila! Truth him."

Normally, I wouldn't hop-to when June barks an order, but I recognize the uncertainty in her tone. Something has gone wrong. She won't stop making eye contact with Caleb. I move around the edge of the room, picking up the mason jar. The drowned acorn shells and floating green bits of herbs aren't very intimidating. I shake them together roughly. The grimoire says that the mixture needs to be at a full froth to reach its maximum effectiveness.

"I knew you wouldn't kill yourself," Caleb whispers reverently to June. He's actively working to stop crying as though that's the thing making her yell at him. His heavy lips stretch flat. "I knew you would never leave voluntarily."

Riley moves toward him, grabbing a fistful of hair from the top of his head and yanking it back until he has no choice but to look at her. "So you decided to make her go? You're a sick fuck, Caleb Treadwell."

"What are you talking about?" he asks, his eyes going wide. The scaliness that I spotted on his arm has started to crawl up the side of his neck. The skin around the silver chain is shredded and raw. "You're the ones who faked your deaths."

Riley lets go of him like his hair has caught fire. "What?"

"No, we didn't," Dayton says, placing an indignant hand to her chest.

"Yeah, you did." Caleb frowns around the room. "You're here. You're alive. Aniyah's writing an article about how this was all a hoax. Bitch is going to take the Rausch Scholarship in a sweep when it goes national."

"Don't call women *bitches*, you fuckface," Riley says.

"Wait," I say, holding the mason jar aloft. I should have thought to bring a colander. There's a chance he's going to choke on an acorn cap before we get the information we need. "What does Aniyah Dorsey have to do with this?"

Caleb tries to shrug but can only twitch his shoulders since his hands are tied. "She saw Dayton walking downtown the week after she supposedly died. There have been other sightings, too. At gas stations, at school. Angel, Sky, Diamond, and Dawn have been having meetings with the school shrink because they told everyone that June is haunting the cafeteria. I thought it was tabloid bullshit until I got the message from June. She was the only person who knew about the necklace, so it had to be her."

Riley yanks at the ends of her hair, frustration vibrating around her. "You saw part of my skull and you think we're just fucking with you? How would we even pull that off? Real life doesn't have CGI."

He shakes his head, his usual smile appearing. "It doesn't matter. June is alive."

"Stop saying her name like that," Riley snaps. She yanks the mason jar out of my grip and throws the lid to the floor with a ringing clatter. She thrusts the glass against Caleb's lip. A thin stream of the potion dribbles down his chin.

"Caleb," June says tightly. "Drink it. Please."

He shuts his eyes and chugs the frothing mass, sputtering when the acorn caps bump into his teeth. When he finishes, he has an airy white foam mustache. "Is that a new kind of kombucha? It needs fewer chunks."

"How fast is it supposed to work?" Dayton whispers to me.

"No clue," I whisper back. "I guess we'll know when he starts admitting things."

Caleb licks the foam off his lip and cranes his head toward June. "Are you mad I didn't come looking for you sooner? I would never have guessed you were staying in an abandoned house. I thought maybe a hotel? Definitely somewhere with running water. You deserve so much better than this shithole."

Riley looks over at me, one eyebrow raised. "That's not much of a truth test. This place is the dictionary definition of a *shithole*."

"Caleb," I say loudly, "why don't you wear jeans?"

"I don't like how they press into my stomach," he says automatically. "They leave lines in my skin that make me feel ugly."

"Why don't you like your stepmom?" June asks him.

"She never wanted kids," he says. "After I go to college, I don't think she'll pretend to like me again. She wants to turn my room into a home gym."

"Aww," Dayton says. "You poor thing."

"Fuck a duck, Dayton. Don't pity the murderer," Riley mutters.

"Why are you so obsessed with the Rausch Scholarship?" I ask.

"The winner of the Rausch Scholarship usually gets a bump in their popularity. I want people to like me. I even plagiarized my application to try to beat Aniyah."

Above us, the ground rumbles. It sounds less like an earthquake and more like a thunderstorm. But the sky was completely clear when I was waiting in the woods.

We all look up at the ceiling as though there's anything to see but more cement. I take a step toward the stairs, but Dayton stops me.

"You're the only one of us with anything to lose," she says gently. She holds her palm up. "Give me your walkie. I'll check it out."

I slip the walkie-talkie out of my pocket and hand it to her. I feel a tightness in my chest as I watch her skip up the stairs.

"It's probably just FedEx," Riley says, sensing my concern. "Who knows what else I bought?"

I nod, hoping she's right. After all, what reason could anyone have to follow Caleb Treadwell to an abandoned house?

"Caleb," I say, "where were you the night of Saturday, October seventh?"

He swings his head to look at me. His relief at seeing June hasn't made him any happier to talk to me. His mouth twists into a sneer. "My dad and stepmom were on an overnight trip to Napa. I was with June for most of the night. She called Dayton for a ride home at around midnight or one."

June moves too quickly for me to stop her. She topples over the grimoire, pulling the ceremonial dagger out. She must have hidden it there when I was outside. The ruby in the handle flashes as she whips the blade toward Caleb, the silver tip pressing into the raw patch of skin at his neck. He hisses in pain, tears starting to roll down his cheeks again.

"It's just your eczema," she whispers. She tosses the blade away, and her nails scrabble for his collar, stretching the cotton down toward his shoulder. Red welts and broken skin trail over his collarbone. She looks over her shoulder at me. "It's not a curse, Camila! It's a rash!"

"I told you it was a rash!" I say.

"You made it sound like he grew scales or was shedding his skin like a snake!" she says. She turns back to him, pressing her fingertips to his chin. "It wasn't you, was it? You didn't hurt me?"

"Of course not," he weeps. "June, I missed you so much—"

She leans forward, setting her forehead against his. "I missed you, too. I'm so sorry. I had to know for sure that it wasn't you. I can't remember . . ."

"What the fuck?!" I shout, but June and Caleb don't look at me.

The walkie-talkie clipped to Riley's pants gives off static and then Dayton's voice. "Hello? Um. There's a problem up here."

Riley turns her back to the rest of us, whispering into the speaker. "If it's raccoons again, I told you to use the broom and chase them out of the house. Binx can't fight them. They have thumbs. He doesn't. It's not a fair fight."

"No, it's people," Dayton squeaks. "Old people. Like, a lot of them. On motorcycles."

"On what?" Riley asks.

Underneath the sounds of Caleb's wet nose breathing, I can hear the rumble of engines revving. A lot of engines. And then a bang, like a heavy book falling to a hollow floor that makes me shiver and jump.

A gunshot.

The walkie-talkie static dies.

"Go to the woods and wait there," I say to June and Riley. I can feel them both start to argue with me, but I hold up my hands. "Stay out of sight unless it looks like I need help."

I don't wait for them to agree. All of us scramble up the stairs while Caleb shouts after us. The candles in the kitchen have mostly guttered out. The back door is open, and I run through it and down the porch steps. The air is bracingly cold against my sinuses, and it freezes my brain.

At the base of the driveway, there are motorcycle headlights burning blindingly bright—a dozen suns attached to roaring engines. Women stand next to their motorcycles, some still in their helmets, some not. Dayton is gone, and I pray that she escaped the gunshot.

As my eyes adjust, I see a woman at the front of the motorcycle gang holding a long black shotgun. Her hair is braided into a long rope that might be white with bleach or time. As I take a step toward her, she motions to the others, and they shut off their engines. The sudden silence seems to have echoes of its own.

"Hey, Toby," I say, my boots crunching in the dirt. Sweat builds between my fingers. The sight of the shotgun terrifies me—this is the first gun I've seen outside the glass cases in Walmart's sporting department—but I have less to fear than the dead girls. No one goes to jail for shooting a zombie. I'd have to really fuck up for Toby to decide to kill me in cold blood. Even Cross Creek PD couldn't ignore a shotgun blast to the head. I don't think.

"Evening," she says with a chivalrous tip of her head to me. "It's a shame you have to meet the rest of my coven this way, but we're here to put a stop to the aberrations you brought to our town."

"Oh yeah?" I ask. I can feel the girls pass out of my protection. Good. I hope they keep running. "You . . . what? Sensed a disturbance in the Force?"

"I watched a three-hundred-dollar chunk of hematite leave my store," Toby says stiffly. "What could you possibly need that much grounding for? I know you didn't think it was just pretty. You knew what it could do. And there have been sightings of the three dead girls all over town. In broad daylight. At your school more than once!"

"You're a big fan of the *Fairmont Informant*?" I say.

I look at the women behind Toby. Dayton was right. They're mostly older, none younger than forty. No one else seems to be armed, although who knows what's hiding in the bags and hidden compartments of their motorcycles. Maybe they all have switchblades tucked inside their boots. One woman removes her helmet as I look at her, revealing fluffy blond hair and a pinched expression that hits me like a slap in the face.

My jaw drops, and I realize I must look like a kid seeing Mickey Mouse take his head off at Disneyland.

"Dr. Miller?"

"Hello, Camila," she says. "I'm sorry I couldn't tell you I am also a practitioner of the craft. I'm not allowed to discuss my religious beliefs at work. I wish you had accepted my or Toby's offer to come to us with your problems, rather than taking matters into your own hands. While magic of this scale shows that you wield an incredible power, you've also proven reckless and wholly untrustworthy, two things that a bruja cannot afford to be." She says *bruja* with the first two letters rolled and the end with a staccato flourish on the *ha*.

Oh lord. She must be one of those white women who orders in Spanish at Mexican restaurants.

"I'm a witch," I say coldly. "Brujería was beaten out of my ancestors by Spanish missionaries a couple hundred years ago. There's nothing but scared Catholics behind me."

"Multiple students have come to me saying that June appeared to them as a ghost," Dr. Miller says, continuing her favorite game of ignoring everything that comes out of my mouth. "I thought it was a shared delusion—"

"Shocker," I say.

"But the details were too specific. The smell of her broken skin, the way her eyes glowed white. And then I saw you leaving campus with two girls in the car. The blond girl in the baseball cap you were with at the school memorial and one with brown bangs, fitting June Phelan-Park's description. I had to tell the coven. You've put the whole town in danger, Mila."

"They don't eat people. This isn't a monster movie."

"They're an abomination," Toby says.

Different religion, same words. It might as well be Riley's mom wearing that motorcycle jacket.

"Where are the undead?" barks one of the other biker witches. Her face has wrinkles so deep I could lose a finger in them, but her hair is coal black. "They need to be put back to rest to return order to the universe."

"The whole universe?" I snap. I'm so tired of adults using hyperbole to try to keep me in my place. I'm not crazy. I'm not too angry. I'm fine just the way I am. I have the power to bring back the dead and force the truth out of the mouths of murderers. "The whole Milky Way Galaxy is out of whack because there are a couple of girls on a living holiday?"

"It's against the will of the Goddess," Toby roars.

"Then why did She let me do it?" I scream back.

The back door of the house bangs open again. Whether it's wind or Caleb, I don't know. The coven leaps toward the noise as one. I take the opening and run as fast as I can in the other direction, disappearing into the trees. I move in a zigzag, ducking branches and skidding on twigs. Rough bark scratches at my palms. The heels of my boots cut deep into the dirt as I scramble around thick tree trunks.

I trip and fall face-first to the ground, my cheek slamming into the dirt. My teeth rattle. Pain makes my vision blur. Army-crawling forward, I look over my shoulder to see if any of the older witches followed, but there's nothing but darkness and the shadows of gnarled trees behind me. Everything smells like crusty leaves and moist dirt. I feel like I've walked into a horror movie and some slow-moving dude with a knife is about to pop out from behind a bush.

Instead, there's another gunshot blast. Mice scratch in the branches above me, and birds scream in the sky. Raccoons skitter, fleeing to their den. Everything in the woods knows to be scared of the shotgun.

I flatten my back against a particularly wide oak tree and close my eyes tight, rooting around inside myself for the connection between me and the girls. They're out of range, but not by much. I move with more purpose, playing hot and cold with myself, although it's hard because every snap of a twig makes me feel like I might puke, which confuses my magical radar.

I reach for the rubber band on my wrist, snapping it with every step.

You started this, Flores. You have to stay focused.

Eyes open.

I hear the crunch of footsteps before I feel the shudder of a single girl passing the threshold of my magic. Even in the darkness, I can see white eyes coming toward me. The broken veins and blood vessels in her face don't fade until Dayton clasps her hands in mine.

"You need to get out of here," she whispers harshly.

"I can't," I stress. "Those witches are very serious about killing you guys."

"We're already dead, Mila. But you aren't." She shakes my hands sharply, like she's trying to get the wrinkles out of my palms. "If a shot misses us and hits you, there's no one to bring you back. Riley already got out of the woods. June and I will be okay. We don't feel pain! We'll find you when it's safe, okay? We can sense each other. It'll be fine."

But what if it isn't? I want to ask. *What if right now is goodbye forever?*

I don't think I can bring them back if their heads are blown off. I think that's the whole point of Toby's shotgun.

"Go!" Dayton pushes away from me. "Go right now, Mila, or I swear to God, I will be so mad at you! Forever. Even when you come join us in heaven."

I swallow, feel for the lump of my keys in the pocket of my jacket, and take off back the way I came. All the way up the driveway past the motorcycles with their lights on and their owners swarming the farmhouse. Into my car.

Toward Laurel Street.

☠   ☠   ☠

The air outside the Greenway funeral home is heavy with dryer scent. I know from seeing my reflection in the window of my car that I'm a mess, even worse than the night I brought the girls back from the dead. Face dirty. Leaves and twigs and filth matted into my frizzy hair. Eyeliner and mascara gooped into the corners of my eyes.

At the top of the long driveway, I lean against the hearse. The black metal of the side door is cool against my pant legs. My body already aches where it whacked into trees and the ground. I pull out my phone, unsurprised to see a crack bisecting the screen. Even so, seeing the flaw in the glass brings a lump to my throat— phones aren't cheap, and my parents struggled to make sure that my sisters and I had one with a decent plan. They'll be furious when they see that I've marred mine. Why wasn't I more careful?

A tear splashes onto the crack as I pull up Xander's contact information. I can't wait for him to answer a text. I press call.

"Mila," he says after two rings. "What's up—"

"I'm outside," I say thickly. "On the drop-off side. Can you come out?"

"Of course. I'm on my way."

I don't bother trying to look less fucked up in the moments between the end of the call and when the door creaks open. Xander appears, dark eyebrows drawn together in concern. Riley used to pluck his eyebrows once a month to keep them from meeting the middle. He would take one of her shifts in the showroom in exchange.

He's wearing a bulky gray sweatshirt and black pajama pants. It's *late*, I suddenly realize. He might have been asleep.

"I'm sorry," I say as he steps down onto the driveway. "I know it's late. I didn't know where else to go and—"

"Hey." He swoops forward, too fast for me to stop him. He pushes the tears off my cheek with the pad of his thumb. "Are you okay? Did you walk here through the woods?"

I bite the tip of my tongue until my spit thins, making the lie more palatable. "Sort of. I had some witch stuff that went kind of . . . sideways." I scrape the tears away from my eyes with the tips of my fingers. "Really sideways. I think I fucked everything up."

He wraps his arms around me, holding me against his chest. "It's okay. Whatever happened, we can fix it, okay? Can it wait until tomorrow, or should I go put on shoes?"

I think of the girls finding shelter for the night. Dayton made me promise that I'd take care of myself, and it's too dark to go looking for them anyway. I'd be putting myself and Xander at risk if I went back to Yarrow right now. I don't want Toby's coven to think he has anything to do with the resurrection spell.

"It can wait," I finally say, but I'm so quiet I don't even know if he can hear me. I tip my head up and say it again with more confidence than I feel.

"Good. Come on in." He steps aside, ushering me through the doors. "My parents are already asleep, but you can get cleaned up, if you want. Do you want to grab a shower and some water? You have mud . . . everywhere."

I look down at myself, knowing he's right. I'm caked in patches of dirt from my boots upward. If I tried to walk into my house right now, my mom would bolt out of bed on instinct and spray me down with the hose before I was allowed to set foot on the carpet.

"My mom's already taken her Ambien," Xander says, guiding me with a delicate hand on the small of my back through the showroom and up the stairs toward the apartment. "So you know nothing could wake her up. I can throw your clothes in the washer, and you can borrow a pair of pajamas from me."

I glance back at him as I climb the stairs. The adrenaline is starting to evaporate out of my bloodstream, leaving me too weak and tired to be embarrassed. "That's really nice, but there's no way your pajamas are going to fit me."

"Oh, right," he says, unconcerned with his miscalculation of the size of my waist. "Go ahead and start your shower. I'll put a robe on the doorknob for you."

I nod my agreement. He reaches down and squeezes my hand before dashing off toward the laundry closet.

I could find my way to the hall bathroom with my eyes closed, which is good because there aren't many lights on. Just a pinpoint in the kitchen and the glow of a computer in Xander's room. Otherwise, the apartment is quiet and still. All the flowers that were here last week are gone, not a single empty vase or spare white petal remaining.

Riley's bedroom door is closed, and I imagine her safely behind it, flexing her left wrist as it heals itself at my presence. The image is so clear in my mind that I can't stop myself from peeking inside. It's empty, of course.

I wish she were here. I wish I knew she was safe.

In the bathroom, I strip and set my jacket with my clothes outside the door for Xander to put in the wash for me. I rinse my boots in the tub, watching clumps of mud swirl down the drain before I step in myself. I turn the water up to scalding and set my face directly into the stream. The shampoo on the rack is Riley's. The idea of using it skeeves me out, so I opt for a dandruff two-in-one that must be Xander's, scratching it deep into my scalp.

Does Caleb really think that the girls faked their deaths? I should have been quicker with the truth spell. I should have made sure that he was innocent before I left the basement. I should have protected the house better. I shouldn't have let Dayton convince me to leave the woods. How am I going to sleep, not knowing if any of them are safe?

The echo of the shotgun blast is stuck in my ears. I scrub at the skin under the rose quartz necklace as though I can smooth out the fear flooding my heart.

When the steam is blindingly thick and my skin is close to boiling, I turn the water off and pat myself down with a towel, feeling around the outside of the door for the robe I was promised. It's dark gray and warm from the dryer, and it settles over my body like the skins of a thousand stuffed animals. It is the height of decadence. Thank the Goddess for Mrs. Greenway's expensive taste.

Trailing water droplets from the boots I'm carrying, I pad down the hallway to Xander's room. My jacket is neatly folded next to his closet door. He lies on his stomach on his bed but leaps to his feet when he sees me in the doorway. Nervous energy crackles between us, although I don't know which of us is more uncertain right now.

"Thanks for the robe," I say. I feel exposed—makeup-less and damp and obviously upset. Without my usual armor, I feel dangerously close to helpless. "I might have to steal it from you."

"It's my dad's," he says.

Of course it is. I wouldn't fit into Xander's robe. If he has one. It would flop open around me like a cape.

"It's clean," he adds in a rush. "Fresh from the dryer."

"That explains its downy softness," I say, patting the collar awkwardly.

He looks down at the knot on my sash, and maybe I'm imagining it, but his hands twitch like he's planning how to untie it.

"You can stay in Riley's room for the night, if you want to be alone," he says. Ever the gentleman. His lips are plump with earnest concern for my well-being. "Do you want to?"

I drag my gaze up to his eyes. It's no help, of course. "Do I want to . . . ?"

"Be alone?"

"Can I be alone in here?" My pulse is loud, but it's been loud all night. You can only be so scared before you hit a plateau. Inviting myself into Xander's room for the first time isn't scarier than the shotgun being toted around the woods, hunting my friends.

"Yes." The word comes out as a sigh. He reaches out and squeezes the tips of my fingers. "Do you want anything? Water? Dinner? Ice cream?"

I shake my head. "Can we just . . . I don't know. Sit? I want to feel normal."

It's not normal to follow Xander to his bed, to hear the door click shut behind us. It's not normal to agree to watch the TV show on his laptop, even though I've never heard of it before. It's not normal to have him lie down beside me, to feel the hesitation in his muscles before he reaches up to comb his fingers through the knots forming in my wet hair.

The warmth of his breath curls into the space behind my ear as he murmurs, "Is this okay?"

My toes curl in his sheets, and I nod, not trusting my voice. Because I don't know if it's okay for friends to spoon or for my heart to gallop as he continues to stroke my hair. But I know that I want this, that I've always wanted it.

I'm so aware of every shift of his body beside me that it becomes the only thing in the world. His arm resting below my ear like a pillow. The restlessness in his feet. The long, slow drag of his breath. It all reverberates inside me like a thousand wishes.

Is this the move that pulls his body to mine?

Is this the second the dam breaks?

I get tired of waiting, so I twist myself to look up at him. The black pools of his pupils have eaten the blue of his eyes, making him look at me with new darkness.

"I tried to stay away from you when Riley was alive," he says, his voice a quiet rumble. His Adam's apple bobs above me. "I didn't let us stay alone too long. I didn't want to get between you two, so I didn't let you see me seeing you. But I did see you, Mila. And I think you were seeing me, too. Not just Fairmont me. Me at home and at work. Me smelling like embalming fluid."

I almost laugh. "It's not a great smell, but it is a you smell."

"I've never had to hide from you." He smooths the hair out of my face. "I don't ever want to have to hide from you."

I pull his face down to mine.

His kiss is like a light switch turning on. It's gentle, slanting mouths pressed together and warm breath exhaled through noses. Legs twisting together and hands exploring the skin exposed by the robe sliding off my shoulders. The friendly rhythm that had us dancing in circles at the farmers' market turns frantic and wanting. Hands that grip as often as they caress. I'm not trying to memorize him tonight; I'm trying to feed on him.

The sash of the robe I'm wearing slackens with one jerk of my thumb through the knot. The cotton and fleece of Xander's pajamas slides over my bare skin, making me shiver and sweat. There are distant thoughts of things I should be worried about right now: my nipple size or pube density or which way the bulk of my stomach is pointing, but he kisses me deep into the mattress, his hands roving over me. There is an inequitable amount of nudity here, though. Blindly, I grope for the hem of his sweatshirt and pull it upward.

I can taste the *no* on his lips, but everything is moving so quickly. The fabric of his sweatshirt snaps over his head, mussing his hair. His lips freeze against mine when I go to kiss him again.

Consent revoked.

Permission denied.

I sit up on my elbows, clarity coming back to me like a tidal wave, bringing shame on its heels. I pushed too far. I didn't ask. I'll have to work to get his trust back. I assumed and was wrong and . . .

The only light in the room is the laptop that got pushed against the edge of the bed frame at some point during our jostling. It drapes us in an eerie silver light, unnatural and robotic. Which makes it all the stranger to see the shadows pushing up and out of Xander's shoulders. The round heads of so much acne. Like the zit I felt on his back at the farmers' market.

Except they aren't zits. Because zits, for all their varying shapes and sizes, don't come flat-topped or long-stemmed. Zits never grow dense and tan against otherwise flawless white skin.

Because they aren't zits. They're mushrooms. Cremini. Portobello. Button. Toadstool. Clusters of them—smooth and porous and brain-like. His entire back is overgrown with mushrooms, each no bigger than a quarter.

No. It can't be true.

It's another fuckup of my magic, like June and Dayton coming back from the dead or Caleb not confessing to the murders.

Please, God, no.

The words fall out of my mouth as I throw on Mr. Greenway's robe and roll off the mattress, not taking my eyes off Xander or his fungi.

"That which rots you marks you."

NINETEEN

"**MILA, IT'S OKAY,**" he says, his voice even and calm, like there's nothing wrong, like there's nothing growing on him. "I didn't want it to come up like this, but I meant it when I said that I don't want to hide from you. It's magic, right? This is the thing you fucked up tonight? *It's okay.*" He stresses it hard and puts his hands up, trying to calm me like I'm a cornered dog. "I don't know what you were trying to do, but it's all going to be okay. I know you can get rid of them."

I can't. You can't cut the rot out of someone's heart.

I grab my boots and my jacket and start running, tying the robe closed as I go. Xander's footsteps follow me down the hall, down the stairs, through the showroom. He calls my name, but I don't turn around. My hip knocks over an urn, which bounces on the carpet behind me. I throw open the side door and almost run into Riley.

Her eyes are white. This must be the perfect lighting, because the blackened gash in her head dead-ends in a swath of bone. Her skull.

She really isn't bouncing back as fast anymore.

Behind me, Xander's scream rips at the night's silence.

My boots knock into Riley as I push past her and keep running.

The ever-blooming green grass in front of the funeral home scratches my bare feet as I scramble toward my car. Even with my pulse in my ears like a drum, I think I can hear Xander or Riley behind me. I have to move faster. I have to get away. I need time to think. I need time to figure out how this could be anything but what I know it is.

Xander couldn't have murdered June and Dayton and Riley. There's no way. June and Dayton were his friends. Riley was his sister, for fuck's sake. They liked each other way more than I like my sisters. He couldn't have drowned her in the creek.

The spell must have misfired. Just like the resurrection spell. Just like Riley not being able to cast spells anymore. It's a mistake. My mistake, like he said. Or something else entirely. A curse put there by someone else. Toby. Dr. Miller. Riley, getting back at him for something minor that happened before she died that she never had a chance to put right.

But if I really believed any of that, I wouldn't be running.

I'm just getting to my car when I hear the roar of an engine. The hearse speeds backward down the driveway and screeches up the street, leaving black marks in the road.

Innocent people don't run, right?

Riley walks across the front lawn, her shoulders hunched and her white eyes sparkling with tears. I didn't know she could cry in her corpse form. The cut in her forehead is starting to stitch itself shut.

"What are you doing here?" I ask, although I'm scared that I already know.

"I followed you out of the woods," she says.

"Tell me you didn't know about Xander," I say as she steps onto the sidewalk across from me.

She takes a step forward, and I stumble back. "Mila, please listen."

"Tell me he didn't kill you!" I shout. I don't care if I wake everyone on Laurel Street. Everyone in Cross Creek. "Tell me he didn't kill all of you."

"No one killed me," she whispers.

"What are you talking about?" I snap. "Xander has mushrooms growing out of his skin. Did you see them? If that isn't the rot coming out of his heart, then what the fuck is it?"

She looks up at me, and I can almost see the outline of where her pupils would be if her body would finish healing itself. "I need you to listen to me now, okay? Let me get all the way to the end. Can you do that?"

I swallow, hugging my boots and my jacket to my front. I wish I could put the jacket on, but I don't think it'll fit over the plush sleeves of the robe.

"I really didn't remember when you first brought me back," Riley says, her voice as delicate as it gets. It still carries its natural roughness even when she's fragile. "Everything was a blank. But I've been getting pieces. Normal stuff, mostly. Homework I never turned in and texts that I got from you. There were some glimpses of what I thought was the creek. Rocks. Water sounds. But I didn't want to remember dying. I thought it would make me more scared of having to face it again on Sunday." She hugs her broken wrist, rubbing the white makeshift bandage between her thumb and forefinger. "I guess it didn't matter if I wanted to remember or not. It came back."

"You remember dying?" I ask, matching her whisper. I don't even know if I want to hear the rest, but we've always shared our heaviest secrets with each other. That's what best friends do, help bear the weight of existence.

"I remember everyone at school talking about Dayton. About how when my dad went to get her body, she was only wearing one of her shoes. People in my trig class tried to find a formula for how hard her body would need to fall to create the force to lose a shoe. But it didn't make sense. June's and Dayton's wounds weren't consistent with a long drop. Dad said they suffocated to death. You can see it in the burst veins in Dayton's face." She reaches up, unconsciously tracing patterns in her cheeks. "When Xander was at June's funeral reception, I went into his room to steal his phone charger. It was plugged in behind his nightstand. But when I reached down to unplug it, something was in the way. I pulled the nightstand away from the wall, and this little black sneaker fell out. It was so small, I thought it was a kid's shoe."

My stomach clenches like someone grabbed it in a fist. Is the shoe still upstairs? Did Xander find a better hiding place for it? Or did he tuck it back behind his nightstand?

"I didn't show it to my parents," Riley continues, glancing over her shoulder at the dark funeral home. "It was just a shoe. It didn't have Dayton's name on it or anything. But my phone was dead, and I couldn't stop thinking *what if.* I knew I could find Xander at June's wake, and he could tell me that it was nothing. A random shoe. A dumb joke with one of his dumb friends. He would tell me I was wrong, and I'd apologize for snooping, and we'd be fine."

She pushes on, aiming her face downward. I think she's looking at the sidewalk, but it's hard to tell without pupils. "I took the bike path through Aldridge Park because I remember Xander saying that he and June used to meet there. It was the halfway point between our houses. I ran for so long before I realized I was still holding the shoe. I'd run for blocks because of a fucking shoe, and I was holding it in my arms, cradling it like I had to keep it safe. And it was all suddenly so ridiculous to be so scared of a shoe that I just burst into tears. I didn't want to accuse Xander of anything. I was just scared and shaken up because people I knew were dead. People do crazy things when they're grieving. So, I went off the path to throw the shoe into the creek."

I think of how slippery it was when I had to get the creek water for the resurrection spell. The algae built up on the rocks. The gush of running water.

"The creek was hella high because it had rained for a couple of days that week, and the slope was all rocks. I couldn't see that well because I was still crying. But I managed to throw the shoe. I watched it splash near the other bank. But then I lost my balance. I slipped and fell and skidded all the way down to the water. I felt my wrist break right before my head went underwater for a minute. I remember how slimy the water was in my nose. Another rock caught me here." She uses a knuckle to point at the slowly healing cut across her forehead. "And I must have passed out. Then there was nothing. But it wasn't murder. It was an accident. I was stupid and I fell and I died."

I touch my face, surprised that there are no tears. I thought maybe after a week, I would have fresh tears to shed for her. But her death feels so far away when it's coming from her own lips.

"The shoe had to be Dayton's," I tell her. "Why else would my spell bring her back, too? Why does Xander have mushrooms growing out of his skin?"

She sobs into her broken wrist and shakes her head, miming an inability to speak. I take a step toward her, grabbing her shoulder with one hand. The color floods back into her eyes at my touch. Red veins and green-gold swirls and a pinprick of black in the center.

"It can't be him," she sobs. "It can't be my brother. He must have had a good reason. Or even a bad reason! Something that doesn't mean he killed June and Dayton. You *know* him."

"I know that he's covered in mushrooms."

She jerks away from me, turning back into a corpse. "Then you screwed up! You've screwed up before!"

"I didn't screw up so bad that I made him murder June and Dayton! I guess you can thank your parents for that."

"Fuck you!" she spits. "He's my brother, Mila! He's the first friend I ever had. I know him better than you ever could. He wouldn't do something like this. You're wrong. You think just because you did one big spell that you're good at this, but you're not. Everything you've touched has gone to shit! Look at what you did to me!" She holds her arms out, showcasing her broken bones and bloated skin. "You think *this* makes you a good witch? You should have left me in the fucking ground. You should have left all of us alone. Don't ruin Xander, too."

Her chest shudders and heaves. She looks so pitiful, and I hate her for it. She's chosen to protect her brother rather than be on my team. She's leaving me alone, again. Only this time it's on purpose.

"The coven was right," I say softly. "You're an abomination. My best friend—my *real* best friend—wouldn't protect a murderer. So whoever you are—whatever you are—you can go straight to hell. Because you aren't the Riley Greenway I wanted to bring back."

I leave her crying in front of the house she's not welcome in anymore, the gash in her forehead spreading wider and wider the farther away I get.

I don't sleep.

Fully dressed and with a belly full of Pepto-Bismol to keep the panic-pukes to a minimum, I sit on the edge of my bed, looking for the number for the police department. But even after I've found it, I keep scrolling. Googling. Checking other sources. I wind around the internet in a Fibonacci spiral until my mind quiets to a cool gray fog. Only then can I call the police department with an anonymous tip that Alexander Greenway was seen in Aldridge Park the night of the Fairmont Academy double suicide. I give the skeptical voice on the other end of the line Xander's license plate number and his exact height and weight.

I let my family see me while they eat breakfast and feed them lies about studying at Starbucks as my excuse to leave. I don't care if any of them believe me. Izzy asks for a Frappuccino she knows that I won't bring back.

Denim jacket on. Boots laced. Back in the car.

I don't know where to look for June and Dayton, so I start in the woods again. The trees are less oppressive in the daylight. I find scars in the bark of a trunk hit by a gunshot blast, but there's no blood or brains around it. The house is empty. The white fabric that bound Caleb's arms is in a heap on top of the useless sigils. Even Binx is nowhere to be seen. He must have slunk out during the invasion last night. The red grimoire is missing.

I drive around town, parking at random and walking into places I know that June and Dayton used to frequent. Starbucks. A fancy sandwich restaurant. Overpriced clothing stores where the employees smirk at me for even daring to walk through the doors.

I get hungry. I buy a fancy sandwich. It tastes like sawdust. Everywhere I turn, I'm scared that Xander will pop out or that the coven will find me or that June's and Dayton's bodies will be lifeless by the time I get to them. Have the cops already been to the Greenway Funeral Home? Has Toby's coven found June and Dayton? Is Caleb still pouring out non-murderous secrets?

Caleb.

Caleb isn't the murderer. He is an asshole and apparently not above academic fraud, but he's not a murderer. Fuck. I owe him an apology. Or a charm bag? He was so thrilled to see June last night, maybe he'll know where she is.

I pull out my phone and navigate to Caleb's Facebook. He has no updates today. I send him a message.

ME: *Are they with you?*

I'm pretty sure that having spent an evening together with a group of zombies, I don't have to clarify who "they" are.

My phone beeps as Caleb's response comes through.

CALEB: *At my house. Come by whenever. 824 Frentz Street.*

Even as I'm entering the address into my maps app, I know this could be a trap. Caleb and Xander could have worked together. Weren't they both in honor society? They could be waiting to slip a noose around my neck as easily as they did to June and Dayton. But I have to take the chance—I owe June and Dayton that much. I'm the one who took them out of the ground.

Frentz Street isn't as fancy as I would have expected. The houses are mostly one-story and squished sort of close to one another. Caleb's is a white house with a pointed roof and a blue door. It might actually be a dollhouse that wished to be a real house. I park across the street in case I need to make a run for it.

As I raise my hand to ring the doorbell, a shudder runs through me. The girls are here.

The blue door swings open, revealing a smiling Dayton. The bruising on her neck has been covered by a thick pink pashmina that I've seen Ms. Chu wear to school before. The color almost offsets the marbling of her corpse skin.

"Oh, thank God!" she coos. Her face turns pinker the second her fingers wrap around my wrist, pulling me inside. The veins on her face pop right back into place when she lets me go to lock the door. My magic is only working in defibrillator blasts now. "We were so worried that those old ladies found you last night. They were driving in laps around town, looking for all of us. It was so scary. Luckily, Caleb was able to free himself from the basement before they searched the house. He found me and June walking over the bridge and brought us back here. His parents are out of town for the weekend, so we have the whole place to ourselves. I slept in the principal's bed last night! I never in a million years thought I'd say that!"

"How do you know you're safe here?" I ask.

"One, we're already dead. And two, we asked. Truth spell, remember? We asked all kinds of questions about us being murdered, and he doesn't know anything."

She leads me through the narrow hallways of the house. There are mass-produced paintings of flowers and pictures of babies in buckets on the wall. In the living room, there's a large canvas printed with a picture of Ms. Chu and her husband on their wedding day. Ms. Chu is in a white blazer with a matching skirt. Caleb is in none of the pictures.

"Go ahead and make yourself comfortable," Dayton says, gesturing to the least comfortable-looking couch I've ever seen. Its tufted back seems to be glaring at me. She skitters into the kitchen, throwing open a glass door and calling into the backyard, "Guys! Mila's here!"

I can't help but imagine how normal this would be if everyone involved were alive. June and Caleb walking in from outside, their hands nervously entwined. Dayton bustling around, passing out sodas and bottled water. Just four normal teenagers taking advantage of an empty house. Except that two of us have broken necks. Only one of June's eyes has color, the other wiped clean. I try not to stare at the white one, even as it narrows at me.

"Riley isn't with you?" she asks, sitting daintily in a gray wingback chair like it's her zombie throne. She also has a scarf looped around her neck. Hers is blue and tied tightly enough that her neck doesn't wobble.

I take a long drink of water from the bottle Dayton handed me. The cold floods down my throat, pricking at my spine. "No. I need to talk to you guys about that. Last night, Riley said that she got some of her memories back. Have either of you recovered what happened to you the night you died?"

"I don't remember personally," June says slowly. She aims half a smile at Caleb, who is sitting in the stiff wooden chair beside her. "Caleb helped fill in some of the details, though. I was here that night."

I must look as puzzled as I feel, because Caleb sets his soda between his knees and steeples his fingers. "June and I are dating. I mean, we were before she . . ."

"We actually went out in sixth grade for, like, a month," June interrupts brightly. "But we reconnected in honor society. It was sort of concurrent with me and Xander, though, so we kept it quiet."

"Wait," I say. "If you were dating Caleb for months, then why would you help us investigate him? The spells, luring him to the house, keeping him hostage. He was—is?—your boyfriend."

She flicks her wrist. "My memories were foggy. I remembered that we were sort of together, but I also remembered telling him that I wasn't ready to tell anyone about us. Since we weren't, you know, the same level of popular. I wanted to take some time to boost his rating on campus. It'd really help if he won the Rausch Scholarship. Everyone wants an invite to the gala." She takes her lower lip between her teeth. "It was a total dick move on my part. So, when you had all this evidence that he'd killed us, I assumed it was because of something I did. People say that I push them too hard." She winces a smile in Caleb's direction. "He was sort of guilty until proven innocent. Especially since I didn't remember giving him my necklace."

"The night they died, we had just told Dayton about us," Caleb says, nodding toward Dayton, who beams at being mentioned. "She volunteered to pick June up from here and have a sleepover, so June wouldn't get in trouble for missing curfew."

"I never had a curfew," Dayton says primly. "My parents trusted me to make good choices."

"But after they left here, I don't know what happened," Caleb says. He slurps soda from the lip of his can. "The next thing I heard, they were found in Aldridge Park."

I arch an eyebrow at him. "And you decided to pretend to be super fine with your new girlfriend committing suicide?"

He smiles at me in return, his usual snide baring of teeth. "What was I supposed to do? Cry in class? June didn't want people to know about us. I honored that. I talked shit when everyone else was talking shit. I was wrecked when I thought she was gone. But Aniyah started asking questions, and Angel, Sky, Diamond, and Dawn started missing honor society meetings so that they could talk to the school shrink. Five people thinking that June and Dayton were still alive was too many to be a coincidence. And it wasn't. They are alive." His head droops. "Sort of."

Dayton leans over to me, whispering loudly. "We explained the Sunday-deadline thing last night. He's sad about it."

"Can't you do something to fix it?" Caleb asks me. He grips one of his knees until his knuckles blanch. "You were powerful enough to bring them back. Why don't you do it again with a better spell?"

June fingers the tasseled end of her scarf. "Caleb. Stop. We talked about this. We're not meant to be here longer than seven days. It's fine."

"It's not fine," he says through clenched teeth. Spit bubbles pop in the corners of his mouth. "You've had time to make peace with this, but I haven't."

"It's not your choice," she bites back.

"My death, my choice," Dayton says to no one.

"I don't want to live on more borrowed time," June says. "My body is rotting. Even having Mila here isn't putting us back together anymore. I don't want to see how much worse it gets. And where would we live? A week in an abandoned house is more than enough. Sunday night is our time to go. We were only here to get revenge anyway." She reaches over and steals one of Caleb's hands. "And we shouldn't have kidnapped you. It was a misunderstanding. So, now we have two days to say goodbye with nothing else to worry about."

"Actually," I say shakily, "there is something else to worry about." I take a deep breath. "I'm pretty sure Xander killed you."

"Okay. *Xander Greenway* killed us." June titters in that popular-girl-pacifying-a-loser way. Her mocking smile mirrors Caleb's. "You also thought Caleb was the murderer, so your track record as a detective is not great."

"But you are an excellent witch," Dayton adds quickly. "The truth spell lasted for hours. Caleb just kept telling us the funniest things all night."

Caleb shrinks into his chair and hides his face behind his soda.

"I'm serious," I say. I explain what happened when I left the woods. The mushrooms on Xander's back. Him stealing his parents' hearse and running away. Riley's confession that her death was an accident.

"She basically admitted that she knew Xander was responsible, but she wanted to blame me anyway," I say, wiping my nose on the back of my hand. Hot tears slide down the curve of my cheeks. "He had Dayton's shoe. The one that was missing from the crime scene."

"You said it was just a little black shoe," June says. "It's not like Dayton's mom wrote her name in it. He could have a shoe fetish. That doesn't make him a killer."

Dayton pats my knee, very briefly recovering her living appearance. "You and Riley had a fight. That's all. Friends fight all the time. June and I fought over who should wear what scarf this morning. She said the blue would make my face veins look worse, and I got super mad at her. But, in my heart"—she sets a hand on her chest and pats it twice—"I knew she was right."

"This isn't a fight about a scarf," I say. "Riley wasn't murdered. The spell was only supposed to bring back the wrongly dead. That's why it brought back you guys. You were killed. She wasn't."

"And even if Xander was the one who hurt us," June says, the *if* as heavy as a stone, "you've already called the cops. There's nothing else you can do now, Mila. I know you want to do this superhero-witch thing and save Cross Creek from evil, but you also need to chill." She bats her eyelashes at Caleb. The effect is odd with her mismatched eyes. "Do you think we could order a pizza? Let's be normal for the day."

I want to feel normal. It's one of the last things I said to Xander. One of the last things I'll ever say to him.

Dayton lets me curl up in her lap and cry.

TWENTY

A COUPLE OF hours later, I wake up alone on the uncomfortable couch in Caleb's living room. The shining black screen of the
TV mounted to the wall reflects my body, twisted into the back of
the couch. The sun is starting to set, leaving the living room dim
and dreamlike. Tomato and garlic and chocolate fill the air, and
my stomach rumbles, remembering the pizza and lava cake the
girls insisted I eat before I passed out.

I drag myself off the couch. I can hear June's voice in the backyard and the splash of water in the kitchen. I ache like I've been
repeatedly punched. Which I have been—by the ground in the
woods, by the worst couch on earth, by the truth of how close I
was to a murderer last night. How safe I felt with him until the
laptop illuminated his back.

Mushrooms. God, that spell is so fucked up.

Dayton is standing in front of the sink. Opalescent suds cling to her bruised skin up to the elbow. Her hands are scrubbing a dish in a wide circle, but her focus is on the window facing the backyard. Through the glass door, I can see June and Caleb playing with a small mound of fluff on legs. The dog wags its tail, overjoyed as June tosses a tiny ball for it to fetch.

"You don't want to join them?" I ask Dayton.

She looks over her shoulder at me and scrunches her nose. "They deserve some private time, and playing with the dog is about as close as they can get. I think they were sleeping together when June was alive, but it wouldn't be right if they did it now. We're technically corpses, so, you know, necrophilia and all that."

"Right." I cringe.

"I thought maybe she convinced me to do it," she says suddenly, her hands swirling under the water. "We've been friends for so long, and I love her, but she has this way of seeing the worst parts of you. She's right. She does push people. She doesn't mean to, not really, but she still does it. I was so scared that she'd shown me something about myself that I didn't even know was there, something that could make me . . . I'm sorry that someone felt like they had to kill us, but selfishly I'm so relieved that it wasn't me. And it's nice that June got to have Caleb back for a little bit."

Outside, Caleb scoops June up by the waist and carries her across the lawn. Her bare feet kick the air, but her mouth is wide and laughing. I almost don't notice the strange pallor of her skin or the parts of her that randomly start bleeding.

"Does it bother you that you didn't find a long-lost boyfriend?" I ask Dayton, prying my attention away from June's happiness. It feels too much like being kicked while I'm down.

Dayton dunks her hands back into the water and pulls up a chocolate-stained plate. "Oh, no. That's too much to live for. She'll be so much sadder tomorrow night when we have to go back."

I edge around to lean on the counter next to her. Water sinks into the waistband of my jeans. "And you won't be?"

She sets aside the sponge and scrapes the chocolate off with her thumbnail. "Sure, I'll be sort of sad. I'll miss Gatorade and swimming and having friends." She flicks a smile at me. "I'll miss you and your grumpy face."

"I'll miss you, too," I say quietly. I don't know when it happened, but it's true. I will miss her. And June, for all her judging and shit-talking.

And Riley. Of course. Her dying almost broke me the first time. What's going to happen tomorrow night when I know that she's gone for good?

"But I already miss things from my real life," Dayton says, cheerfully continuing to scrub and talk at the same time. "Like choir and my family and being able to walk around without scaring people. That first night back, you said we weren't really back to life. Just sort of visiting. I had a good visit. I'm ready to go back to heaven."

"You don't think God is going to be mad at you for being a zombie for a week?"

She rolls her eyes at me. "God doesn't get mad at you, Mila.

No matter what your mean old witches say. Will you put some music on for me while I finish the dishes? Something I can sing along with."

I pull my phone out of my pocket and squint at the screen, struggling to see anything but the crack in the glass. I have a missed call from the landline at the Greenway Funeral Home. I put the voicemail on speaker.

"Mila, this is Monica Greenway. I'm looking for Xander. Is he with you? He said that the two of you have been spending time together, and I have a pair of, well, fuller-figure jeans in my washing machine. Your mother says you're out studying this afternoon. If you hear from Xander, tell him he needs to return home immediately. We received a very strange phone call . . . Anyway, pass this along if you see him."

Fuller-figure? Come on. She could have just said *jeans*. Mrs. Greenway trying not to call me fat is so much worse than her coming out and saying she thinks my body is gross. Her euphemisms are more hurtful than June's actual insults.

"A strange phone call?" Dayton echoes. "From who?"

"The cops, maybe? Or Riley?"

"It would be strange if her dead daughter called."

I blow out a breath, opening my texts to respond to Mrs. Greenway to tell her that Xander isn't with me. Hopefully the cops have already tracked him down, but I won't let myself be an accidental alibi, especially since my mom is blabbing my whereabouts to whoever asks. Above my last conversation with Xander, there's a message from a number I don't have saved in my phone. It has a Creek County area code.

UNKNOWN NUMBER: *It's Aniyah. Don't erase this, please. Something fucked up is going on with the Greenways. Stay away from Xander. He's lying to you.*

MY PHONE: *Can we meet up and talk about this? Tomorrow night?*

UNKNOWN NUMBER: *Yes! Where?*

MY PHONE: *The abandoned house on Knapp Road. 8 p.m.?*

"No, no, no," I say out loud. "I left my phone in my jacket when I was showering last night."

"So?" Dayton asks.

I reach over her and the sink full of murky water and bang on the window until Caleb and June look up. I motion for them to come inside. They do, leaving the yapping fluff outside.

"Xander told Aniyah to meet him at Yarrow House tonight. We have to go get her!"

"Wait, what?" June asks.

"She thinks Xander used her phone to lure Aniyah to her death," Dayton says.

I send a panicked message to Aniyah's number.

ME: *Call the cops. Don't go in the house. Get as far away from the house as you can.*

The clock on the oven says it's a quarter till eight.

"Fuck!" I snap the rubber band on my wrist so hard that the glue gives and the elastic flops to the floor. "Fuck, fuck, fuck. We gotta go. Leave the dishes!"

"Mila!" Dayton says, flicking the soap off her hands. "Why would he wait a full twenty-four hours to get Aniyah alone? Why wouldn't he have her go right away if he really believed she had information worth dying over?"

"Because he thought we were going to spend last night fooling around, and that was obviously more important than killing the editor of the *Fairmont Informant*!" I shout.

"Is that the newspaper's name?" June asks. "For real?"

I don't have time to waste. I grab June's and Dayton's wrists and pull them out of the kitchen before their necks can even un-break.

"Wait!" Caleb calls after us.

"Stay safe!" June calls back, her long legs fumbling along behind me. "If we're not back in half an hour, call the cops!"

"Thanks for the pizza and pashminas!" Dayton adds.

June only asks me to slow down once as I drive us to the edge of town. She seems to realize from the scream-barking sound I make in lieu of words that her request has been denied. I push my Toyota within an inch of its life, the gas pedal cutting a trench into the floor mat.

"It doesn't even make sense, Mila," Dayton says from the backseat. "I might not remember dying, but I remember Xander. We were friends. He and June came to my last show-choir concert. He brought flowers. You don't bring flowers to someone and then murder them."

"I'm sure someone has, at some point, given flowers to someone they've murdered," June says. "But I don't think Xander is one of them. Have you considered that the mushrooms on his back were there because you're not as good at magic as you think you are?"

I let them chatter among themselves. I don't blame them for their denial. It's the same mental gymnastics that made them not believe they were dead until the first time I stepped out of the magical perimeter in Walmart. Or that made Caleb think that their corpse forms were makeup. Or that made Aniyah believe that they'd faked their deaths.

If only one of us is going to be thinking clearly, I'm fine with it being me. My focus is perfectly level.

Another girl is not going to die. I won't let it happen.

Bringing the girls back from the dead wasn't enough. The revenge curse wasn't enough. The truth spell loosened the wrong lips. All the magic I've done—have ever done, will ever do—will be for nothing if Xander hurts Aniyah Dorsey.

The car jostles and bumps down the driveway. I park as close to the porch as I can get. Normally, I want to stay under the radar, but tonight I want to be as conspicuous as possible. Let everyone driving by know that there are people inside. That we need help. That the cops should definitely beat down the door.

The hearse Xander stole is nowhere to be seen, but he could have easily parked up the street and walked down. He wouldn't want to be spotted.

I climb out of the car, wishing I had a weapon or something. But if Aniyah can walk in unarmed, then I can, too. At least I have zombie backup.

Dust kicked up from the driveway coats the inside of my nose and tickles the back of my throat. From the outside, the house is as silent as ever. It looks no different than it did when I walked through the woods this morning. I'm struck by the realization that I don't want to go inside. That I would be happy to never see the inside of this house again. It doesn't make me feel safe or welcome. It's the hole where I've been throwing my secrets.

But I have a job to do tonight.

There's nowhere to step on the rotting porch that doesn't come with a screech or groan of wood, so I walk with my usual sense of purpose. Boots on the ground. Collar up. Zombies behind me.

I step through the back door. There are no lit candles. Everything beyond the doorframe is blackness. Instead of the normal stench of mold and raccoons, the abandoned kitchen is an assault of undiluted fragrance. Orange and sage and cedar and cinnamon. As glass crunches under my boots, I realize that it must be the remains of the essential oil vials that Riley and I spent so much money on. Toby charges fourteen dollars apiece for them.

June and Dayton stop behind me until I fumble for the flashlight app on my phone. No one complains when I keep the light aimed at the floor, the most likely place to find a body. The sunken living room is as we left it—unlit candles sitting on top of stacks of books, empty Gatorade bottles built into squat pyramids.

There's a noise upstairs. June, Dayton, and I flinch in unison, moving back toward the kitchen.

"I know you're down there," Riley's voice floats down, even before she hits the top step. In the spotlight of my flashlight app, she's even more ghoulishly gray-skinned and bloodied. "I'm not healing a lot, but I can feel your magic, Mila."

"Why are you here in the dark?" Dayton asks as Riley descends the rickety stairs.

"Why are you here at all?" June asks.

"Where else was I supposed to go?" Riley asks. "You guys ditched me. Mila thinks that I came back *wrong*. It's not like I can go back to my family. I came here to sleep until I die again. I have a candle in my room upstairs, but it went out when I was napping."

"So, Aniyah isn't here?" I ask, squinting at the bowed ceiling.

"Um." There's a cough from the back door. The four of us spin around and see the outline of a fat body in the doorway. Aniyah Dorsey, alive and well. "I waited in my car until I saw you drive up. Are there no lights in here?"

Dayton scrambles to find a lighter. She lights a taper and hands it to June, who helps her light all the candles around the living room. As the room starts to glow, Aniyah takes a horrified step back outside.

"What the fuck?" she screams.

"That's rude," June croaks. I think she's exaggerating how hoarse her voice is with her broken neck. She's starting to sound like my gremlin impression. "You'd hate it if people screamed when they saw your face."

"Yeah, well, I don't look like a corpse!" Aniyah says, one hand on the doorframe, ready to launch herself back to her car.

"We are corpses," Riley snaps. "So come in, since you had to go digging around, making up stories about how we faked our deaths."

"Our deaths were very real," Dayton says, flashing a glimpse of her neck bruise from under her pashmina. "Obviously."

Aniyah walks in on trembling legs. She edges around the room the same way that Binx does when he's wary of the company he's keeping. She tucks her hair behind her ears and pushes her glasses up, making absolutely sure that nothing is obstructing her view. I notice that she's carrying her school bag. She clings to one of its straps.

"Is that your evidence?" I ask, jerking my chin at the bag. Now that she isn't in immediate danger of being murdered, I pity her less. I want to know what she thinks she knows and send her back to her parents before Xander or the cops show up.

She swallows and nods. "Pictures of June at the Celebration of Life. Dayton walking downtown. Riley in the front seat of your car. A copy of Riley's death certificate, signed by her dad, who must have faked it . . ." She stops and holds up a hand. "I'm sorry. What is that awful smell?"

"The house," June says. "The raccoons. Our insides decomposing and the smell coming up out of our throats."

Aniyah hugs herself. "Mila, did you invite me to talk to the literal undead? You couldn't have just *told* me that there are actual fucking zombies in this world?"

"There probably aren't zombies other than us," Dayton says thoughtfully. "Off the record, Mila is a very powerful witch."

"But not great with the direction of spells," June adds.

"Aniyah, I didn't invite you here at all," I say, dragging a hand through my hair. "I'm pretty sure Xander wanted to lure you here to hurt you. So, now that you've seen that the girls are real-dead not fake-dead, you can drop the article. It'll make you look foolish and hurt a lot of people who miss their dead loved ones. Go home, lock the doors, and if you see Xander, call the cops."

"Why? If his parents didn't fake Riley's death, then why would he have beef with me at all?" Aniyah asks with more defiance in her voice than in her curled posture. "So the article didn't work out. It's not like I care what the most popular boy in school thinks of me. I'm not scared of him."

"You should be," I say.

"I'm not going anywhere until someone tells me what the hell is going on," she retorts. "Beginning to end, full detail. You can't just spring zombies on me and then not explain how they got here."

"Your curiosity is not worth dying over," June says. "This is where your article ends. We didn't fake our deaths. You were stupid to think we could have. Now get out before you get murdered, too."

I can see candlelight reflecting in the wetness of Riley's eyes as she moves her gaze over her shoulder. Toward the door. The undulating flame makes her eyes look wild where they should be expressionless.

Cold dread settles deep under my skin, spreading all the way out to my fingertips. My lips and eyelids are buzzing with fear that I have to choke down whole.

"He's here already, isn't he?" I ask Riley under my breath. "He's been here with you all day."

Tears spill onto her waxy cheeks. "He didn't have anywhere else to go."

I swallow. "Aniyah. Once you clear the porch, run as fast as you can. Text me when you are home and every single door is bolted shut. This isn't a joke. I need you to get out of here alive, okay?"

But the broken porch steps are already shrieking under the weight of footsteps. The silhouette in the doorway is distinctly Xander's, from the part in his hair to the field of mushrooms blooming across his torso.

His voice floats out of the darkness. It freezes my bones as it whispers, "Mila?"

TWENTY-ONE

XANDER RUSHES INTO the living room. His chest is pumping like he's been running. The mushrooms have spread across his chest and down his stomach, covering the front of him in fungi that end abruptly at the elastic band of the black pajama pants I saw him in last night. His feet are bare and caked in mud and blood.

I wonder if the blood is his.

June and Dayton make a dead-girl wall between Xander and me and Aniyah. Riley stands to the side, rubbing her broken wrist.

Xander pauses on the threshold of the living room, visibly recoiling.

"Mila," he says, making eye contact with me from over June's shoulder. "Are you okay?"

"Is *she* okay?" Aniyah asks, pushing past the zombies. "What the fuck is wrong with your skin?" She looks over her shoulder at me. "Is he dead, too?"

Her attention is diverted for a second too long. Xander sinks his hand deep into her hair, fisting his fingers around the roots of her barrel curls.

"Don't!" Riley shouts.

Arm shooting out, he flings Aniyah sideways. Her head cracks against the handle of the open basement door, and she crumples to the ground, lying very still.

"No!" I try to rush forward to get to Aniyah, but Xander meets me halfway, his hands wrapping around my forearms. His lips curl into his most disarming smile, the one that makes his eyes sparkle like sapphires. But that sparkle means nothing. It's just glitter with no substance.

"Mila," he repeats. He pushes my hair out of my face so hard that I can feel strands breaking. "Riley told me everything. She told me it was an accident. I'm not mad. You'll fix it. I'll help you fix it. I know you didn't mean to bring them back. You didn't know what you were doing. I told you that I'm not mad about"—his eyes flick down to his chest, but he looks away quickly, his jaw tense—"any of it. I saw that you took June's lip gloss out of Riley's room that night I gave you the necklace. I'm not mad about that either. You didn't know it was special. Just like Riley didn't know not to take my shoe. I should have told you sooner what the lip gloss meant to me. And what you mean to me. You wouldn't have had to do this on your own. I should have been there to help."

The lip gloss. I can only faintly picture it now. Too fancy to be purchased in Cross Creek. The plastic melted down to a goo before the grave swallowed it.

It was June's. And if Dayton had ever borrowed it, it would have her DNA, too.

Stomach acid splashes all the way up to my front teeth. I yank my arms back.

"You can't help me," I say. "You killed June and Dayton."

"That's what you're mad about?" He goggles at me and spreads his arms wide. "Jesus Christ, Mila. Look at me!"

The floorboards squeak. Xander turns to see June and Dayton leaning over Aniyah, trying to help her to her feet.

"Get away from her," he warns, taking a threatening step. I see something red glinting in his pocket. The handle of the ceremonial dagger, bobbing. It isn't sharp enough to tear through the deep fleece pockets, but with enough force behind it, it could draw blood. I wonder if he meant to use it against Aniyah. Was he going to bother staging her death as another suicide?

Riley jumps in his way, putting her hands up to stop him but not actually touching him. "Let them leave," she pleads. "Just let them go. You don't need them."

"Shut up, Riley," he sneers, maneuvering around her. "You don't know what you're talking about. You spent a week living with them!"

She circles around him again, her voice breaking. "You were friends with them for years!"

Dayton holds her hands out to help Aniyah get to her knees.

"I said leave her there!" Xander snarls. I've never noticed the vein in his temple, how it leaps up and down when he talks. There's another one pulsating in his neck. He reaches for the closest taper and throws it into the kitchen. It misses the girls but lands among the shattered glass. The essential oil erupts into flames, a perfect line of fire that slices across the kitchen and licks at the doorframe.

Of course. He's too smart to not have booby-trapped the exit. He meant for Aniyah to die here.

And now we all could die here.

"Xander!" Riley says, wrapping her arms around her stomach. It's hard to tell since she can't actually turn colors, but she seems queasy. "What are you doing?"

What's left of the cabinets in the kitchen crackles and pops as the fire starts to eat up the walls. Herb brushes and twig pentagrams that I strung together hiss before they catch fire and fall to the floor. Dayton, June, and Aniyah rush away from the flames, knocking over some of the empty Gatorade bottles in their wake.

"Mila," Xander says evenly, as though he can't taste the greasy smoke. "You need to get out of here. Now."

"Where am I supposed to go?" I yell. "You just lit the motherfucking kitchen on fire!"

"And you're trapped here, too!" Dayton says, putting herself between me and Xander. She thrusts her hands on her hips. "Do you hate us that much?"

He examines her face, almost surprised that she's there. "I don't hate you. You don't exist to me anymore."

Sweat builds in my palms and pools in the small of my back. For now the heat is bearable, making Yarrow pleasantly warm, for once. But it won't take long for the living room to catch. This whole place is a stack of kindling. Smoke is starting to gather against the swollen ceiling like slimy brown ghosts. It's being sucked upstairs to the window that Riley pulled the boards off of.

The window that is now the only way out.

"I should have done it sooner. I shouldn't have wasted so much time. There would have been less cleanup before. Before the scholarship and the attention. Before we had friends to lose," he says, shaking his head. He runs his fingers through his hair, making his mushrooms flex. "It was never going to stop. All they did was cause pain. Undermining and cutting everyone down. Hurting so many people." He looks over at Riley, not seeming to care that her skull is glistening in the candlelight and her white eyes are leaking tears onto her gray skin. "I had to stop them. It was killing you, Ry."

She shakes her head, a hand coming up to cover her mouth. "No. Oh God, please, no."

Aniyah takes a step back, toward the kitchen fire. I can see my own need to run reflected behind her glasses. I catch her eye, make her look at me for long enough to see how very serious I am about getting her out of here alive. I jerk my head toward the stairs. Her mouth slants up on one side to say, *Are you fucking serious?* I widen my eyes—because, yes, this is the most serious I have ever been in my life—until she takes a breath and starts to inch away.

"Every time you thought it was going to get better, it started all over again," Xander says to Riley. "The ballet lessons you couldn't take and the parties you weren't invited to. Even when your name was on the shortlist for the Rausch Scholarship, Dayton started telling people that the committee wouldn't vote for you because they'd be too scared of what you'd pick as the theme. She said maybe you'd choose witchcraft or dead bodies."

"I heard Dan Calalang say it first!" Dayton protests.

"Then maybe he needs to be next!" Xander snaps. The vein in his neck throbs, a balloon close to bursting. He stares daggers at Dayton, and when he speaks again, his voice quivers. "We have a family business here. We provide a service that everyone needs. We're supposed to live here forever. I'm supposed to take over the business from my dad. But how can we survive living across the street from people like you? Trying to live our lives when people like you will always whisper about us in the grocery store and keep us out of the PTA and make sure that everywhere we go, people know that we're freaks. Because no one was ever going to stop you. They didn't stop you when you had Riley kicked out of ballet. They didn't stop you from having your parents change my Rausch gala theme from science to luau."

Out of the corner of my eye, I see Aniyah freeze in fear, her foot about to reach the first stair.

June must see her, too, because she folds her arms over her chest and gives a theatrical scoff, flipping her hair so hard that it makes her neck bulge on one side.

"Science was too nerdy," June says loudly. "People had so much fun doing limbo. You can't blame me for giving people what they wanted."

In a blur of movement, Xander has her face in his hand. His nails sink into her cheekbone hard enough to make his arm shake. Her lips pucker like a fish in his palm. But while his grip stays firm, his face slackens. Tears glaze his eyes, and finally his voice breaks. "I tried with you, June. I tried to be nice. I tried to be a good boyfriend. I tried to get you to stop. But you wouldn't let me fix you. You wanted *me* to change. You treated my life like it was trash that you were sorting through. You made fun of my family. Letting you get close to me just made it easier for you to hurt us. It was a mistake. I gave you too much ammunition. And then you cheated on me with Caleb Treadwell. You couldn't stop humiliating me. What did you think would happen at the end? How much did you think you could hurt people before they hurt you back?" His thumb digs so deep into her cheek that I'm scared it'll break the skin. Before it does, he moves away from her in disgust. Tears slide down his cheeks. "Hanging was too good for you. You two were everything wrong with Cross Creek."

I know that June and Dayton were those people. Snobby and elitist. Narrow-minded and shallow. But there's so much more to them than that. There's laughter and compassion and hope and love and a joy for lives they can't live anymore. And no matter what they said about Riley and Xander, they didn't deserve to die. I've seen them grow in just one week. The June in Xander's story isn't the same girl who would cause a distraction so that Aniyah could creep up the stairs. The Dayton he's painted as exclusionary isn't the girl who let me sleep in her lap. They never got a chance to show people how capable of good they were. And now they never will.

June watches him like he's a wild animal, keeping her attention just over his shoulder instead of making threatening eye contact. She stays very still, knowing that any response is the wrong response.

"You took our lives from us with your endless fucking gossip, and I took them back from you." He rubs his hand over the cut on his thumb, over and over again as though willing it to stay open. "I should have stopped you the second you started all this. Because it was always Dayton to start, too stupid to know when to stop talking. It was your mom who got my parents kicked out of the PTA, wasn't it? It was your ballet class that Riley wasn't allowed to join?"

"I didn't know," Dayton says, wringing her hands together. "I promise I had no idea how much I'd hurt either of you—"

"You didn't care!" The words are mangled, not quite a roar or a sob. "If you'd cared, this wouldn't have lasted for years. Twelve years of torture. Of a reputation we didn't deserve. Every town needs a funeral home. Everyone has to bury their dead. Why shouldn't it have been our family? Why did it make us outcasts? Because two girls decided to whisper *what if* in the ears of everyone who would listen. What if we were up to something freaky? What if we were dangerous?" His lips curl away from his teeth in a wet sneer. "When you died, I was free. Riley was free. Cross Creek was a better place. Everyone will see that. After summer vacation, people will start to forget you. They'll move on. They can be happy—truly happy—for the first time. Thanks to me."

Aniyah has made it upstairs. I can hear the crunch of floorboards, and I pray that the second story can keep its structural integrity long enough for her to get out. Even if I don't survive, she needs to. It's not her fault she got dragged into this. I brought it down on us.

What's Toby always saying about magic coming back times three?

A ceiling beam in the kitchen snaps and crashes to the floor. The fire leaps into the living room, quickly swallowing the closest stack of books and momentarily distracting Xander.

Dayton swoops toward me, shoving me as hard as she can toward the stairs. "Let's go! One of us can still die, you know."

I start running. Xander spins back but is punched by June. The blow cracks against his temple, followed by another to the nose. She has her dukes up like a professional boxer, protecting her neck and bobbing on her toes. Dayton flies up the stairs, her pink pashmina flapping behind her. I follow her, and Riley launches herself onto Xander's back, holding him in place. I hit the top landing blind. I've never been up here before, and the light from the fire downstairs hasn't reached this far. By the time it does, it'll be too late.

June pants up the stairs behind me, yanking me toward the third door on the left, the bedroom over the living room with the slumping floor. On the floor, there's a sigil written in chalk, an unlit candle, and a single mushroom as long as my thumb. Its flesh is shriveled, the cap turned in on itself. The bottom of the stem is blackened with dried blood. I have to look away before I throw up.

The night sky is visible through the open window. I can almost, but not quite, taste fresh air. Before June can shimmy through, Riley rushes into the room. With her hair knotted and her face wet with tears, she appears unnervingly fresh from the creek.

"I'm sorry," she sobs, holding her stomach like she's trying to keep her guts from pouring out on the floor. "I didn't want to believe it. I didn't know how bad it was. Please, believe me. Please. I didn't want to believe he could do this. I thought it might have been an accident or a misunderstanding. I thought I was remembering it wrong. I wanted to be wrong. I'm so sorry."

"You couldn't have known," I say. Although, honestly, I will say anything to get everyone through this window. My fight-or-flight has switched on hard, and I am ready for liftoff. When June doesn't look convinced, I push her back toward the window. "June, none of us knew. And as the two people here who got nude with the murderer, we don't get to judge. Now come on."

Glaring at me with her one colored eye, June grabs Riley by the hair and throws her out the window. I know that Riley can't technically die, but I still yelp when I see her rolling down the roof, followed by a snickering June. God, dead girls play rough with each other.

I am halfway through the window myself when fingers wrap around my ankle and pull me backward. My head bangs against the windowsill on my way down. Pain splinters through the base of my skull, at once burning and numb. Xander stands over me, backlit by the fire that has finally started to spread up the stairs.

"You wouldn't leave me here alone. I knew you wouldn't," he says, his voice like honey thick enough to drown in. Delusions are like that, I guess. Syrupy sweet and heavy enough to keep you submerged.

I sway to my feet, more punch-drunk than seductive. I can't believe that we'll both get out of this alive. The fire is starting to creep around corners, covering the room in its hazy glow. Dingy brown smoke pumps through the air, burning my eyes and singeing my lungs. Smoke inhalation is a thing that kills you, isn't it?

Maybe Xander wants us to die together to prove once and for all that I'm Not Like Other Girls. That I can be martyred instead of murdered, as though they aren't the same thing.

Or maybe there's no logic at all. I'm expecting a lot from someone who set a flaming trap without having an escape plan for himself. Even now, he isn't throwing himself to safety. He's hit the end of the road, and he isn't budging.

And he wants me to go with him.

I can feel a deep, dark part of myself flutter with the compliment. Somewhere inside me, sixth-grade Mila whispers, "*He could drag any girl to her death to be with him forever, and he chose me.*"

Sixth-grade Mila really thought that the only person better than Edward Cullen was Alexander Greenway. Part of me has always been lured by the monster inside him.

Even though the smoke is starting to make me feel sluggish and the back of my head throbs, I can fight. If he kisses me, I can bite the tongue out of his mouth. Dig my thumbs into the corners of his eyes and burrow until I find brain.

Is that what he thought about when he was alone with June? Is that how he rocked himself to sleep at night?

Am I better because it would be self-defense if I did it?

When I do it.

If I can do it.

The thing in me that wants to live speaks for me. "Of course not. I've been waiting for you my whole life, Xander. There's never been anyone but you. "

The best lie is always the truth.

He wraps his arms around my waist. The mushroom caps that I drew out of his broken soul press into my chest, squealing against the buttons of my jacket. The sound sets my teeth on edge, but Xander mistakes my cringe for a hug. He curls his head into the dip of my shoulder, the same as he did on the bench at the farmers' market. He sighs against my neck, cooling the rose quartz. I set a hand on the back of his head, my elbow cushioned by a flat toadstool. With sweat clinging to his back, he feels like a wet Nerf ball. Porous. Slick. Spongy.

There isn't enough air. The smoke would be thick enough to choke me if I could remember how to breathe. But the whole world is on fire, not only this house.

One of my hands strokes his hair as the other travels to the waistband of his pajama pants. My thumb traces the pleats in the elastic until my nail catches in the seam of the pocket. There it is—smooth, round metal and the bumpy plastic of a fake ruby.

"Did you ever really like me?" I whisper, my voice as weak and unsure as if I switched languages. Asking could kill me—there isn't enough time, I know that—but what about not knowing? When you're facing down the moment you'll be able to cite as ground zero of your post-traumatic stress—if you should be so lucky to live long enough to get to *post*—then why not collect all the information?

"I love you," he sniffles. "I've always loved you. I would kill for you."

And the awful thing is that he means it. Literally. He could fix my life the way he fixed his and Riley's. He would stab or strangle or poison anyone who hurt me.

Toby.

Dr. Miller.

The Nouns.

My parents.

My sisters.

"Then you can die for me."

I pull the ceremonial dagger out of his pocket and rear back, bracing both hands on the handle. I bring it down with every ounce of strength in my body. The blade slides into Xander's shoulder easily, and I keep shoving until I feel the metal bite into the moldy wood of the wall.

The sound of his scream crackles in the air like a broken log. Inside his mouth, I can see his tonsils have turned to smooth white mushroom caps. There's nothing left but the rot.

Blood rises up between the mushrooms, slipping between stems and caps, spurting onto the sleeves of my jacket, flecking against my mouth. I rub my lips together, tasting hot pennies and dirt.

He looks from the hilt of the dagger to me and back again, a moth on display in a burning museum. Pinned, but breathing. We both know that I could have aimed for his heart. That he could rock the blade out of his skin to free himself. But he's trapped for a moment, and that's all the time I need to get myself and Aniyah and the others to safety.

I look back at the sigil on the floor, the shriveled mushroom lying beside it. I can imagine Riley's hand wielding the chalk, chanting spell after spell over the mushroom. "The mushrooms were never a curse. I just made you see what you've been hiding. Magic can't get rid of what's inside of you, Xander. I could never fix you."

"Camila." He says my name like it's hope itself. Like it could be enough to change my mind.

I don't say goodbye.

It's a long way from the roof to the ground, but I have no choice. I land in the dead grass and roll up like a potato bug.

Yarrow House is erased, piece by piece, in fire as orange as a sunrise.

TWENTY-TWO

MY FINGERNAILS ARE filthy against my pillowcase. I can feel the itch of a scab knitting together where my head hit the windowsill. The stench of smoke and licking flames is stuck in my hair. It's probably baked so deep in my skin that a part of me will never leave Yarrow.

My mom's hand is on my shoulder. She tells me there's been an accident.

I pretend to be asleep until she leaves.

TWENTY-THREE

I WAKE UP again with a sharp elbow in my back and milky breath in my face. My sisters are on either side, squishing me into a Flores-girl sandwich. I open my eyes into Izzy's.

Over my shoulder, Nora is asleep, her mouth open wide to let a torrential downpour of drool fall onto my pillow—the one *with* a pillowcase, thank God. What I thought was her elbow boring into my back is actually the nose of Pua the pig, smashed between us.

If Nora is bringing back something she stole from me, shit has gotten very real.

I roll my head back to Izzy.

"Mom told you?" My voice is as raspy as Riley's. My tongue tastes like smoke and blood.

She sucks her lips in and nods. Her eyes are damp. I wonder how long she's been watching me sleep, getting more and more scared instead of waking me up. Nora has never been afraid to wake any of us up if she needs the slightest thing—water, a snack, attention—but Izzy bears everything like it doesn't touch her. She tries so hard not to be a typical middle child that she reaps almost none of the benefits of it either.

"I'm not going anywhere, okay?" I tell her. "I know that a lot of people have been dying, but that's not going to happen to me. Not like that."

A tear splashes onto the tip of her nose. "You aren't wearing your rubber band."

I glance down at my bare wrist. "It broke yesterday. I'll put a new one on today. Wearing it was a good idea. It's been helping a lot."

She sniffles and nods. "I knew it would be."

"So humble."

She takes two big lungfuls of air, and more tears fall down her face. "I'm sorry Xander died," she whispers.

I'm not, I think.

Skin crawling, I can feel the phantom weight of the dagger in my hand, the squish as it moved through his body and into the wall behind him. I didn't kill him, but I let him die. He chose to stay in that burning house. I'm an accessory to his death. But I could have been his last victim.

It was self-preservation in revenge's clothes.

I nudge Izzy's knees with mine. "Go back to sleep."

I pet her hair until her eyelids get too heavy to stay open. She sleeps like Nora, throwing her elbows around and breathing loudly through her mouth.

At some point, there will be questions. Xander's body was found in the charred shell of Yarrow House. The coroner will have to start with all the mushrooms growing out of his skin before they worry about why he was in an abandoned house when it caught fire. Then there will probably be cops and voicemails from Mrs. Greenway. I might tell her to keep the clothes I left in her washing machine.

Today, I don't want to answer any questions. It's day seven of the spell.

I leave my sisters to sleep in my bed. Tomorrow, I'll tell them to stay the fuck out of my room again. Today, it's nice to know that they're safe.

Lucky Thirteen is closed on Sundays. I asked Toby why once—it's not like she has to go to church—and she told me that everyone deserved a day to themselves. She picked Sunday because it was when her friends could ride with her.

This was before I knew that sometimes Toby's friends assemble on Friday nights to hunt zombies.

I stand outside the little yellow Victorian, not quite in knocking distance of the door. With the shop closed, the building has transformed back into being someone's house. A house with a shotgun inside.

I dig my fingernails into the lines of my palm, one by one. Toby and her friends and her shotgun ruined my Friday night. I can claim part of her Sunday.

I knock on the door. When I don't hear movement inside, I knock again, harder. I'll stand here all day. I'll make a scene if I have to. I have business with that old witch.

The door swings open, and I take a surprised step backward. Dr. Miller cranes her long neck toward me, her fluffy hair wild around her face. She's wearing a pink bathrobe printed with multicolored hearts, each as big as my hand.

"Camila," she says, way less surprised to see me than I am to see her. She points toward the sign in the front window: *So Mote It Be, We're Closed.* "You'll have to come back after school tomorrow."

"I'm not here to shop," I say. "I need to talk to Toby. Is she, uh, here, too?"

She gives me a pitying smile for even having to ask. Toby is here. They are here together. Dr. Miller and Toby live together. Huh.

"I don't know that she'll want to visit with you right now," she says. She drops her voice down to a whisper. "I know it doesn't look like it, but her feelings were truly hurt when you stole from the shop and did magic without her help. It will take a long time to build that trust back."

"Xander Greenway is dead, Dr. Miller." I cross my arms over my chest, but the bravado can't carry me through. My sinuses burn and my voice cracks as the reality of it settles over me. "He killed June and Dayton, and last night he died trying to kill me and Aniyah Dorsey. And it's the last day of the resurrection spell, so I'd like to get some stuff cleared up before I go see my friends for the last time."

A hand flies to her chest, pressing down the lapels of her robe. Her mouth flops open like a fish struggling to breathe out of water. She looks at the sleeve of my jacket where Xander's bloodstains look like splattered paint. There are footsteps behind her, and I see Toby appearing at the base of the stairs that are usually roped off.

"Cora? What's going on? What's the—" Toby stops talking as she sees me. Her forehead creases. "Mila, we're closed."

Dr. Miller steps aside, swinging her head back and forth in disbelief. "No, she needs to talk to us. There's a lot we don't know. Come in, Camila. Please."

Toby's chin tucks back into her neck in confusion as I step over the threshold. Unlike her usual gauzy and revealing outfits, she's wearing red flannel pajamas that cover all her tattoos. It might be the first time I haven't been able to see her cleavage. "What are we supposed to do? Play wise old crones and have tea?"

"Another child is dead," Dr. Miller hisses. "So, yes, go put the kettle on."

Toby's frown deepens, but she turns on her heel and leads the way through the store and behind the register where their home starts. The living room is an explosion of sky blue wallpaper covered in cherubs and giant velvet couches that could easily seat their entire coven. We turn into a very narrow kitchen, dominated by a giant carved wheel of the year on the wall where other people would have a clock. Toby goes to an electric tea kettle while Dr. Miller urges me forward toward a set of French doors.

Instead of going outside, we step onto a closed-in porch that runs along the entire back of the house. Bundles of drying herbs hang against the windows, probably plucked from the garden on the other side of the glass. The morning sunlight is misty here. I wonder if Dr. Miller brought me to this room because the smell of drying lavender is so strong. Lavender is good for healing.

Dr. Miller takes a seat on one of many rattan furniture monstrosities, none of which look particularly strong. I choose a loveseat with sun-bleached cushions and keep my attention on the garden outside, naming plants in my head until Toby comes in and grumpily plants a tea tray on a wicker side table.

Dr. Miller reaches for the bright turquoise teapot and pours steaming liquid into the three matching cups. She passes me a cup. The tea isn't dark enough to be real black tea, but it's also too pale to be chamomile. I take a sniff.

"It isn't acorns, is it?" I ask, thinking of the potion we forced on Caleb.

"Do you need assistance in telling the truth?" Toby asks, her voice edged in a growl.

"It's Tension Tamer," Dr. Miller says lightly. "I have a weakness for store-bought teas. Toby thinks it's a waste of money since the shop sells herb blends." She holds her cup in both hands and draws it close to her chest. She remembers to put on her counselor half smile. "What happened, Camila?"

"Why don't you start with your decision to steal from my store," Toby says, leaning back in her seat. "And then continue with doing magic that is a violence to the Goddess—"

"Toby," Dr. Miller says with more sharpness than I would have guessed she was capable of. "That's not helping."

I hold my tea under my nose, watching the swirls of steam writhe and undulate upward. It's like a ghost of the smoke that still paints the inside of my nose and mouth, the slimy brown smoke of old wood burning down around me.

So, I tell the story, the whole thing. Starting with Riley's accidental death and the grimoire showing up at Yarrow House all the way through to limping into bed this morning with Xander's blood still on my skin. Dr. Miller only stops me a couple of times to ask for clarification. Toby doesn't say anything at all, but her tea sits untouched on the table.

"Tonight the girls are going to go back to the graveyard," I conclude. "And I want your coven to be there."

"We won't help you keep them around," Toby says, her brows drawing together. "They might be your friends, but that doesn't change how they got here."

"I don't want you to help them stay," I say. I wish I could make them stay. I wish I could give them their lives back, but they don't belong here anymore. Their visit is almost over. "I want you to watch them leave so you'll believe that they're gone. And if anything goes wrong, you can help me make it right. There was no spell in the grimoire for putting them back."

"It's very mature of you to ask for supervision," Dr. Miller says.

I bristle at the idea but take a sip of my tea to hide it. "I did what I had to do for Riley. And June and Dayton. I'm not going to apologize for it, but I want to make things right. The iron rose hematite should come back after the girls go. It's in Riley's grave right now. I can cleanse it and give it back to the shop. Or I can work it off, I guess. It's not like I'll have anything else to do." I offer a weak smile and a shrug. "All my friends are dead."

Toby examines me. I know she's an old lady in flannel jammies, but the intensity of her gaze is still vaguely terrifying, like she can see secrets oozing out of my skin. But I don't have secrets from her right now. Right now, she and Dr. Miller know more about me than my own parents.

"How are we supposed to trust you again, Mila?" Toby asks. It isn't accusing or angry. She honestly doesn't seem to have the answer. And I get it. Because I also don't know how I'm going to come back from raising the dead and leaving a murderer to die. I can't picture tomorrow at all.

"The same way I'll learn to not be scared you're gonna pull a shotgun on me again," I say. "I'm going to give you a chance to make good. And I think I deserve a chance, too."

TWENTY-FOUR

WITH A HANDFUL of movies and a bag from the drugstore, I drive to Caleb's. When the front door opens, I'm greeted by Dayton blowing a party noisemaker. The long green tube of paper unravels toward my face with a honk.

"You're here!" she cheers, the noisemaker clenched between her teeth. She has a hard time smiling and talking and keeping it in her mouth all at the same time. "We didn't want to wake you up too early since you had, you know, a hard night. But it's our last day, and Caleb got us a bunch of treats!"

She pushes me inside. The kitchen counters are packed with chips and bags of cookies and cereal and liters of soda. There are sweating Starbucks cups on the coffee table in the living room, where Caleb, June, and Riley are unironically playing a round of Uno.

"Our funerals sounded like they sucked," Dayton says, skipping by me to launch herself into a pile of pillows and blankets under the TV—a huge improvement over the uncomfortable couch. "And Ms. Chu and Mr. Treadwell don't get back until late tonight, so Caleb set us up with a tiny going-away party!"

"It's nothing much. Mostly just emptied out the pantry. Everything's an upgrade after you live in an abandoned house," Caleb says, his tongue wedged into the corner of his mouth as he examines his cards. He jerks his head toward the coffee table. "I got you a caramel Frap, though. Riley said it was your drink."

"It is. Thanks. I brought movies," I say, holding up the reusable shopping bag. "And I grabbed some bleach for you, Riley. If you wanted to do your roots before tonight."

She looks at me for the first time. At least I think she does. Her head lifts over her cards, and her mouth opens slightly. "Really?"

"Yeah." I shrug. "I think as long as you're holding on to me, the wound on your head will stay closed so you don't have to worry about getting any chemicals on your skull. You don't have to. I just thought you might like the option since there's running water here?"

Riley gets to her feet and leads the way to the bathroom between the master bedroom and Caleb's room. It's nautical themed with a decorative wooden anchor and blue-and-white stripes painted on the walls. I've never pictured where Ms. Chu poops, but this would not have been my guess.

I put the box of bleach on the counter as Riley settles herself onto the lid of the toilet. She fusses with the sleeves of her shirt, pulling them down over her fingers as I mix the various bottles together. It makes me think of all the times I've done this before. Riley has always worn her hair unmanageably long, making it difficult for her to wade through and catch all the brown bits in the back. She always gets super antsy as the bleach starts to sting her scalp and talks faster and about incrementally sillier things to keep her mind off it.

Now that I think of it, picturing where the principal poops would have made an excellent addition to the bleach distraction game.

When I have the disposable gloves on and the bleach mixed, I stand between her legs, combing her hair back. She reaches out, settling her hand awkwardly on my leg. I watch her left wrist pop back into place. She rolls it with a sigh of relief and looks up at me with hazel confusion.

"Why are you doing this?" she asks.

I put the first blob of bleach onto the brown hairs in the center of her forehead, smoothing it back into her hair. The smell is instant and harsh. I lean back and turn on the bathroom fan with my elbow.

"When you were dead," I say slowly, "this was the thing that kept me up at night. I couldn't stop thinking about you being buried with your roots showing and how pissed you'd be if you knew."

"Aren't you mad at me? After the stuff I said to you the other night—about being bad at magic and how I wish you hadn't brought me back. It wasn't even true. I am glad that I got to see you again. And I don't even know if I could do magic before. You're right, we never had proof or anything."

"We never needed proof," I say with a shrug. "I never needed magic to work until I had to bring you back."

"I was just so angry and so scared," she says softly.

"We had a fight," I say, echoing something Dayton said to me yesterday. "It's not our first. It's not even the worst one. Remember when you called me *fluffy* instead of fat?"

"Fuck a duck. It was eighth grade! I didn't know anything about body positivity yet," she groans. Her lips press together, and she cuts her eyes at the floor. "But last night . . . Mila, my brother tried to kill you."

"Yeah, but I trapped him and left him for dead." I aim the tip of the bottle behind her ear and squeeze purplish ooze around her hairline. "Aren't you mad at *me*?"

"No," she says, but it sounds uneasy. "I know that he would have killed you. I didn't want to believe it. I spent all day yesterday telling him how chill it's been having June and Dayton around this week. June can be ignorant, and Dayton is sort of flighty, but for the first time I kind of understood why he was friends with them. And then hearing him confess to what he did, I realized that I didn't know why he was friends with them. Or anything else about him. It was like he became a total stranger to me. Except also not? I think he was capable of hurting people our whole lives; he just saved it for now." Tears slide down the sides of her face, and her chin wobbles as she holds in a sob.

"I don't think he ever would have stopped if you hadn't pinned him inside the house."

"He kissed me," I blurt, as I mush bleach-soaked hair between my fingers. "When Toby's coven showed up and I went to your house. Xander let me get cleaned up, and I was in his room, and we started making out. But then I saw the mushrooms and—" I bite the inside of my cheek as my stomach churns. "I wanted him so much, Riley. I had a crush on him for years."

"Yeah," she says with a sniffle. "I know."

Surprised, I yank too hard on her hair. She looks up at me, and the apology dies on my tongue when I remember that she doesn't feel pain. "What do you mean you know? I never told you."

She wrinkles her nose. "God, Mila. I'm your best friend. You think I didn't notice that you were basically obsessed with my brother the whole time we've known each other? You know the license plate number on his car."

Embarrassment crawls up my spine, making me want to curl up into a ball and hide. "You never said anything," I say.

"Neither did you. Besides, I didn't want you to ditch me for Xander and the honor society." She turns her attention to the floor. "He was always interested in you, too."

Xander was the gravitational force in my life for so long. My best friend's brother. My secret crush. But he was a story I told myself. Bashful and successful and kind. Perfection watching the world with blue eyes. I didn't know his soul was full of fungus. Does it matter that he loved almond milk and no-show socks and books about aliens if his love was pollution? As grimy and shiitake-brown as the smoke that rose out of Yarrow as it burned down to embers.

He told himself a story, too, as he memorized me in bits and pieces, the same way I tried to keep him. I wasn't the solution to his problems or the decisive force that would absolve him of what he'd done. I wasn't the girl who would be willing to burn if it meant staying with him.

We were both wrong, and we paid for it in different ways.

"Just my luck," I say, my voice shaking and eyes burning. A tear splashes onto my cheek. "I killed the first dude who was ever interested in me."

She wipes her eyes and gives me an icy glare. "You didn't kill him. He lit the fire."

I avoid her gaze and focus on pushing the mass of her hair to one side. "Your brother is dead. Your parents must be a wreck. And it's my fault. Even if I had to do it, I'm still the one who did it."

"And the creek technically killed me," she says with a scoff. "I'm not mad at it. It was my stupid mistake."

"Try telling that to Dayton, who's only had Gatorade for seven days so you won't have to look at a bottle of water."

"You think I haven't tried? She has way too many electrolytes in her system. I'm afraid she's going to get 'roid rage."

"Do you not know what electrolytes are?"

"Magic is real, and you are bleaching a dead girl's hair. Everything we know about science and religion could be a lie."

"Yeah, but it's probably not. I'm pretty sure electrolytes are, like, calcium and other minerals your body needs."

"Then why do we pay so much money for special electrolyte water? Did I spend my entire life getting ripped off?"

"Seems like it." I laugh.

"Hey, Blister?"

"Yeah?"

"I love you. I'm sorry my brother tried to kill you."

"I love you, too. I'm sorry I had to let him die."

It's such a stupid understatement that we both laugh, even though our eyes are still wet and our hearts still hurt.

After thirty minutes, Riley's hair is as unnaturally yellow as ever. She makes me keep my index finger poked into her side so that she can use Ms. Chu's blow-dryer and admire herself in the mirror. When we finally leave the bathroom, she is once again a very gnarly looking corpse with very shiny hair. But she skips across the living room and flings herself into a pile of pillows, obviously very pleased with herself.

Seeing her so happy, even for a second, is worth every single moment of this week.

Riley, June, Dayton, Caleb, and I watch a slew of movies and TV shows, eventually devolving into watching single scenes that make us laugh. I eat leftover pizza and lava cake for dinner. June has three grilled cheese sandwiches and a bowl of Cinnamon Toast Crunch while going through the notes I rescued from her locker. She writes replies on the back of each of them, mostly apologies. Dayton uses Caleb's laptop to fall deep into a Tumblr rabbit hole. We have a dance party in Ms. Chu's bedroom while listening to "Uptown Funk" ten times. We watch the sunset while laying in the grass of Caleb's backyard.

It feels a lot like what I would do if I knew the apocalypse was coming.

Caleb's parents are minutes away from pulling up in the driveway when we get the last dish into the dishwasher and the pizza boxes smashed down into the trash can. Dayton, Riley, and I hover next to the front door, giving June and Caleb a sliver of privacy around the corner. Still, their voices float back to us. None of us try that hard not to listen.

"You have to be here when they get back," June says.

"I don't care. What are they going to do? Ground me?" Caleb's voice is rough with the macho bullshit that I'm used to him pulling in chemistry. I sort of forgot that's how he normally talks to me.

"I don't want you to watch me die. It's bad enough you have to remember me like this." I imagine she's referring to her corpse-form, maybe even going so far as to do that thing where her head wobbles too much on her bendy neck.

"Look," she says, suddenly serious. "The last guy I made popular ended up killing me. Maybe it's not as fun as I think it is. Just . . . be happy. And don't kill anyone, okay?"

There's a soft wind of whispers. The whistle of words so private that they won't even turn a corner for us.

June leaves the house silently, her white eyes as wet as spilled milk.

☠ ☠ ☠

Motorcycles roar up to the kissing gate under the willow tree. The Cross Creek coven silence their engines as they walk their bikes between headstones. Tonight, they wear matching jackets that have the words THE QUARTER MOONS IN A TEN-CENT TOWN embroidered on a giant patch on the back. Toby leads the pack, of course. Her helmet is hooked to the side of her seat. There's a huge white pentacle painted on the back of it.

June, Dayton, and Riley shiver closer to me. None of us can bring ourselves to stand on top of Riley's grave, even though there isn't anyone inside it. Yet.

"It's okay," I murmur. "They promised to play nice. They need to watch you go so there are no more misunderstandings. Or shotguns."

Toby parks her motorcycle next to a giant angel statue. She peels off her jacket and her leather gloves and drapes them over her bike seat. Despite the cold, she's wearing a white peasant top. Her tattoos show through the fabric like dark stains.

"Merry meet," she says.

"Hey," I say.

Riley throws up a hand. "Hi, Toby. Other witches. Blessed be."

There are some begrudging *blessed be*s from the other witches. I wonder if they're mad about being out late on a work night. Or at all. I don't know how late old ladies party.

Toby reaches into the saddlebag on her motorcycle. My breath catches as she draws out the old red grimoire.

"Take this with you," Toby says, shoving the grimoire into Riley's hands. "I spent a day looking over it, and the shit in there doesn't need to be floating around the land of the living. That is hardcore black magic."

Riley recoils, craning her neck away from the book as though she's thinking about throwing it somewhere. "I kind of figured that when it made my brother's body explode into mushrooms."

"Jesus Christ." Toby sucks the spit off her teeth and hooks her thumbs in the belt loops of her jeans. "You guys are lucky you didn't end the world with this shit. I told you to be careful, didn't I?"

"We've all done magic we're not proud of," says one of the other witches, a black woman with tight braids swirling against her scalp in a conch swirl. "Toby, didn't you spend three years trying to drag your soul mate to you?"

A gray-haired woman laughs huskily. "Oh no. You can't fuck with fate like that."

Dayton widens her white eyes at me, apparently shocked to hear cursing coming out of the elderly. Even zombies can be scandalized, I guess. I give her a shrug.

Dr. Miller, in pink-and-white leggings more suited to yoga than midnight motorcycle riding, pinches her hands together daintily. "I'm sorry if we scared you girls the other night."

"You mean when you tried to literally hunt us?" June asks coldly. It's particularly threatening in her pitted voice.

"If you didn't want to be hunted, you shouldn't have gone skipping around town without decent disguises," Toby says airily.

Dr. Miller slips into her pacifying therapist voice. "It's normal for witches your age to attempt big, messy magic and have it go wrong. That's why it's best to practice in a group."

"A lesser witch would have brought back shadow versions of the girls. The mindlessly hungry, without conscience or memory," says the woman with the conch braid.

"The kind of zombies that make *The Walking Dead* look like It's a Small World," Toby growls.

Dayton sucks in a gasp. "I'm scared of both of those things."

"I guess you haven't looked in a mirror recently," says the gray-haired woman.

"Hey!" June snaps, aiming a blackened fingernail at her. "We're about to die, so have a little respect."

"Why?" Riley mutters with a scowl. "She'll be joining us soon."

"We only have a couple of minutes left," I say, loudly enough to keep any of the Quarter Moons from thinking about starting a fight with my zombies. "Do you mind if we have a minute alone?"

I shove the girls farther down the slope of the graveyard, tripping over my boots as I try not to stomp on any flowers. I check my phone. Five minutes until midnight.

"Okay," I say with a sharp sigh. "Here are the rules. No crying. No promising to watch over me from heaven. Nothing that we wouldn't do on the last day of school. I mean, we probably wouldn't have seen each other again after senior year anyway, right? It's like we're all going off to college."

It isn't. And we all know that it isn't. But I'm not going to stand here and cry until the graveyard slurps them back up.

"Oh, I wish we'd made life yearbooks," Dayton says, pressing her fingertips to her lips. "Mila, I would sign yours: *Love, your guardian angel.*"

I tsk at her, sounding unforgivably like my own mother. "That is heaven talk. Forbidden."

"That's not fair," June whines, tilting her head back in a theatrical pout. Her neck flops too far, and she has to yank on her own hair to move her head back into place. It is disgusting to watch. "You didn't mourn me or Dayton at all the first time."

"True," I say. "But I will have the rest of my life to miss you."

"Fine," June says. "You are way too practical for a Libra."

"All right," Riley says, hugging the grimoire to her chest. "I'll start. Um. Keep in touch?"

"Don't ever change," Dayton adds with a grin.

"Have a great summer," June says. "But I'd really mean: *Have a great life, loser.*"

"See you later." My sinuses burn. I force myself to smile. "Oh shit! Hold on."

I scramble to unclasp the necklace from around my neck. I forgot what it was like to walk around without its gentle weight pressed into my skin. I swing the chain around Riley's neck.

"Here," I say, fumbling with the clasp. How did Xander make this look so easy? My thumbnail can barely open the damn thing. "Take it with you. Your mom would be so pissed if she knew."

She laughs, and it's wet and husky and so very much hers, even though it's coming out of cracked, gray lips. "Fuck a duck. She would hate it. That's awesome."

The four of us take one last moment together. The urge to rip the grimoire out of Riley's arms and find the recipe for putting off this goodbye is almost too much to bear. But our paths are diverging, and all I can do is be grateful that we had this week that I extorted from the universe.

I'm a witch. I'm always grateful.

The girls wander to their graves. They kick off their stolen shoes and set their toes in the dirt. The coven edges nearer again, sensing midnight. It is the witching hour, after all.

Since there isn't a choir here, I pull up a karaoke track on my phone. The computerized instruments sound like they're being played inside a tin can, all metallic dissonance and echoes. There are way more flutes than I think are really necessary, and the piano sounds more like a wheezy organ. But Dayton doesn't seem to mind. She smiles dreamily and opens her hands, conjuring the song out of herself.

"I'm always chasing rainbows, waiting to find a little blue-bird . . ."

After the last verse, her notes are still floating on the air, trapped in fog, when the earth trembles and the graveyard goes silent.

TWENTY-FIVE

ALEXANDER GREENWAY WAS buried next to his sister. The singular news article on the *Cross Creek Examiner* website didn't mention the books that burned with him or the remnants of three fancy dresses with traces of formaldehyde. There was no report of Xander's body having any wounds or anomalies. Looking too deep into one of those things would mean having to answer for the others. I think that no one involved in the investigation wants to know how Xander got his sister's burial dress out of the grave or why he was covered in fungus or why he showed no signs of struggle.

Or our police department just sucks?

Either way, his death was ruled an accident, but everyone at Fairmont Academy is treating it like the fourth suicide.

To be fair, they've had too much practice to do anything else.

Ms. Chu isn't eulogizing today. Neither is Mr. Greenway. He hired another funeral director to come in and perform the service. Having both of his kids die in the span of one week has obviously been too much for him to take. His face is as gray and shadowed as Riley's was the last time I saw her. Mrs. Greenway is in a haze like she's sleepwalking. Suspicion and silent accusations seem to stand like a force field between them and everyone else. Their pew has no family members, just members of the church Xander and Riley never attended. I think I recognize Dayton's parents.

I'm sitting with my family, sandwiched between my sisters. Mom seemed pretty sure that I'd try to walk out of the service, so she trapped me. I don't blame her. I probably would walk out of this if I could. I already know that this will be the last time I ever walk through the doors of the Greenway Funeral Home. Everything—from the yellow wallpaper to the too-thick carpet—makes me think of the sharpest edges of knowing Riley and Xander. The scab they left on my life might never fully heal, but I can at least avoid infecting it.

After another awful performance by the show choir, I skip the receiving line with the totally real excuse that I need to get to work. My hours at Lucky Thirteen flex since there are very few customers and I'm not being paid, but my parents don't know that. I told them that working there is helping me make peace with Riley's death. I've even started toeing the line and referring to it as "her suicide," even though I know that she didn't mean to die. It makes them feel like I've made emotional progress. It makes them less scared of me.

The graveyard took back Riley, June, and Dayton but kept the iron rose hematite, so I'll be working off my three-hundred-dollar debt to Toby by stocking shelves and tying together different kinds of herb brushes. On top of my new weekly meetings at school with Dr. Miller to discuss my PTSD and depression—apparently wanting to stay in bed for weeks at a time and not talk to anyone isn't the healthiest coping tool?—my life is suddenly full of those meddling old witches.

The sky is blanketed in white, the sun's light and warmth smothered by clouds. I stop at the edge of the bright green lawn to button up my jacket. I adjust my cuffs over the seed-bead bracelets I've started making again. Dr. Miller thought it would be a good idea to return to some of my non-magical hobbies so that I don't accidentally fuck with the balance of the universe again out of sheer boredom. It feels good to craft. Counting out the tiny beads is almost meditative. And they're prettier than wearing a hair tie on my wrist every day.

Binx prances out of the neighbors' shrubs and rubs himself against my ankles, his tail swishing through the air. I scoop him up, rubbing my thumb behind his ear until he purrs. "You think the Greenways are going to remember to feed you now? Mrs. Greenway wouldn't even let you live indoors."

"So witches really do talk to cats? Does he talk back?"

Aniyah Dorsey is walking down the driveway toward me. Her silver frames have been switched out for sunglasses. She's wearing all black, down to her lipstick. It makes her teeth look especially white when she flashes me a smile. I resent how cool she looks. She doesn't look like she just went to a funeral; she looks like she just buried someone.

"I didn't see you in there," I say, gesturing toward the house with Binx, who makes his grumpy mooing sound.

"I snuck out the side door during the slideshow when Chloe Wellington started scream-crying," she says. Her tongue wedges under her upper lip. "I didn't want to see him again anyway."

I understand the feeling. It's hard to see his face and not see a monster. I guess people have been trying to warn us forever that the boogeyman would be just some guy. *Man* is in his title, after all.

I know that I couldn't have saved him, even if I'd wanted to.

Maybe one day the guilt will be easier to bear.

"You doing okay?" I ask Aniyah.

"Since running for my life out of a burning house with a group of zombies from a mushroom demon that I can never tell anyone about? Yeah. I only wake up screaming sometimes. Otherwise, I'm hella chill." Her lips purse, and she tips her head up toward the sun, her hair swishing around her back. "It's getting easier, but only because it's starting to feel fake."

I nod. "Nightmares have a way of doing that."

"And we're the only ones who even know that it was real."

"Us and Caleb Treadwell."

"Oh shit." She hops with excitement, then has to right her sunglasses. "Did you hear he had to pull his Rausch Scholarship application because he plagiarized the essay?"

"I'm out of the loop at Fairmont right now. Rumors don't really make it to you when you don't have any friends," I say.

"Uh, I'm telling you the rumor right now. Consider yourself in the loop."

Dr. Miller has been harping on me for not giving people a chance. By *people*, she mostly means Caleb, who has invited me to join the honor society despite my mediocre grades. I think he pities me because I'm partially responsible for Xander dying. Dr. Miller thinks that he just misses our dead mutual friends and is trying to be nice.

If I spend the rest of my life avoiding people who could die on me, I'll be alone for a long time. And what are the chances that I'll immediately befriend another murderer?

You know what? I really don't want to know the statistics on that.

"You don't have an older brother, do you?" I ask Aniyah abruptly.

"Nope. One younger sister. She's thirteen, so she's kind of an asshole."

"Tell me about it. Mine are eleven and fourteen. They're the worst." I hoist Binx closer to my chest, holding on to him like a surly security blanket. "So you . . . what? Wanna start the fat brown girl clique?"

She cocks her head at me. "Doesn't that sound dope as hell?"

Honestly? It really does.

ACKNOWLEDGMENTS

This book has been my most collaborative effort to date. Allow me to thank all my witches. (No, I will not ever get tired of witch puns. Hex-cuse me.)

Las Chicas Malas Brujas:
Anna-Marie McLemore, Tehlor Kay Mejia, and Candice Montgomery, who beta read and listened to me whine and never once told me to shut up. I love you all so much. Someday, we'll get those four houses next door to each other. Tamales and ponies and wine for everyone!

The Badass Lady Authors Coven:
Cori McCarthy, Amy Rose Capetta, and Jenn Bennett, who are less a coven and more a list of very nice mentor authors who all take my panicked DMs when I don't know what books are anymore.

The Red Sofa Coven, My Minnesota Witches:
Thank you, of course, to Laura Zats, my most incredible agent who also might be my guardian angel. Also to Erik Hane for putting up with Laura and me listing terrible titles in our group thread. And Dawn Frederick for leading the way in all things bookish.

The Razorbill Coven:

Thank you to Ben Schrank and Tiff Liao for believing in me and giving me the chance to write the fat Latina Wiccan story I've spent my entire life researching. Marissa Grossman and Alex Sanchez for always being a phone call away to help me iron out plot ideas—from red herrings to mushroom monologues. Corina Lupp, who designed this book, inside and out, and Michael Frost, who photographed that bitchin' jacket. My awesome marketing team, especially Casey McIntyre.

The Wordsmith Coven:

Kate Frentzel, my copyeditor, and my proofreaders Krista Ahlberg and Vivian Kirklin, who saved all my readers from my sloppy idioms and repeated misspellings. Thank you the most.

The Harbor Family:

Forever and always. You may not be witches, but you are magic.